W9-AFL-311

DECEPTIVE CADENCE

DECEPTIVE CADENCE

Eugenia Zukerman

The Viking Press / New York

4/1981
Music

Copyright © Eugenia Zukerman, 1980

First published in 1980 by The Viking Press
625 Madison Avenue, New York, N.Y. 10022

Published simultaneously in Canada by
Penguin Books Canada Limited

LIBRARY OF CONGRESS CATALOGING IN PUBLICATION DATA
Zukerman, Eugenia.
Deceptive cadence.
I. Title.
PZ4.Z938De   [PS3576.U24]   813'.54   80–15021
ISBN 0–670–26236–6

Grateful acknowledgment is made to the following for permission
to reprint copyrighted material:

Harvard University Press: An excerpt from *Harvard Dictionary of
Music* by Willie Apel, 1969.

Simon & Schuster, a Division of Gulf & Western Corporation: A
selection from *Yma, Ava; Yma, Abba; Yma, Oona; Yma, Ida; Yma,
Aga . . . and Others,* by Thomas Meehan. Copyright © 1959, 1960,
1961, 1962, 1963, 1964, 1965, 1966, 1967 by Thomas Meehan.

Printed in the United States of America

Set in Linotron Palatino
Designed by Sharen DuGoff

For my parents,
Shirley and Stanley Rich

Cadence: A melodic or harmonic formula that occurs at the end of a composition, a section, or a phrase, conveying the impression of a momentary or permanent conclusion. . . . The deceptive cadence is an authentic . . . cadence whose tonic chord is—deceptively—replaced by some other chord. . . . *See also* masculine, feminine cadence.

—*Harvard Dictionary of Music*

DECEPTIVE CADENCE

When Tibor Szabo disappeared he left behind him several thousand devotees rustling their programs in the Philharmonie in Berlin, concert managers calling each other around the globe, a file stuffed with recording and concert contracts up to and including 1984, a large bank account in Liechtenstein, a sister in Cleveland, a mother in Switzerland, a girl in every port, a woman named Sally, and a flat in London with a shiny silent Hamburg Steinway.

"Meine Damen und Herren," a voice finally intoned through a loudspeaker to the crowd at the Philharmonie, "ladies and gentlemen, we regret to announce that Tibor Szabo will not be able to perform tonight."

Two thousand two hundred and seventy-seven people sighed, some in anger, most in disappointment, before proceeding to the box office to obtain their refunds.

When Tibor Szabo disappeared he left behind him the legends, the promises, the commitments, the pressures of a spectacular international concert career.

"What do you think happened?" a reporter from the *Daily Telegraph* asked Szabo's good friend Werner Rawlings, the novelist.

"He's like Houdini," Werner said, a smile creeping catlike onto his face. "Bound, gagged, and locked inside a piano, he found a way to get out."

"And where do you suppose he went?" the reporter prodded.

"That," said Werner, "is not the point."

It was July 1976, and the worst heat wave in recent years scorched London. The city blistered by day and throbbed at night. In the glare of a relentless sun, people carried on, wilted but brave, fainting and swearing at the changeless sky. Beastly, bloody awful, insufferable— swarms of complaint stung the air, angry but ineffective, and despondent eyes turned upward for signs of rain. There were none. By night, choked with heat, no one could sleep. There was nothing to do but wait, and one did, draped over a terrace railing or window ledge, sprawled on the parched grass with collar open and drink in hand, or just wide-eyed on one's bed. Doors opened, tables were moved outside, drinks were poured. The English were awake, there was nightlife al fresco, and London began to look like Naples, like Rome, like the Riviera, certainly more Mediterranean than British.

"Lovely," Werner Rawlings sighed as he walked slowly down Walton Street at ten p.m., the temperature hovering at 98, the air still as cement. He enjoyed the heat and the movement it forced, the sound of voices, of people drinking and eating. His white gauze shirt was damp, clung to his skin, and perspiration ran down his back. He wiped his forehead with one sleeve, brushing back a mass of wet curls, and turned into Lennox Gardens Mews, keeping close to the wall that separated it from the gardens of the houses on Ovington Street and made the mews half-garden, a flowered thicket tucked into the wilds of Kensington. Werner stopped across from number 32. No reporters or cameras lurked near the window boxes, so he crossed the cobblestones, sucked in his stomach to reach into the pockets of his tight-fitting white pants, and took out Tibor's key. He listened at Szabo's door. A toilet flushed, a door closed, a plate broke, a woman laughed, but that had to be the Americans next door. Werner turned the key and walked in.

He held his breath, heard nothing, and slipped into the sitting room to close the curtains securely before switching on a lamp. He blinked in the light and noticed with regret that nothing was out of place. He had hoped for some sign—the piano smashed, papers and music scattered across the floor, a signal, something. But the room was neat and tidy, cared for, clean; as left. Covered with a Spanish shawl, the Steinway stood in the center of the room, like a horse in stable, waiting patiently. Scores and records surrounded it on bookshelves, and a portrait of Stephan Vlostid, Szabo's teacher, hung on the wall, perfectly straight. In that room, where Werner had spent hours, days, listening to Tibor play, talking with him, drinking with him, now in that hot airless space there was no sound, not even an echo.

Werner turned, and after a moment's hesitation in which he decided he had no right and then decided he had every right, he climbed the stairs to the bedroom. Light from the streetlamps in the mews threw shadows on the large unwrinkled bed and across the eighteenth-century captain's desk Tibor had blithely paid too much for. Harrods was conveniently just around the corner, he'd said, and besides, the desk drawers locked. Sliding his hand with difficulty into his back pocket, Werner took out a slim silver penknife, flicked it open to the smallest blade, and stalked the desk like a hunter. He tried the top left-hand drawer. Locked. He inhaled, placed the tip of his knife blade into the ornate gold lock, and with the finesse

3

of a professional clicked it open in one effortless attempt. It was a deep drawer, crammed full. He dug in, flipped through a folder marked "1976." It contained a copy of Tibor's itinerary through December, five tightly spaced pages of hotels, airplane schedules, rehearsal times, concert arrangements, fees; a letter from Michael Klein, his manager in New York; three handwritten perfumed notes; a gas bill; a royalty check for £10,000 from Deutsche Grammophon; a photo of Tibor Szabo shaking hands with Herbert von Karajan; a clipping from the *Süddeutsche Zeitung* with the headline SZABO—PIANISTENWUNDER; and a catalog, "History and Politics in the West since the Sixteenth Century," from Heffer's bookstore in Cambridge.

Useless. He closed the file and reached deep into the drawer, pulled out an old photo of Tibor's mother, hands on her hips, her head tilted to the side, a straw hat covering one eye. A straight nose and high cheekbones linked her face to Tibor's, but it was her broad grin, charming the viewer while holding him at bay, that confirmed the connection. Next Werner found a small red address book filled with names, all female, and after each name a plus or a minus. He smiled, put the book on top of the desk, and reached for another photo, another letter, then tried the next drawer, his penknife opening lock after lock. Nothing but public photos, business and fan letters, old itineraries, concert programs, used plane tickets—the spoils of earlier tours.

Trust him to lock up the trivia, Werner thought, and he slumped onto the desk chair, his head tilted back, his eyes coming to rest on the wall where the photo of Sally stared back at him. Framed in silver, she glowed on the wall like an apparition, an image fixed for a moment, illusive as a cloud formation, meant to dissolve. Even in black and white, even in shadow, her eyes penetrated, she demand-

4

ed attention—as much now as three years before when Werner first met her.

"This is Sally Fraser," Tibor had said in a tone both proud and vulnerable, and he had stepped back, looking delighted, while they shook hands. If her peculiar handshake startled Werner, her eyes dazzled him. Their color was blue edging toward violet, a deep lavender so intense and radiant he had the sensation of looking into the eyes of some rare tropical creature.

"I'm so pleased to meet you," Sally said, her voice soft but assured. "Tibor has told me so much about you."

"All lies," Werner bragged.

"I hope not," Sally said, her eyes narrowing beneath translucent lids.

He watched the photo, expecting it to vanish, but Sally stared back, steady as an icon fixed in place.

"There were others," he whispered at her, "hordes of them." He picked up the address book he had taken from the desk, flipped the pages, and names flew past, Natasha, Heather, Anna, Gabrielle, Kirsten, Angelica, the pluses and minuses merging together like crosses in a religious text. But these were only acolytes, and the object of worship was nowhere to be found. Werner stood up, fingered the leather binding, and tossed the address book back like a small fish into the depths of the open drawer. Dizzy from the heat, he held on to the edge of the desk, swayed forward. Drops of sweat from his forehead landed with a pinging sound on the file marked "1976." He wiped it dry, smudging the numbers.

"Just as well," he muttered to himself. It's not recent, what you're looking for, is it? he thought. Or is it? You haven't a clue what to look for anyhow, do you? A suicide note? Not bloody likely, not Szabo. Just find him, find the poor sod, before—

He pounded his fist like a stamp across the blurred

numbers, closed the desk drawers, and ran back down the stairs. In the sitting room, reaching to switch off the lamp, Werner impulsively stretched out his hand to straighten the covering on the piano and noticed an open score on the music rack. He sat down on the piano bench and studied the page. Scratches in blue and red ink scarred the paper, fingerings written in pencil, erased and crossed out, penciled in again, crawled over the notes, like spiders, and on top of the right-hand page, in large red capital letters, was the word CALM. Tibor had taught Werner to read a score; he should recognize this piece. Yes, Liszt's B-minor Sonata, last page. At the bottom circled in blue was the F-major chord Tibor had shown him, the one preceding three pianissimo B-major chords at the very end. The crescendo slashed beneath it was underlined in red.

"It is impossible," Tibor had said, flashing a grin. "On the piano you cannot make a crescendo on one chord—there is no way. Liszt was a maniac. The only thing you can do is crescendo physically, convey the expansion with your body, create an illusion. You see how unsatisfactory music is, how impossible?"

"But you found a solution, one that works," Werner offered.

"When you can't play it, fake it." Tibor winked, mercurial as always, one minute dark and gloomy, the next exuberant, elated. There had always been a balance, always.

He'll get over it, Werner assured himself. He'll be OK, and he closed the music, turned out the light, and strolled down to the restaurant on the corner for a cold lager, if they had any left, and a look around.

Sitting at a table in the open courtyard of the Jacaranda, where he'd been frequently with Szabo, Werner tossed breadcrumbs into the stone pond in the center, watched goldfish flick orange tails, small ripples spread. The waiter appeared with a lager, apologizing for its warmth, wiped at his forehead with a white cloth, and said, "I am sorry to hear about your friend Maestro, such a nice man."

"You know the press," Werner said. "They exaggerate to make a story. Szabo's on holiday. He'll be back."

"Smart man, your friend," the waiter said. "He probably go to the mountains to get away from the heat, no?"

Werner nodded, sipped his tepid drink, and looked around at empty tables topped with crumpled napkins, drained glasses. It was nearly closing time.

"I hate to bother you," a voice said, accompanied by a small woman holding a half-empty glass, who slid into the chair opposite him, "but didn't I hear you mention the name Szabo?"

Werner looked into a heart-shaped face. The large round eyes were ringed like a raccoon's with heat-smudged mascara.

"Hi," she said, "I'm Mary Beth Peters from Boston, Mass. Glad to meet you."

"Rawlings," Werner said, raising himself slightly out of his seat to reach for her hand.

"Are you a friend of Tibor Szabo?"

"Yes," Werner said.

"Well, so am I. I met him backstage at Symphony Hall a few years ago. He was very charming, very friendly."

"Was he?" Werner asked, sitting up straighter, leaning forward.

"Very. We spent some time together. One night, to be exact." Werner opened his mouth to say something either protective or explanatory, but decided on neither. Mary Beth continued, "Listen, I have no regrets, it was great. I just wanted to tell you, since you're a friend and you must be concerned about him, not to worry."

7

"Why is that?"

"Because I know where he is," she said, grinned, and stirred her drink with a red plastic stick.

Werner grinned back, hoping to encourage her. Any information was better than none. "Where is he?" he asked.

"He's in the U.S.A."

"Any particular place? I mean, it is a rather large country."

Mary Beth chewed on the blunt end of her swizzle stick. "That one night, we talked a lot. I should say, *I* talked a lot. I suppose you could say I have that tendency. Anyhow, I asked him lots of questions, you know, like what's your favorite food, what's your favorite city, and I even asked him if he ever got fed up with playing the piano. He said yes, sometimes he got so tired and fed up he just wanted to go crawl in a hole like a bear and sleep forever. So I asked him where he would go, and he said he had a plan all worked out. He said a friend of his, a lady, some lawyer, had a cottage in Connecticut, somewhere up in the northwest corner. Anyhow, he said it was so beautiful, overlooking a lake, with oak trees, it reminded him of home, of Hungary. He said he had a key and he'd just go there and hibernate for a while."

"How interesting," Werner said, having thought of that vague possibility himself, having even placed a call to Estelle Stillman, Szabo's lawyer in New York.

"I've had the police look already," Estelle had said, "but there's nothing in Connecticut. Just writers and chipmunks."

Werner faked a yawn, and said he was tired, he had to be going. "I enjoyed chatting with you, Miss Peters."

"Please," she said, "call me Mary Beth." Werner stood up and slid money onto the table. "M.B., if you like," she added, raising her hand like a stop sign. But Werner vanished through the door, down Walton Street, breaking into a run at Beauchamp Place. There will be no escaping the Mary Beths who know where Tibor Szabo is, he thought, no avoiding the women with stories to tell, conclusions to draw, illusions to feed. And yet, as he hailed a taxi, he couldn't help being amused and repelled by the image of all Szabo's ladies, waiting by their respective telephones, thinking, It is me to whom he will turn in this, his hour of need.

"Liszt was a maniac," Tibor tells her, waits a second, remembering he said the same thing to someone else at some other time, but he cannot think when, where, or under what circumstances, time and place flowing together until the only time is the present, the only place is the one he is in, New York City, the only day is today, April 16, 1976. He pushes the button on his Seiko digital watch, purchased at the Tokyo airport transit lounge, and bright red numerals glow for a split second. In thirty minutes he will be onstage at Carnegie Hall, but his performance has already begun.

"You see," he says and pushes the score of the Liszt B-minor Sonata onto her lap, sits beside her on the couch, and points to the impossible crescendo.

"It looks so hard," Amanda says of the hieroglyphics on her lap. "I don't read music, but I see what you mean." She gazes intently at the page while Tibor admires her profile, soft features that curve one to the other, nothing angular or jarring, and a cascade of chestnut hair flowing down her slightly arched back.

"Relax," Tibor orders, as much to himself as to her.

Amanda tries to smile, closes the score, and says, "You're the one who should be nervous."

"Me?" Tibor laughs, standing up. "I'm anxious, yes, excited, but nervous? That is for the others."

Amanda reaches for her notebook to write it all down, but Tibor takes her hand, pulls her to her feet, and says softly, "I'd better get dressed. Will you wait for me?"

"Of course," she says, and he kisses her hand before disappearing into the bedroom of his suite at the Navarro Hotel on Central Park South. Amanda Blake looks at her watch and opens her purse to check her ticket. Eight-thirty p.m., it says.

It can't be eight-ten, she thinks, checking her watch again, putting it to her ear. What if he's late? Should I tell him what time it is? Is it my fault for insisting on this interview?

She paces around the room, admiring the white roses from Angel, the red ones from RCA, a basket of fruit from CBS, candies from the hotel management. She picks up her notebook and jots it all down for *Vogue*: "His favorite piano, sent over by Steinway. Scattered on it—music, his latest recording, publicity photographs, piles of unanswered letters, a book about chess, *What's Your Next Move?*"

Before the mirror of the antiseptically white bathroom Tibor brushes his hair, slicks it back with water, knowing it will defy the effort anyhow. "A pithed frog," he whispers at himself, thinking of the bottled specimens he saw as a child, lining the shelves of his mother's laboratory, lips thin and tightly drawn back, yellow eyes bulging, cold clammy skin. He squirms and wishes, momentarily, for the small sharp pin that stops the brain. He blinks at himself, sticks out his tongue, then yells, "Where the hell are my cuff links?"

Amanda rushes in to help him. His cuff links are found and twisted into place, and he lets her adjust his tie. Standing near him, watching him get ready, sensing the tautness of his thin but muscular body, the moist heat rising from him, she is terrified and excited, as if locked into an empty room with a stallion.

They arrive at Carnegie Hall just in time. Tibor bounds up the stage-door steps, unbuttons his coat, rubs his hands together, and smiles at his manager, Michael Klein, who opens the door, his face gray as the wall. "Why do you look so worried?" Tibor asks. "It's only eight twenty-five. Is there a concert tonight or something?"

"Hungarian gonif," Michael says, slapping Tibor on the back, laughing but wanting to kill him. Carnegie is sold out, stage seats included, and there is not exactly time for jokes.

"Tibor!" a woman dressed in silk calls. "Darling, my tickets. They were supposed to be at the box office, but they're not."

"Sid!" Tibor yells. "Where are you?"

The manager of the hall darts into his office like a hounded rabbit, tickets in hand. "Sid," Tibor calls after him, "take care of Mrs. Stillman, please," while a mob, insensitive to the possibility that Tibor might need a moment of quiet reflection before his solo recital, surges toward him shouting, "Tibor!" "Tibor!" "Mr. Szabo!" They know that in five minutes Szabo is scheduled to touch the piano keys and transform their evening, maybe even their lives, but without a ticket, it will all be missed.

"Larry!" Tibor calls to a tall usher in a blue uniform who guards the door to the backstage area. Larry reaches out a blue sleeve and pulls Tibor through the crowd. "Larry," Tibor whispers in his ear, "don't let anyone up to my room, just . . ." and he indicates Amanda, who struggles to reach his side.

"Michael!" Tibor calls over bobbing heads. "Michael!" A silver-haired man pushes through and is introduced to Amanda. "Michael, Amanda, Amanda, Michael. I want her in Box Twenty-five."

"I have a ticket," Amanda says, trying to be helpful, but Tibor ignores her and repeats his request.

Michael pleads with him. "But Sid just put Mrs. Stillman in the last seat in Box Twenty-five."

"Michael, fix it," Tibor insists, pushes Amanda in front of him, waves good-bye, blows a few kisses, and takes her up with him to his dressing room.

Michael follows, stops at the door to the stage, and peers out to see how the hall is filling up.

"Jammed," he mutters to himself. "Thirty thousand dollars' worth of tickets sold, it's eight-thirty, the public is waiting, and Szabo is upstairs with some chippie." He reaches into his pocket for the reassuring packet of Tums, calms himself down, and goes up to the Green Room, which is brown, opens the door to Tibor's dressing room, which is green, and asks Tibor if he needs anything. "Coffee, anything at all?" Then he discreetly leaves, letting Tibor do the farewell-I-play-for-you number he has over-heard so many times. Why do they fall for it? Michael wonders. But then again, he thinks, I'm not Szabo.

"Come here," Tibor says to Amanda, reaching out his hand to pull her onto the couch next to him. "I play for you," he whispers stagily. He smiles. He means it every time he says it, even though he says it often. He knows that she will feel no small rush of emotion at the thought that he will play for her, only her, above anyone else in that enormous adoring crowd. He feels no small rush himself, but not in the heart. It is in the stomach, pressing, grinding, churning.

Amanda leaves the room just in time for Tibor to reach the toilet and empty the contents of his stomach neatly into the bowl. He flushes. Leaning over the sink he turns on the faucet, feels the cool metal of the tap against his teeth, and groans, more for effect than from need, then pops a mint into his mouth.

Someone knocks at the door. "Coming!" Tibor yells.

"We're ready," an official voice calls back.

"Give me two minutes," Tibor says and ignores the protest. He emerges from the bathroom and eyes the upright piano in the corner of the room. There is no time to touch it. Besides, it would be bad luck. He walks back and forth, smooths his hair, takes a deep breath, checks his fly. He cracks his knuckles, flexes the cold fingers, blows on them, then looks out of the small hidden window overlooking the stage below. Faces, a sea of faces, float around that big black ship of a piano. People are taking off coats, looking at programs, greeting each other, getting settled. A couple seems to be arguing about seats. The woman reaches into her handbag, drops it, and as the contents scatter under seats and bodies bend down to help with the collection, Tibor quietly sings the opening passage of the Chopin Ballade. He watches lipsticks and keys being dropped back into the lady's leather bag, and when she snaps it shut, he turns and stares for a few seconds at the closed door, the final barrier between himself and that stage, that treacherous territory he has tracked so many times before. Each time the terrain is different, each time is the first time, but he is an expeditionary, accustomed to risks, ready for anything. A delicious dread flows through him, his nostrils widen, he inhales deeply, presses his left shoulder to the door, turning the knob with his right hand, and takes the stairs down to the stage two at a time.

In Box Twenty-five Amanda admires the hall, wedding-cake tiers decorated ornately in white and gold leaf, lush wine-colored velvet. The atmosphere is palpable with excitement. Michael sits beside her checking his watch and his antacids just as Tibor races onstage like a thoroughbred through the starting gate. He is a favorite. The audience thunders applause. Pleased with themselves to be here, his fans know this concert will be a winner. Tibor makes that promise with his first bow, his left hand lightly touching the edge of the keyboard with complete assurance as he bends forward to acknowledge their cheers.

Steady, he tells himself, clutching at the slippery black

wood for support as he bows, taking a deep breath with his head down as far as possible, trying to force some air into his constricted lungs. He is underwater, drowning, the pressure unbearable. His lungs might collapse any second.

Tibor's head rears back at the end of the bow and his black mane shivers. He sits down quickly and sounds the first octaves even before the clapping stops. Some call that arrogance. Most call it magic. He calls it survival.

MEET THE ARTIST

Tibor Szabo was born in Budapest in 1943 and began his piano studies at an early age. During the Hungarian Revolution of 1956 he and his older sister fled to Vienna. He then lived in Paris in the household of the late pianist Stephan Vlostid, with whom he continued his studies. In 1961 he won first prize at the Concours International de Piano in Paris and later that year made his debut with the London Symphony Orchestra playing the Brahms D-minor Concerto, Sir Malcolm Sargent conducting. "A phenomenon," the London *Times* reported of that debut, "a Titan. Here is Herculean pianism tempered with the poetry of an Orpheus." His debut in the United States in 1962 is legendary. Last season Mr. Szabo gave more than 100 concerts in sixteen countries. He is a favorite at the major international festivals and is one of the most widely recorded artists of our time. Now a British subject, he lives in London during the brief periods when he is not on tour.

Friday, April 16, 1976, at 8:30

TIBOR SZABO

Piano

CHOPIN   Ballade No. 2 in F major, Op. 38

SCHUMANN   Fantasy in C major, Op. 17
Allegro fantastic e con passione
Moderato, ma energico
Andante sostenuto e mezza voce sempre

Intermission

LISZT   Sonata in B minor
Lento assai—Allegro energico
—Grandioso—Andante sostenuto
—Allegro energico

Exclusive management: Michael Klein, Inc.

Steinway Piano

Mr. Szabo records for EMI, CBS, DGG, and RCA RECORDS

NOTES ON
THE PROGRAM

Chopin's Ballade No. 2 is dedicated to Robert
Schumann; Schumann's Fantasy Opus 17 is dedicated to Franz Liszt; and Liszt's Sonata in B minor to
Schumann. Judging from the mutuality of these
dedications it would seem that a warm confraternity
existed among the major composers of the high
Romantic era. It was, in fact, in the spirit of the time
for ideas and homages to be exchanged. Chopin's
four ballades for piano, written in the 1830s, are
thought to be inspired by the romantic Polish poets,
particularly Mickiewicz, who, like Chopin, lived in
exile in France after the failed Polish revolt of 1830
against Russian domination. It has been said that
"Switez," by Mickiewicz, a poem about a town
being engulfed by an enchanted lake (perhaps a
metaphor for the loss of Poland's national identity),
is the literary inspiration for **Chopin's Ballade No. 2
in F major.** A·; a musical illustration, the opening
passage describes the mood set in the drama: "If at
nightfall you approach the lake and turn your gaze
upon its waters, you will behold stars above and
stars below with twin moons. . . . You will be
suspended in an abyss of blue. But he must be a

bold man who will go to the lake when it is dark. What a devil's dance does Satan lead there!"

Chopin breaks the calm tranquil mood with violent and frantic figurations. Dramatic tensions are built with a plastic handling of motifs and figurations, until the conclusion is reached, and the music, like the town, is swallowed up, left (in A minor) desolate, silent.

Despite Schumann's dedication to Liszt and his intention to contribute the proceeds of the Fantasy's publication toward the creation of a monument to Beethoven in Bonn, it was really Clara Wieck who inspired the piano masterpiece that is **Schumann's Fantasy in C Major, Opus 17.** "It is a deep lament for you," Schumann wrote to Clara, whom he had been forced to give up in the summer of 1836. "I have never written anything more impassioned than the first movement." Although filled with despair, the Allegro is mixed with peaceful introspection, fading at moments into silence. The opening theme, like a sustained cry, is given impetus by turbulent motion in the left hand, until a second theme ascends hopefully through the dramatic and lyric extensions of the first. The movement ends in a mood of resignation and with a quotation from the final song in Beethoven's cycle *To the Distant Beloved.* The Moderato is bold and heroic, rich in harmony and nearly manic in intensity. It is in the third movement where a quiet resolution is achieved, evoking the profundity of the Adagio of Beethoven's *Emperor* Concerto, and echoing the motto from Schlegel with which the Fantasy was published: "Through all the tones that sound in earth's fitful dream, one gentle note is there for the secret listener."

Liszt never performed Schumann's Fantasy in public, and nowhere in Schumann's voluminous writings on music is there a reference to **Liszt's Sonata in B minor.** Schumann did not welcome Liszt's dedication to him, since the great esteem both men felt for one another's work when they first met had not survived long.

Liszt was concerned with what he called "the mysterious language of tone," which he felt could project a state of soul. His Sonata in B minor has in fact been called the forerunner of the symphonic tone poem. The work is in one fluid movement, with eloquent recitativelike sections, angular fugal themes, gentle lyrical melodies. It is a carefully constructed work, with five thematic elements controlled and manipulated, interchanged and, ultimately, transformed. The work's range of expression is great, with portentous descending progressions, restless and nervous dotted rhythms, and lyrical motifs which, in the coda, converge into a meltingly poignant utterance.

GIDEON SCHREIBER

"Riveting presence," Amanda scribbles on her program. "There is an aura around him. Face transfigured, almost beautiful. Hands sweep across the keyboard, now gentle, now brutal, fast as hummingbirds. Head drops back, mouth moves slightly. Is he singing or moaning? His eyes close. He possesses the piano, controls it, knows when to tighten the reins, when to pull back. He is master, totally assured. . . ."

Fucking piano, Tibor thinks. Should have chosen the other one, this is a tub, a hulk, can't get a decent sound. . . . Thoughts sink, and he is resuscitated by the feel of the keys, the solid bench beneath him. He breathes again, easier, the Ballade spins out from his hands, and he concentrates, sustaining sound, floating. Wild broken chords after the lilt of the opening Andantino rage from his arms like thunder. He can do it all, it is easy now, he is Szabo. Until he is actually there, onstage at the piano, Szabo is someone else, someone he reads about, whom people speak about, until the moment itself, and he is able to find himself by losing himself in the music.

He finishes the Chopin, feels good, smiles, and takes three bows. Waiting in the wings for latecomers to be seated, he peeks out through the small window of the door to the stage.

Maybe the piano isn't center stage, he thinks, wondering if it has been moved since his morning rehearsal, when it was set to his exact specifications for optimal sound.

"Hey, Bob," he calls to the stagehand, "did you move the piano?"

Bob throws his arms in the air. "Me, Maestro, would I do that to you? It's set just like it was this morning."

"OK, cool," Tibor says, looking back out the window and squinting up toward Box Twenty-five. A woman with long hair leans forward in her seat in the front row, probably Amanda, and if not, it is still a good omen. He checks his fly, smooths his hair, takes a sip of water from the glass offered him by Sid, wipes his hands on his trousers, and storms back onto the stage for the Schumann, ready for battle, sure of his ground.

As if for royalty, he bows elegantly toward Box Twenty-five, listens to the applause, and lets it echo. He takes time to adjust the piano bench, he fiddles with a cuff link, he bows his head and takes a deep breath, exhales and begins. The Fantasy is a piece he knows with every inch of his body, he feels it inside himself as an entity, and while he plays, that intimacy is evident to everyone, even those who are in the hall just for the event of a Szabo recital, even those who cannot possibly understand it. As the first movement progresses, concentration and intensity increase, the audience draws close like moths to a flame. Tibor is aware of this in the corner of his mind, feels the public hover near, but he is never interrupted, his concentration never breaks. He sweeps through the second movement with momentum, unerringly spans the terrifying skips at its end, and in the third movement slows to grandeur, and a final statement that is fervent yet majestic. Applause startles him. He stands up, automatically bows, and heads for the door.

"Bravo!" a man standing up onstage yells as he passes. Tibor looks at him, surprised by the effusively clapping hands and the man's cheeks splotched with excitement.

"It was OK," he thinks, emerging, waking up, "but it wasn't that good," and he walks on and off stage, bowing, smiling, and finally exiting up the stairs to his dressing room for the twenty minutes of intermission.

An elderly man stands at the door to Tibor's dressing room. He leans on a cane, shakes his head from side to side.

"Jancsi!" Tibor holds out his arms, embraces the frail man, pats him gingerly on the back.

"How are you, are you OK?"

"Me? After the Schumann how could I be bad?" Janos Hartog squeezes Tibor's arms, pats his face, and steps back to look at him.

"You really thought it was OK?" Tibor asks, knowing it was but wanting to hear it from Janos, a friend from Hungary, a violinist.

"OK it was not. Incredible it was. Fire was coming out of the piano!"

Tibor claps Janos on the shoulder and notices he is looking tired, his eyes are watery, his skin waxen. Not the Janos he used to play Beethoven sonatas with in the living room of the apartment in Budapest, with smells of applecake coming from the kitchen and his father's pipe smoke curling into shapes above the sofa. Janos apologizes for coming at intermission. "But such a crowd after, for an old man, it is too much. Forgive me."

Tibor kisses him on both cheeks. "I'll call you," he says. "We'll play chess."

"Sure, call me," Janos says, winking. "I'll beat the pants off you."

Tibor knows he will not call, intends to, wants to, knows he should, but there is never time, not now, not anymore.

Amanda appears at the door, flushed, wondering if she really should have come backstage at intermission even though Tibor told her to. She smiles at him, hoping she can find something to say that will not sound trite. Tibor looks at her expectantly.

"It was extraordinary," she says, and spans the abysmal distance between feeling and words with a kiss on his wet cheek. He tastes of salt.

"Bravo, boychick!" Michael says, entering the room. He leans back impresarially and beams at his artist as Tibor unbuttons the first few gold studs of his shirt. The front of it is drenched and his throat gleams with sweat.

"You'll catch a cold schvitzing like that. Bring a shirt so you can change at intermission. Bring two," Michael suggests.

"What are you worried about? I'll get sick? You'll lose your twenty percent?"

Michael pretends to swat Tibor with the back of his hand. The kid can say what he wants, do what he wants. When you can play like that, you've got license. Michael pulls down the vest of his black pinstripe suit, checks his watch, and announces, "Five minutes."

"Before what?"

Michael chuckles and intercepts visitors at the door, herds them back into the Green Room, whispering, "I think he needs a few minutes alone."

Tibor cracks his knuckles. Liszt creeps into his thoughts snatching at his calm mood.

"Shall I leave?" Amanda asks.

"No," Tibor says, emphatic if distracted, and he reaches for the anchor of her hand. "I want you to be with me, now, and later."

Careful, Amanda warns herself, and eases away from him with comments about the program. "I never realized all those composers were such good friends, that they actually wrote for one another. I'm not sure that kind of exchange exists anymore. It must have been quite wonderful, don't you think?"

Tibor presses her hand to his lips and looks at her intently. His brown eyes, speckled with gold and rust, make her think of a kaleidoscope pointed at autumn leaves. A tilt of the head and the color changes, now amber and brown flecks, now orange and gray. It makes her dizzy.

"I think it's clever programming," she says, trying to steady herself.

"The idea wasn't mine," Tibor says, biting playfully at one of her fingers, making her blush. "It was Werner

24

Rawlings's idea. He's a friend of mine. He points out all that garbage to me, and I heap it together. I don't know if it works."

"It does. I think so anyhow."

"I'm glad." Tibor kisses her, his tongue darting between the even rows of her teeth, puncturing her caution, sinking her resolve, pushing her from the gentle waves of flirtation into the swift current beneath.

He is tentative at the beginning of the Sonata. The mood of the opening eludes him, and he takes the Allegro energico too fast. He is agitated and cannot concentrate. He struggles. His left foot juts out, he cannot control his movements, he is frantic, his head is detached from his body. The audience is mesmerized by his obvious struggle. He is exposed, like a shelled crab.

"Go on, go on." Tibor prods himself into the Grandioso and holds on to the recitativo passages like an exhausted swimmer to the sides of the rescue boat. A second wind, he goes on, it's all right, getting better, he is strong again, he feels himself sucked down into the whirlpool of the presto section, but he knows how to handle it, to dive to the bottom, rise to the top, and then float into the coda, taking the public with him.

After the last single quiet low B, the audience rumbles like an earthquake just starting, then rises to its feet, roaring now in full force. Tibor hesitates, beached, gasping for air. He puts one hand on the upper lip of the keyboard's lid and lowers his head. He stands and with blurred eyes and a ringing in his head acknowledges the cheers, smiles, and finally bows. A woman rises from a stage seat and reaches out one red rose to Tibor. He takes it, bends to kiss her hand, bows, and the audience screams.

Tibor smiles, glides through encores—the glitter of Liszt's "Feux follets," the drama of the Agitatissimo from

Schumann's *Kreisleriana*, the dolor of Chopin's Mazurka opus 63, no. 2, in F minor.

After the lights in the hall go up, the first bear hugs, the first backstage kisses swarm into the Green Room. "Congratulations!" "Brilliant!" "Bravo, Tibor!" The line of well-wishers twines around the staircase and out to the lobby. Voices buzz, elbows and shoulders move and squirm; the friends, the flesh-pressers, the admirers, the truly moved, the truly moving want to touch him.

Record jackets are presented for his signature, flash-bulbs pop. A concert manager from Holland congratulates him and presents him with his card, a Belgian journalist asks for an interview, a brief one, just a few minutes, and a woman in a fox jacket kisses him on both cheeks, sighing, "You gave me such pleasure, such pleasure."

A serious young man presses Tibor's hand and says, "Harold Waldbaum. I wrote to you, Mr. Szabo, do you remember? I wonder if it would be possible to play for you?"

"I would like to hear you," Tibor says, "but I am leaving in the morning."

As the boy tries to smile Tibor says, "Well, maybe next time I'm in New York. . . ."

"When will that be?" the boy asks. But throats clear, people in line press forward, impatient for their turns, other hands reach out for Szabo before he can answer.

"Bravo, thanks, bravo, thanks, bravo, thank you." Amanda listens to the chant of inadequate words while waiting patiently in the hot, smoky room. She looks at a wall hanging of deer leaping across an open field and listens to Michael Klein talk to Johnston T. Midford, record producer from CBS.

"Look, John, he is counting on those six days for a holiday. He's going to the Canaries."

"I know. And we've found a church there, an old Spanish gem not far from Las Palmas with great acoustics.

26

We can fly down some portable equipment, and Tibor can record, just for one morning. All the rest of the time would be free."

"Good of you."

"I know he loves to work. He might like the idea. Ask him."

"He needs a rest. I won't ask him."

"He owes us those sessions. You might remind him."

"You'll get your sessions, but not in the Canaries."

Both men stand back, horns unlocked, the battle to continue by telephone. When the crowd thins out, Tibor takes Amanda into his dressing room, sits beside her on the couch, and leans back, with both arms draped over the back. He closes his eyes. He is tall and sturdy, but seated now he appears small, boyish, makes her want to stroke his forehead, brush back the lock of hair that always falls in his eyes, despite his habit of flicking it back with a twist of his neck. She watches beads of sweat collect on his forehead, gather above thick, dark eyebrows. His long lashes flicker, and his oval eyes, turned down slightly at the corners, make him look tired, or decadent, or maybe both. A rose color suffuses the hollows under high cheekbones, and his sharp straight nose points to dry feverish lips. Amanda imagines pressing a wet cloth to his face, feeling warm features move beneath her hands.

Keeping his eyes shut, Tibor allows himself a few thoughts about his performance. It was OK, not terrific, just OK, although the Schumann had moments, no, one moment, to be exact. The rest was shit. Never mind. It's over, done. He sits up quickly, apologizes for keeping Amanda waiting, and asks her if she is tired.

"Me? Oh no, not at all, but you must be exhausted."

"As a matter of fact," Tibor says, moving closer, "I've never felt less tired."

"You're amazing."

"Why is that?"

"Do you really need me to tell you?"

"Yes."

"Well, first of all, you just played a recital at Carnegie Hall, a long and arduous program."

"Did I?" Tibor teases, kissing her on the temple, brushing her cheek with his lips.

"And," she continues, smiling, "you greeted your public graciously."

"Did I?" he asks, sliding one hand behind her waist and up along her back.

"And yet," she says, "you still seem to have a great deal of energy left."

"Oh yes," Tibor agrees, pressing against her, "energy, great energy."

Standing at the top of the stage-door steps, a camel's-hair coat draped over his shoulders like a cape, his body leaning forward, he waves and smiles and signs autographs before sliding with Amanda into the shiny black Cadillac limousine for the trip to the inevitable reception.

"If I say something," Amanda begins somewhat tentatively, as they turn up Park Avenue, "about your performance, will you laugh at me?"

"Possibly. But don't be offended. I'm Hungarian."

"OK, then. I felt one thing when you played, I had one thought beyond the music."

"What was it?"

"I felt glad to be alive."

Tibor laughs. He can't help it. "Sorry," he says stroking her arm. "I *am* glad you liked it, really." There is no point telling her that he played like a pig, that he felt miserable in the Liszt, that only the Schumann, and only one moment of it, was up to his own standard. No, if she is glad to be alive, who is he to spoil it for her?

"He's ruined everything," Michael Klein mumbled to himself as he walked the five blocks between his office on West Fifty-seventh Street and CBS Records on West Fifty-second, the July heat buzzing around his ears like a fat lazy fly. He calculated his possible losses. Two Szabo tours next season, six weeks each, average gross each visit two hundred grand, his take, twenty percent. He could be out eighty thousand dollars if Szabo was gone for good. He passed Sam Goody's record store and saw a CBS display in the window. "SZABO!" it said in large silver letters, next to a huge color photo of Tibor in an overcoat, collar up, mist in the background, his dark eyes piercing through the plate-glass window, staring right at him.

So where the hell are you? Michael thought and realized he'd gone two blocks too far. He kicked at a crumpled soda can, walked back to Fifty-second Street, and whirled through the revolving door at CBS, cold air splashing his face. He signed in, took a pink visitor's card, handed it to a guard, and punched at the elevator button. Johnston T. Midford was in his office on the eleventh floor, on the phone. Trim in a white linen suit, red tie knotted like a large jewel, he was calm and contained, his chiseled features cool as marble. He motioned for Michael to come in, put his hand over the receiver, and said, "It's the *Daily News*. They want to know where to find Szabo."

"Tell them to look in Carnegie Hall," Michael growled. He pulled a Kleenex from a tortoiseshell box and wiped at his face. Circles rippled out from the small black stones of his eyes, and his cheeks were puffed. One more sleepless night and I'll collapse, he thought, and tugged at his seersucker vest, then blew his nose. Flattened by Vinnie Gianinno's fist when they were kids in the Bronx, it made him look like a fighter, a tough—hardly like the best impresario since Sol Hurok. But Michael Klein understood and loved music, knew what was good, and his list of artists was small but prestigious. Without Szabo, he thought, the emphasis will be on small. He sniffed, and listened to Midford assure the press they would be notified the minute news was available, and gracefully say good-bye.

"Michael," John said like doctor to patient, "you'll have to simmer down, handle this with care. Did you see the *Times?*" he asked, and handed it to him.

"Front page?" Michael groaned, crumpled the paper into a wad, pulled it open again, staring at it in disbelief. "Will you look at this goddam big headline? PIANIST DISAPPEARS. Why the hell didn't they give him front page when he played at Carnegie Hall—PIANIST PLAYS?"

"Read it," John ordered.

Michael skimmed through. "Tibor Szabo, widely considered to be the greatest pianist of his generation . . . at the peak of his artistry . . . Werner Rawlings, the novelist, who saw him just before his disappearance, said that Szabo was 'extremely agitated' . . . fear a suicide attempt."

"Suicide?" Michael whispered, looking back up at John. "He wouldn't dare."

"You and I have no control over it, I'm afraid. But I'll tell you this, Szabo never struck me as a depressive."

"He wasn't," Michael said, wiping at his forehead. "He was on top of the world, he was—"

"Why are you using the past tense?"

"Christ," Michael said, "you're making me nervous. I'm sure the kid is OK. Scotland Yard just called my office. They've checked immigration at Heathrow, and he didn't leave London yesterday or today."

"Since when does he have to leave England in order to blow his brains out? Besides, he can drive a car, can't he? What could have been bothering him, anyhow? Was he in some kind of trouble? East-West spy stuff, anything like that?"

"Don't be crazy. Of course not. No. It has to be something personal."

"And serious. Was there a woman?"

"There were hundreds. I never saw him with the same one twice."

"That doesn't mean there isn't one special lady in his life. Call Estelle Stillman. She's a close friend, after all, and his lawyer."

"I've talked to her. There's no one, and believe me, she'd know. She had a call from his friend Rawlings in London. He has another cockamamie idea—some Hungarian gypsy fiddler who thinks he may have gone to Budapest. They're checking it out. It doesn't look hopeful. I've called his general manager in London, his local managers all over Europe. No one has heard a thing, no one has a clue and it's been days."

John rubbed at his head. "Strange, isn't it, how you can work with an artist, listen to him pour his guts out in sound, and never know him at all."

"Well, it's an impossible relationship. I mean, the artist is the whale and we are little fish, latched on for a ride."

"You might feel like a parasite, Michael, but I certainly don't. Without managers and recording companies where would pianists like Szabo be?"

"Playing pianos. Don't kid yourself, we're expendable. What's nice, though, is when there's an artist who's a friend, I mean a real friend. Remember when Becky died? Tibor was in Helsinki, and two days later he had to play in Milan, so what did he do? He flew all night to come to the funeral. 'You hardly knew her,' I said when he walked into Campbell's. 'She was your wife,' he said, and kissed me and even insisted on driving out to the cemetery in Jersey and damn near missed his flight to Milan. Szabo. There's a mensch."

"It's true. He's admired and well liked."

"Liked?" Michael asked quietly. "I love the kid."

"And the money," John added.

"You make me sick," Michael hissed, as much at himself as at John. "It's disgusting, this business. Since Hurok died, no one cares about the artist anymore. It's only business, packaging, selling. Hurok would have cried."

"We all know Hurok was a great impresario, devoted to his artists, but you're forgetting one thing about the old man. He wouldn't have cried. He would have gone out and found Szabo by now." The intercom on John's desk buzzed. "Who is it?" he asked.

His secretary's voice answered from a small box, "Amanda Blake. A writer from *Vogue*. She says she was with Szabo in April."

John looked at Michael and picked up the phone. "Midford here."

"I'm terribly sorry to bother you, Mr. Midford, I just can't help being concerned and wondered if you might have some—"

"Miss Blake," he interrupted, then rubbed at his bald head as if polishing a rough reply, the muscles in his cheeks rippling. "We're working on it," he said in a controlled voice. "We're all concerned, but we know there is no cause for alarm."

Alone in her apartment, Szabo's recording of Chopin nocturnes playing softly in the background, Amanda hung up, flushed with embarrassment. It was obvious that she should not have called, but when she read the newspaper she had been overcome with worry. Szabo had absorbed her thoughts, her constant fantasies since their night together in April—one night, but a night that still seemed so vivid she could close her eyes and take herself right back to the concert, the party, the hotel room. She remembered details, sounds, colors, even the toilet seat in the master bedroom of the Stillmans' apartment, with specks of gold, little black poodles, and in ornate script the words "Oui, Oui, Madame." The Stillmans' collection of Corot sketches, Courbet landscapes, Picasso lithographs, great-master drawings, etchings, and oils stops at the door to the master bedroom. There, poodles take over, poodles in varied poses on the wallpaper, poodles in porcelain on a white and gold dresser, poodles in glass, a proliferation of poodles, leading Amanda to the bathroom to wash her hands under faucets of golden poodle heads with pink poodle soap. She combs her hair and looks at herself in the mirror. The thought occurs to her to bark. She smiles as she observes the familiar pretty face in the mirror, the face Arnold calls cute, the face Tibor described to her as "exquisite, fine-boned, and totally aristocratic." She dabs some rouge on her cheeks and walks regally back into the dining room.

"This one is Mimi, this one Fifi, and this one is Rubinstein," Estelle Stillman is saying, pointing to her three living poodles.

"And why is that one Rubinstein?" someone asks.

"Because he's the pee-anist!"

Tibor laughs the loudest. He loves these parties, good food, good wine, talk, any kind of talk after a concert. He needs to wind down, to be surrounded by people who love him. And he is loved.

"Ah, here she is," Ben Stillman says, catching sight of

Amanda. All eyes scan her as she enters, willowy in a green dress and flowing hair. Estelle takes her in like a speedreader—Tibor's type, not an original, not a rival.

"Are you a musician?" Ben asks.

"No, a journalist."

"In fact," Tibor announces, "she's writing an article about me, a profile for *Vogue*." He pounds his chest and turns sideways. "Which should I give her?" he asks, "right or left?"

"How nice," Estelle says to Amanda over the laughter, "to be able to get close to your subject." Estelle rings for the butler, sips her wine, and folds her arms across a mocha silk dress. Her short brown hair is carefully brushed back, dramatically streaked with gold, and twined around her long sun-browned neck is a strand of small pearls, a treasured gift from Tibor. He was nineteen when he presented it to her, she, thirty-two. She and Ben were so enchanted by his legendary debut in New York that they had invited him to their house in Bermuda for a few weeks. Ben had been unexpectedly called back to New York on business. What happened was legendary, too, for Estelle. From time to time, when there is no Amanda around, and if Tibor feels like it, they replay their Bermuda passion. What has remained constant is that Estelle is still his lawyer, "the best and most beautiful," as Tibor assures her.

"How long have you and Ben known Szabo?" Amanda asks her over the blanquette de veau.

"Since his New York debut in 1962."

"Was it really as special as they say?"

"Absolutely. He came out onstage, this tall, gangly boy with shocks of jet-black hair and such eyes, such expressive eyes. He played the Rachmaninoff Third, and from the first note the audience knew he was something incredible. When it comes to the truly great, the public is discerning even if they can't understand it. They sensed it, they knew Szabo was great. They rose up like a giant tidal wave when he finished."

"They still do, but what about Szabo, has he changed, has his playing changed?"

Estelle plays with some spilled salt next to her plate and smiles at Amanda, then gazes across the table at their common interest, who is engrossed in another conversation.

"Yes, his playing has changed. After all, he's nearly thirty-three, he's a mature artist."

"I've heard that a lot of child prodigies do not mature very easily, but Tibor seems different."

"He is. He is lucky and smart and has good instincts." Estelle raises her glass to clink Amanda's, smiles like a cat soaking up sun, and then goes on. "So many prodigies fall apart in their mid-twenties, too much fame too soon, too little perspective. The attrition rate is appalling. Go into any manager's office and look at brochures from ten, fifteen years ago. You'll find names of pianists, the young genius from France, the wizard from Belgrade, names you've never heard of. But Szabo had the strength and depth to survive, just as he survived his escape from Hungary in fifty-six. Has he told you about it?"

"No. He doesn't seem to want to talk about it and I haven't pressed him."

"I'll tell you what I know, which isn't much. He and his sister went alone together at night in November of 1956 through the swamps into Andau, and were then placed in a Red Cross camp in Vienna to wait for news of their parents. Their father had been killed and their mother chose to stay in Budapest. Tibor was apparently in a state of shock, so severe he couldn't talk. He had dysentery and was very weak, and it was Stephan Vlostid who rescued him, so the story goes, took him to Paris, healed him, became another father to him, a teacher, a mentor."

After a moment of silence Amanda looks at Estelle and says, "Quite a story."

"Isn't it?"

"It explains a lot."

"It explains nothing. Szabo would be Szabo with or without a revolution, with or without a mother, a father."

"How can you know?"

"Because I believe we are born with innate character. Yes, environment can alter it slightly, but we are what we are, and Szabo has a very strong, a very natural spirit which can never be defeated."

"What do you think it is, Estelle? May I call you Estelle?"

"Of course," Estelle says, rather pleased that she is impressive enough to make Amanda ask.

"What do you think it is that drives him, that keeps him going at such a pace and such a level?"

"I don't know, I don't even think he knows. The music, of course, his commitment to it, devotion."

"Is he devoted to anything else?"

"You mean people, of course, family, women?" Estelle asks, sensing that Amanda's interest is not purely journalistic. She traces her left eyebrow with her right index finger and decides how to put it. "I would say that he has his devotions, but they tend to change. It's really music that seems to matter to him, the music itself."

Across the table Tibor tells a story and nearly knocks over a candle with a wave of his left hand. Estelle's voice rises above the exclamations of alarm. "Careful," she says, "you can't play the piano with burned fingers."

"I'll do something else then," Tibor says, his eyes meeting hers with the steady gaze of an old sparring partner.

"Like what?"

"I'll be a masseur. Don't laugh! That is a real profession, a useful profession. You relieve people from tension, you give them pleasure, you make them feel good—"

36

"And," Estelle interrupts, "you keep in constant touch with them."

Tibor raises his glass and stands up. "A toast, to our lovely hostess, whose wit and gracious hospitality are exceeded only by her beauty."

"Hear, hear." Estelle leans across the table toward her guest of honor, who jauntily kisses her on the cheek.

"And here's to you," Ben says, rising slowly to his feet, "Tibor, for giving us a memorable performance and for giving us your friendship!" Ben pours more wine. He is rich, a successful man, but mild, kind, and understanding.

"The secret of our marriage," Estelle confides to Amanda, "is the freedom Ben gives me."

The party ends sometime past midnight when suppressed yawns and nagging reminders that tomorrow-you-have-to-get-up-early finally mobilize people to put on coats and say good-bye.

At the hotel Amanda wonders, for a moment, a very brief moment, if it is really wise to go upstairs with Tibor to, as he says, touching her gently on the arm, "continue the interview."

"It has been a glorious evening," she says.

"Ah, and you are tired," Tibor says, his eyes compelling, his hand moving up to stroke her cheek.

She has been with Szabo for two days, notebook in hand, she has more than enough material as it is, and Arnold is waiting for her at his apartment. Gallant and charming throughout, Tibor has been surprisingly interesting, amazingly articulate, and of course, flirtatious. Of course. She recognizes it, his need, his hunger to provoke, to arouse, to prove himself. It's been a very pleasant flattery, this two-day badinage, but now she should go home with her notebook, she knows it.

"Those eyes, those beautiful tired eyes. Let me kiss them, let me kiss you," Tibor urges, his voice deepening, his accent appealing. It is international, she can identify it as a total mix, but the rhythm of the speech is Hungarian, agogic, heavy on the downbeat. "When *I* am *on* the *stage*," he will say, "*here* is *where* I am *com*fortable. *This* is *where* I feel *now* I am *a*live."

She feels very much alive herself, *now*, here on this curb, this man asking her to his room. She enters the revolving door held still for her by Tibor, who follows, his hand pressing firmly against the glass. He stops at the desk, collects his key and messages, and reads them as they go up in the elevator.

He opens the door to his suite, drops his coat on a chair, and puts his arms around her, smells her sweet hair, her delicate perfume. Amanda pulls away and says, "Please don't. Tibor, I'm very drawn to you, but my life is complicated and—"

Tibor holds her hands and looks into her eyes. "You are so lovely," he says, "and I could grow very fond of you."

I doubt it, Amanda thinks, but says nothing. The kaleidoscope of his eyes tilts again, colors change, and she feels a sudden urge to stroke his hair.

"I understand, my darling, I do," he tells her, kisses the palms of her hands, asks her if she'd like to sit down, if she wants coffee, if she wants to ask him any more questions.

"You must be tired of questions."

"No, not really, I just haven't any answers." Tibor removes his tie, opens his shirt collar, rolls up his sleeves, sits down opposite her. Amanda notes the smooth skin of his neck and the veins on his forearms, raised slightly, blue trails she longs to follow. But she is there for a purpose. She will ask him questions.

"I think," she begins, "that one of the exceptional qualities of your playing is courage. You're not afraid to try things, you take risks, you camouflage nothing. Yet when I talk with you, you are guarded, cautious. Can you reconcile these two sides of yourself?"

Tibor smiles, rubs his chin, cracks his knuckles. "Illusion," he says, clears his throat and sits up straighter. "Illusion plays such a large part in music. You might hear my playing as courageous, risk-taking. Someone else might hear those very same qualities and say, 'How sloppy he is, how without style.' You are entitled to your opinions, of course, also to your opinion that I am guarded and cautious as a person. I would rather things were reversed, that you heard my playing as cautious and saw me as courageous."

"I didn't mean to—"

"I know, I know. You don't mean to insult, only to provoke."

"I mean neither. I'm just stating an observation."

"What a good journalist, objective, observant. But you've picked a dull subject, Amanda. I'm only a musician, only a vessel through which music flows. Once the music is heard, it evaporates. True, the musician sets it in motion, he spins it out from dots and lines on a printed page until it takes flight. But then it disappears, and what is the musician left with? Nothing."

"Are you serious?"

"Of course. It's a macabre business, really, playing music. I resurrect dead notes, give them momentary life, and they sink back into silence. It smacks of necrophilia, don't you think?"

Amanda chews on her pen. "I can't tell if you're serious," she says.

"Dead serious. For the moment anyhow."

"Is it the moment that counts for you?"

"Yes. Yes and no."

"You are such a bundle of contradictions."

"Aren't we all?" His chatoyant eyes darken, change to black opals, flecked with light.

"Look," he says, "it's getting late, I've got to pack, and I think our interview is about over anyhow, don't you?"

"I don't know. I think it's just getting interesting. I'm sorry if I offended you."

"You offended me? Of course not." He stands up, runs his fingers through his hair. "It's just that I can't understand who would want to read about a pianist. What is it that's of interest? We practice, we play, we practice, we play."

"Your playing is interesting, your life is interesting, your escape from Hungary—"

"You're not printing any of that crap, are you? Oh, come on, Amanda, lots of people left Hungary in 1956—what's the big deal? I just happened to get away carrying my little gift with me. I didn't ask for that gift, you know. As far as I'm concerned it's excess baggage."

"But surely you must be grateful to have all that talent."

"Gratitude is one thing—of course I'm grateful, it allows me to make music, one of the few redeeming human expressions left in this godforsaken world."

"You make it sound as if your playing has nothing to do with you. Where do you see yourself in all of this?"

"I see myself as someone who plays the piano because that's all he is trained to do, someone who loves music, someone who has a heavy schedule, someone who doesn't want to answer any more questions." He turns away, whirls back, hands clasped. "Amanda," he says, as if in prayer, "I'm tired. I'm sorry."

"Please don't apologize," she says, closing her notebook, "I do understand."

"Do you?"

He looks sad, like a little boy, lost, tired, his eyes are glassy. Amanda wants to kiss his forehead, give him milk and cookies, sing to him.

"Of course I understand," she says, getting up, straightening a rose-covered pillow. "I'll send you the article before we print it. You can delete anything you like."

"Thanks," he says, looking small and shy.

"Good-bye, then, and thank you for everything."

He gets up and walks toward her. He puts his arms around her, draws her face up to his, and begins to kiss her, first her eyes, then nose; he lingers at her upper lip.

"I really have to go," Amanda says.

"I know," Tibor whispers. "We both have too much work to do, and our lives are much too complicated."

"Yes," she says, feeling his hand press against the small of her back, sending tremors through her. "I—"

"Shh," he tells her, "shh, don't say any more, don't think about anything, nothing, ne pense à rien, rien. . . ."

He picks her up, carries her into the bedroom, and puts her gently down on the bed. She feels as if she's underwater, swimming, floating. He is like a dolphin charting his way through familiar waters. She is weightless, drifting.

"Ne pense à rien, rien. . . ." he whispers. She drifts and drifts, the current sweeping her out, the shore far behind. She clings to the dolphin, she rides and rides.

At three a.m. Tibor is smoking a Disque Bleu, looking at the lights in the park below, the statue of José de San Martín, revolutionary and liberator, his horse rearing, bronze hooves pawing at a veiled moon. He turns and admires Amanda's sleeping form on his bed, the globe of her hips, the texture of her skin, the chestnut hair spilled on the pillow. Lovely, he thinks, but he knows he can't sleep until she's gone. He has to sleep alone and he has to wake up alone. It's not just the call from Sally in London he'll get early in the morning. He simply has to sleep alone.

He wakes Amanda, kisses her. He helps her dress and takes her downstairs, puts her, sleepy, into a taxi. He hands her cab fare, her notebook, kisses her tenderly, and

41

promises to call her when he gets back to New York, and sends her home to Arnold. Then he goes for a quick walk around the block, the long block, fast, faster, a little run. Now he can sleep.

After a fourth sleepless night, July 4, 1976, Sally Fraser pulled a thin mauve caftan over her head, wrestled with the sleeves, brushed her damp hair, and piled it on top of her head, sticking a sharp hairpin into her scalp. She yelled. Gorky, her cat, looked up from his basket, cringed as her brush flew past and landed with a thump against the wall. Sally stomped across the room, ignored the mewling cat, and yanked at the telephone, which was ringing with the persistence of an alarm clock.

"Yes," she said.

"It's me, Werner."

"Any news?"

"No. I've talked with his manager, his lawyer, CBS Records, his sister. There's a lot of conjecture, but no clues. The authorities are alerted at all ports of entry into the States, and so far he hasn't turned up. Scotland Yard still insists he hasn't left England. So he's got to be around." He paused, deciding how best to put his next thought. "There's one thing you might be glad to know—in talking to all those people, I could tell none of them knew about Sally Fraser."

"Then I've been left in total obscurity. Cold comfort, isn't it?"

"Don't be sarcastic. It doesn't help," Werner said. "I know you're upset, even angry—it's all understandable—but what we have to do before we sort out our feelings is simply find Szabo. Please help. Was there ever a place he talked about with great longing?"

"Just Hungary. You know the saying, 'A Hungarian is a Hungarian, and home is home'?"

"I've thought of that, too. In fact, I've called a Hungarian friend of his, a gypsy fiddler. He gave me contacts in Budapest. Estelle Stillman is checking on it right now."

"Who's she?"

"His lawyer."

Sally was silent, then asked, "He has a woman lawyer?"

"Didn't you know that?"

"I guess there's a lot I didn't know about him."

"And he about you."

"That's not helpful. You know how guilty I feel. I've never been quite so miserable."

"Sally, I'm sorry. I know. I just feel so frantic, so helpless, so culpable myself. I've got to find him—you understand that, don't you?"

"I'm not sure I understand anything anymore."

"You do. You'll be fine. I'll be over later. Will you be all right until then?"

"Yes," Sally said, and then, as if to confirm it to herself, she said it again, "yes," hung up, and went out for a walk, banging the door behind her.

Morning sun jabbed into her eyes as she followed Willow Road down toward Hampstead Heath, and waves of heat rose up from the sidewalk, swamping her in perspiration. The streets were deserted. The grass was brown and dried petals clung to lifeless stalks in the parched gardens she passed. A large dog stopped near her, his pink tongue hanging out, his sides heaving. She patted his head and crossed over at the corner of East Heath Road, carefully avoiding the spot where she and her mother had been hit by a van twenty-four years before.

Sally was seven when it happened and remembered nothing about it except waking up, her father's pale face

44

leaning over the hospital bed and his distant voice telling her Mummy was dead. Both Sally's legs were broken and her right arm had been crushed. After blood transfusions and endless operations, Sally's legs healed, but although she regained some use of her right arm, that hand was paralyzed, curved into a permanent fist.

Her father, James McKelvy Fraser, devoted all his energy and affection to her rehabilitation. A struggling poet who made his living as a carpenter, he saw in his only child all of his wife's fine qualities, plus something else, some little spark. He helped Sally walk again, taught her to push objects into the fist of her right hand, and to use them. He was patient and persistent, devising projects to help—a replica of the Parthenon made out of wood, with carved figures of men, horses, chariots; a model of Westminster Abbey; a copy of the Tower of London. He taught her to paint, to make furniture, to write poetry, to cook, and she became so adroit and precise that her disabled hand seemed more an eccentricity than an impediment. They went everywhere together, to concerts, theater, exhibitions, poetry readings. Sunday mornings they climbed to the top of Hampstead Heath, flew kites, painted watercolors of the city spread before them. They were apart only when Sally was in school or when James had a carpentry job. She was a good student, but shy and frightened of the other children. If James was out on a job when Sally returned from school, she would drop her books off at home, a small flat on Tanza Road next to the Heath, that large public expanse of meadows and woods that was her private haven.

She had a favorite tree near a part of the Heath called Kenwood, a giant beech, its low moss-covered branches stretched out like comforting arms. Cradled in that tree, she would spin a web of fantasies, elaborate and delicate, sit quietly for hours trapping thoughts, ingesting sights and sounds. Friends commented on his daughter's remoteness, and advised James to remarry as soon as possible, but he and Sally were happy together. It was a contented existence, until Sally turned sixteen, and then her adoring arms thrown around his neck, her nubile body pressed against him forced him to realize it was time to separate. He explained his decision to her as best he could. Then he sold the flat in London, retreated to his family's ancient estate in Kinross, Scotland, neglected since the family fortune dried up years before, and sent Sally off to a school in the country.

Standing beside her cases at Victoria Station, Sally wept and kissed her father's hands, begging him to change his mind. Sunlight drifted down from the iron-and-glass domed roof, outlining her father in a hazy gold light, like a gilded saint. He was tall and gaunt, with a small pointed beard and eyes like his daughter's, blue as the center of a flame, blue as a glacial pool.

"You're too big now, Sal, stop all this sniveling." James hugged her, breathed deeply, and pushed her away, holding her by the shoulders at arm's length. "You will see that this is for the best," he told her, and propelled her toward the train, which coiled and hissed into the station.

In that exile called school Sally could hardly function. Dressing in the morning became an impossible task, and if she did manage to put something on and go to class, it was only to sit in the back of the classroom, mute, frightened. She wrote to her father, imploring him to let her come to Scotland, but he answered with vague statements about courage, which only made her angry and morose. Sessions with Cornelia Bunting, the headmistress, were no help. Miss Bunting peered at her from across a vast oak table and told her to stop feeling sorry for herself, everyone had problems, she was not alone. "Try to find something that interests you, and throw yourself into it, lose yourself."

Painting interested Sally, but the art studio was forbidding and so was Richard Altby, the teacher. A man of forty-two with grizzled hair and eyes pale as moonstone, Richard lumbered around the studio like a polar bear, ponderous, glowering at canvases, patting shoulders when he approved, or growling with displeasure. When he came around to Sally's easel, he stood and watched.

"Are you frightened of me?" Richard asked, twisting a button on his sweater. Sally lowered her head. Her eyes rested on his scuffed shoes, spotted with paint. "Are you?" he asked again.

Sally looked up and hid her right hand behind her back in a pose she hoped made her look confident.

"No," she said, and wondered if he felt sorry for her—a crippled girl, so obviously shy.

"Good," Richard said. "Then we can work together."

Sally blushed. Her temples throbbed with embarrassment and she bit her lower lip to keep from crying. She tried to dip her brush, which she held in her fisted hand, into a bottle of red paint, but knocked it over instead. It smashed on the floor, color spreading out toward her feet.

"Never mind," Richard said. "Leave it. I'll help you clean it up after class."

She stayed late into the afternoon, and like a day lily blooming in his light, Sally opened herself to Richard. He was reassuring, comforting. He convinced her that her handicap was hardly noticeable, that she could control a brush as well as anyone, she needed only to try. He held the hand she called grotesque in his and pressed it to his cheek.

Sally was not the first student Mr. Altby had taken under the frayed wool blanket of the art studio couch, but she was the first he cared about so completely. She was childishly eager, wildly responsive, but her compassion and awareness were strikingly precocious. And then there was the freshness of her firm opalescent skin, her graceful movements, her flickering blue eyes. They planned to live together, but when Sally was about to graduate and enter the Royal College of Art in London, Richard could not bring himself to leave his wife and two children to follow her.

Sally locked herself in her dormitory room, lay on her bed alternately weeping and studying cracks in the ceiling. After a while she began to consider her possibilities. Life without Richard was unthinkable, but after some contemplation, so was ending her own. School was closing for the summer holidays, so she'd have to go somewhere, but where? To Scotland to her father's ruin of a home? She could make herself useful, help fix it up. His letters made it sound like an adventure, but perhaps their vivacious tone came from the presence of Sophie, his "friend," and Sally thought she might be in their way. She did have a scholarship to go to the Royal College; London was big and anonymous, a good place to be alone, to try to forget. But how could she go to art school, when every line, every stroke would remind her of Richard? She walked around her room, picked up a pad from her desk, a piece of charcoal, and tried to sketch. A tear fell on the page, and when she rubbed at it with the side of her hand, the effect was interesting. She began to think about London, the mix of people, the varieties of buildings, the color, light, Hampstead village, the Heath. She would be depressed, but she would be on familiar ground, and besides, there really was no choice.

But in the London of the 1960s, it was impossible to be eighteen and talented and depressed for long. Sally's studies were exhilarating, the atmosphere was vibrant, and she flung herself into her work. When a painting of hers was chosen, along with works by ten other students from the Royal College, for an exhibition, it was singled out and written up in *The Times*:

David and Abishag (4x6) by Sally Fraser is by far the most effective piece in the show. David's face has an expression of unbridled lust, but despite his regal bearing and the opulence of his attire, there is a tentativeness lurking in the eyes giving him a forlorn, frightened look. The voluptuous Abishag is painted with a primitive energy, uneven strokes tempestuously applied. She is alluring, seductive, yet she wears a miniskirt, her coltish legs poke out like a little girl's. Piccadilly glares at the viewer from behind these two Biblical figures, with ads for porn movies and garish neon signs. One small camel stands in a corner of the canvas under a palm tree watching the scene with sad eyes. Fraser's use of figurative elements in an essentially abstract scheme is refreshing, and her eclectic themes, the mythic and the pure pop, are blended together with a disciplined technique to form a provocative combination that reads on many levels.

Sally Fraser refused to become part of any literary-artistic coteries that longed to embrace her. Instead, she worked quietly, alone, and although there were a few friends and some men in her life, she shielded herself with her work and never let them get too close. When her paintings began to sell, she bought a house in Hampstead, four stories on Willow Road, badly in need of work. Her father came down from Scotland with Sophie to help with the renovations. Sophie was quiet and affectionate. A widow with two grown sons, she was a gentle presence and seemed to please James. The three of them painted, papered, and, by putting dormers into the attic, created a studio that looked up the hill across jagged rooftops and winding streets on one side, and down toward the Heath on the other.

Sally worked well on Willow Road, starting every day when the morning was the color of pewter and the village of Hampstead was still. Her cat and a radio kept her company. Music stimulated her vision, she thought, and the radio stayed tuned to BBC 3. One morning while working on a seascape, trying to refine gradations of light and shade playing on waves, she found herself listening to a piano piece. Tone colors glistened, intense darks, brilliant lights, then a coruscation of notes like sun beating on water. She dipped her brush and felt the color flow onto the canvas, just right, just what she was looking for. When the piece was over she stopped to listen to the announcer: "We have just been listening to Debussy's 'Reflets dans l'eau,' played by Tibor Szabo."

Soon after, on a drizzly fall afternoon, she finished work and walked down as she often did to the Hampstead Tea Rooms at South End Green, to read the papers and relax with a cup of tea. Tibor Szabo was there, in one of the large, airy rooms, stuffing an éclair into his mouth when he noticed her sitting near him. He had just finished a recording session of Beethoven sonatas with Zev Barzlil, the Israeli cellist, at the Abbey Road Studios nearby. Sally was leaning forward in her chair, blue cloth draped against her body like folds on a marble statue. She was reading the *Evening Standard*, her face seemed lit from within like an alabaster lamp, and something about her wide mouth, high cheekbones, pale skin, and wavy mane of golden hair still sparkling with rain fascinated him.

"Who's that?" he asked Zev, who lived in the neighborhood and seemed to know everyone.

Zev looked, straightened his emerald cravat, which, as he knew, set off his green eyes and crinkly black hair. "Forget it," he said.

"Why?"

"That's Sally Fraser. A painter. Strange and difficult. I know."

"Then tell."

"I took her out a few times—a concert, a movie, even dinner. She was polite, but icy. If she could refuse bed with Barzlil, what chance have you got?"

"Introduce me," Tibor said. He got up and headed for Sally's table without waiting for Zev. "Excuse me," Tibor said, making Sally look up, "but aren't you Sally Fraser?"

"Yes," she answered, startled by the deep, rumbling voice and by the tall man towering over her with powerful shoulders, enormous hands, and dark eyes gleaming like polished ebony.

He slid into the chair opposite hers and, lying with practiced conviction, said he admired her work and always wanted to meet her. When he told her his name her look of instant recognition pleased him.

"You've been of some help to me," Sally said, then flushed, feeling excited but foolish.

"How's that?"

"It's just a coincidence, really, I don't know if I should tell you, I—"

"Tell me, please," Tibor said, the urgency real, his interest growing with the sound of her voice, the flow of her words. Sally looked into his eyes, felt herself slip into two dark tunnels, full of danger, but something told her to explore.

"I was working in my studio, having trouble with a painting of the sea, and I heard you play on the radio —'Reflets dans l'eau.' The sounds were so evocative, I found myself painting like mad and . . ." Without realizing it, she had raised her right hand, making brush strokes in the air. She noticed Tibor studying her fist and she drew it quickly down into her lap.

"What happened to your hand?" he asked, naturally, and she answered, as naturally, "A childhood accident, just one of those things."

Tibor wanted to reach under the table and take it in his,

feel it small and curled like an infant's, sweet, vulnerable. He nodded instead and said rather stiffly, "It would mean a great deal to me to be able to see that painting."

"Why?"

"It's an amazing thought. I work, struggle to make something, play something that isn't even mine to begin with, and after I've played, what am I left with? But now you tell me I've been part of the creation of something tangible, visible, real. To see that would give me satisfaction."

Sally laughed, but stopped abruptly when a hurt look crossed Tibor's face. "Forgive me," she said. "It just strikes me as odd that we see each other's world as saner than our own. Artists are a crazed, dissatisfied lot. I always imagined that to be a musician must be so satisfying—playing concerts, giving people pleasure."

"There is some of that, yes. But take away the audience, the applause, and you see one man at one piano, alone. And a pianist is the most solitary of all musicians. A violinist, a cellist, a wind-player—he generally makes music in combination with others, and what's more, he embraces his instrument, but a pianist most often plays alone, and he doesn't even hold his instrument; he strikes it, then moves away." Tibor flicked his hair back out of his eyes and wondered why he was telling her these things. He covered his confusion with a smile.

Sally smiled back and asked if he would like to go see her painting now, she lived just up the road. Then, embarrassed by her own lack of restraint, she quickly added, "I mean, some other time."

"Now is the only time," Tibor said firmly. He already had money in hand, his coat buttoned, and her cape held out to wrap around her.

Sally walked up Parliament Hill in the heat, shivered at the remembered sensation of Tibor's hands wrapping her in the cape, fastening it for her under her chin, as if he'd done that for years, taking her arm, and walking with her for the first time into her house. He seemed at home in her studio. He looked at her seascape, stepping away from it, tilting his head, folding his arms. He looked at it for a long time, then walked toward her, embraced her.

"I'm frightened," she said.

"Don't be," he told her, and stroked her hair, rested his chin against her temple, felt it pulse against his skin. Panic fluttered like birds' wings inside her, but he spoke to her softly. "N'aie pas peur, calme-toi, calme-toi." His dark, soothing voice, the sounds of whispered French, smooth as scented oil, relaxed her, and she draped against him like a silk scarf.

Lying next to him in bed, she watched him sleep, traced his features with her eyes, then placed her face next to his to feel the rhythm of his breath beat warm and moist against her cheeks. His eyes fluttered open and he reached for her, took her right hand and examined it, caressed it. Sally watched him; his curiosity surprised her, but she felt at ease as he looked, she felt calm.

"Like a lotus," he mumbled, and kissed her hand. "Curled, delicate pink. Did you know the Greeks made wine from the fruit of the lotus and it was thought to produce contentment and forgetfulness?"

"Is that what you want from me?"

"I have it already. I have forgotten everything but you, and I feel content."

Late the next day he had to go to Zurich. "Come with me," he pleaded. But she couldn't. She had been commissioned to do a portrait, and she wanted to finish it. He left and she felt empty, abandoned, even though the decision had been hers. She forced herself to work in her studio, worrying the entire day that she would never see him again, then telling herself it didn't matter. But he called, he sent flowers, he spoke to her in his exotic voice, deep, urgent tones, and told her he missed her, couldn't wait to get back to London, and when he arrived a few days later, stood at her doorway, briefcase in hand, a lock of hair in his eyes, and smiled at her, it was as if he'd never left.

She tried to travel with him. She enjoyed the concerts. Sometimes she even thought she loved him best when he was onstage, playing for her, speaking to her in his truest voice. But the trips were tiring, there were always too many people around, and after a few days she would get edgy and want to go home. Tibor understood. He shared her devotion to work, understood that she needed her studio, her painting. In a way, it was a better arrangement. He had his freedom, he worked hard on tour anyhow, and it made coming home to London exciting, rushing from the airport to his secret life, his private love. It was perfect for both, for a while, until each needed more of the other, neither could give quite enough, and their time together was spent arguing, pleading, making impossible promises. Both knew that at some point something would have to change, but both put it off, and neither expected it to happen so suddenly, or cause the explosion it did.

Sun pressed down on Sally like an open palm. It was difficult to walk, and there was no place to go. She instinctively headed up toward Kenwood, toward the spot where her dreams were first spawned. When she saw her beech tree in the distance, she felt a pang of sadness, like seeing an old friend who had suddenly aged. Withered in the heat, its branches sagged, its leaves were brown and curled. Sally leaned against the flaking trunk and patted it, felt tears stream down her face, burning her cheeks. She wept as she had when her father sent her away, she wept as she had when Richard stayed behind, and the same knife-sharp pain cut at her, deep beneath the ribs. The events of the last few days had happened so fast, like that crash twenty-four years before, and she couldn't tell whose fault it was or why it had happened. She knew only that Tibor was gone and, this time, would not come back.

Sally rubbed at her eyes with two fists and thought of her mother. "Stop rubbing so hard at your eyes," her mother would tell her.

"But I like the pretty lights it makes me see."

"You can see prettier lights with your eyes wide open. You have to look." Her mother in a blue flowered dress, smelling of blue flowers, leaning over her, planting a kiss like a blue seed on her forehead. The image faded, the pretty lights were gone, and she leaned against the old beech tree, staring out at the Heath with swollen eyes.

≋ There is little visibility at Chicago's O'Hare International Airport. Mid-April and it's snowing hard. Flight 602 to San Francisco is indefinitely delayed. The Muzak incongruously twangs with Hawaiian guitars. Tibor leaves his coat and briefcase in the first-class lounge and chats with the first-class hostess, who today, April 17, 1976, is Dolores. She has just read an article about him in *Time* and she is thrilled to meet him.

Tibor opens his book, *What's Your Next Move?*, and reads: "White gradually obtained a formidable position while Black committed a number of injudicious moves, each trifling alone, but cumulatively the effect was fatal. The stage was now set for White's crushing attack. . . ."

One move at a time is enough. He flips through magazines, eats peanuts, drinks coffee, and then makes phone calls:

No, he cannot attend the Ladies Auxiliary function after the Boston concert in October, please tell them thank you very much but he will have a funeral to go to on that day. No, he will not record such and such with so and so. Yes, he will go to St. Louis on April 16, 1982. No, he will not record in the Canaries, for Christ's sake, it's his vacation. All right, all right, he'll think about it.

He hangs up and thinks about it, his vacation, five days alone with Sally high in the hills of Maspalomas in the Canary Islands, far away from the tourists of Las Palmas, on the other side of the island. They've promised each other these five days, and his friend Karl Arnheim has offered the guest house on his estate. Sun, blue sky, white sand dunes, and Sally beside him. He sees her as he left her, standing at her front door in a purple robe, blinking back large wet pearls that cling to her lashes. He kisses her wet eyes, her nose, asks if she will be all right, and she says yes, of course, yes; then he presses her to him before getting into the limousine and watches from the rear window as she waves, both arms fluttering above her head. She's gone and he closes his eyes to bring her back. Sally.

"Are you all right?" Dolores asks. He's fine, he'll take a walk, but first he promises Dolores he'll come back quickly. She's just found the review of last night's recital at Carnegie Hall in *The New York Times*: "Fire and sovereign technique . . . reminds us of the days when pianists were pianists. Szabo promises and, unlike so many others, he delivers."

Trinket shops, plastic souvenirs, bookstalls. Tibor browses. It's the same stuff, the same stuffed dolls; none of it ever changes. At least there is the game room and the pinball machines. Tibor racks up a whopping score on the Amazing Torpedo. He's been playing these machines for years. Nothing changes, not the look of glee when the lights flash and bells go off, not the dash to the nearly missed plane, not the need to score.

He goes to a coffee shop. He doesn't want any coffee. He just wants to talk to the waitress.

"Yeah?" she asks, stuffing a piece of Juicy Fruit gum into her mouth, before he even slides into the seat.

"Would you be ever so kind," Tibor says in his Hungarian-British best, "to give me a cup of coffee?"

She cracks her gum and reaches for the pot, pours the coffee. She watches Tibor stir his cream in. She cracks her gum again. "Where are you from, honey?"

"London, England, actually."

"No kidding. Really?"

"Really. Where are you from?"

"Here."

"Do you like it here?"

"You must be kidding."

"I'm not."

"I hate it. I'm getting out. I'm studying at beautician school nights, and as soon as I can I'll get out of here. It's my husband—well, I don't know if I should tell you. . . ."

"You can tell me."

She tells him, everything, and he listens like a priest, telling her it's OK, everything will be fine.

Next, a shoe shine. When he's waiting, when he's disgusted, when he's feeling bloody well fed up, there's almost nothing quite like a shoe shine to make him feel great. Tibor mounts the old leather throne, places his feet on the worn brass posts, and waits to be serviced. He watches the shoe shiner flick his cloth, rub his goo, shine his shine. They talk shoe talk and snow talk while Tibor thumbs through a discarded *National Enquirer*. When finished, he walks out, his two shoes clean, burnished, ready for inspection.

Now for postcards. He finds a perfect shot of a traffic jam in the Loop. "Tied up in Chicago," he writes and sends it to Estelle. One for Michael, of the Wrigley Building, and, why not, while he still remembers her name, Orchestra Hall for Amanda.

Back in the first-class lounge Dolores and Tibor have a drink together. She asks him who is his favorite composer. He says he doesn't have a favorite. She says she likes the French composers best, she likes color. He says he prefers the color of her eyes. She tells him he may be snowed in for the night but luckily her apartment is right near the airport. She even has a piano, it's only a little Wurlitzer upright, but still, if he'd like to practice he could. . . .

Information lights up on Dolores's screen: Flight 602 to San Francisco is now available for passenger boarding at gate 32B.

Tibor writes down her phone number in his address book and promises he'll call her up on his way through Chicago next week, but he'd really better take that flight to San Francisco now.

"Of course," Dolores says, helping him on with his coat, and watches him disappear down the corridor. Szabo keeps moving.

At 35,000 feet the seat belt sign is turned off and he is free to move about the cabin. But Tibor is trapped in seat 3-A, listening to Harvey Tomkins.

"With the Philadelphia Orchestra, Beethoven, wasn't it, on PBS? God, you were terrific, really great. I liked that slow part in the middle, really soft and nice. I like good music, but we don't get an awful lot of it in Grand Rapids. My daughter is talented at the piano, really talented, her teacher says so. But I don't think I'd like her to be a professional musician, not really. It must be a difficult life."

"It has its compensations," Tibor says, watching the stewardess as she bends over to hand seat 1-A his drink, her buttocks moving under a tight red skirt, her pink legs stretching. A baby cries and is squeaked at with a rubber toy, the pilot announces the flight path, and Tibor asks the stewardess her name as she hands him a 7-Up, a double scotch for Harvey. They smile at each other, and Tibor excuses himself to stand up, says he needs the toilet. Near the magazine rack he stops Nancy on her way to the kitchen and he asks her if she is staying over in San Francisco, would she like to hear a concert, his? She's routed straight back to Chicago. He looks wistfully at her, grabs a copy of *Time*, and goes into the closet of a toilet.

Flipping to the music section, he reads the article about himself, the one Dolores pointed out, the one he said he wasn't interested in. He scans the superlatives, then unzips and smiles wryly at the sign DO NOT PUT FOREIGN OBJECTS IN THE TOILET. Green disinfectant swirls down the silver bowl. He washes his hands and, for the convenience of the next passenger, wipes the basin dry.

"Sorry, Harvey," he says as he climbs over legs and spills peanuts. Nancy is handing out tiny hot shrimp, but Tibor isn't having any. Instead, he pulls out a score from his briefcase.

"What are you working on?" Harvey asks.

Tibor tries not to groan, forces himself to say Brahms, the D-minor Concerto, then buries his head in the music. Harvey's voice fades and he can almost feel the keyboard, imagine depressing keys for the expressivo pianissimo entrance, thinking of the voicing of the chords, the problem of making the phrase flow, even, liquid. Then there are those fiendish octave trills. He tries the Liszt fingering on his knees; then, when he turns to the Adagio, the difficult slow sustained chords make him smile. He can't help it. He thinks of Werner Rawlings—the two can't be separated; the friendship is founded on those chords.

Tibor had played the Brahms for his debut with the London Symphony in 1961 and at a party given for him after the concert he met Werner Rawlings, a novelist "and a great music lover, knows *everything*, he's too terribly amusing," as Lady Weatherby, his hostess, said during the introduction. He remembers Werner's clear blue eyes, little rosebud mouth, and his smooth cheeks punctuated with two bright spots of pink. He looked like a cherub off a greeting card, but an insolent crown of wild blond curls and a tall rakish body turned the total impression from seraph to satyr. Werner wore a maroon scarf twisted twice around his neck and smoked a Havana cigar, and Tibor liked him immediately.

"The slow movement was *too* wonderful," Lady Weatherby told the two men. "Brahms wrote it just after Schumann died, didn't he? It is like a requiem, isn't it? What friends they must have been. How Brahms must have suffered when Schumann died."

"Ah, yes," Werner said, and as soon as their hostess turned to greet a new arrival, he whispered to Tibor, "He was fucking Clara to console himself."

Tibor laughed and asked Werner if he really thought Schumann's wife had been Brahms's lover. Werner sipped his wine and answered by singing, to a melody from Schumann's Quartet in A major, "Clara, if you don't stay away from Brahms I'll lock you in your room."

The Red Lion Pub, where they went as soon as they could politely slip away from the reception, closed at midnight, and Werner suggested going to his place in Camden Town. They walked down Conduit Street toward Berkeley Square, laughing, slapping each other on the back. Tibor did an imitation of Lady Weatherby, pursing his lips, eyes rolled heavenward, while Werner tried Lord Weatherby, virtuosic throat-clearing included.

A taxi dropped them off at Inverness Street in NW 1. They stepped over a few squashed tomatoes, smashed apples, and scraps of colored paper left over from the fruit vendors who set up stalls there each morning.

"It ain't Mayfair, mate," Werner said in a cockney accent, and opened the door onto a steep staircase carpeted in frayed green. On the wall leading up were three paintings of the same naked woman, legs parted, head rolled back, identical except for the large stenciled letters LOVE in a different color on each canvas.

"Care for a cuppa?" Werner asked as he turned on the

bare light bulb hanging over a long wooden table on which a typewriter, books, papers, and a few apple cores were scattered. Tibor squinted in the sudden harsh light and looked around at an enormous room, high walls stacked floor to ceiling with shelves sagging with the weight of books and records. Beads and bits of ornaments hung from nails on the bookshelves, and on the floor leaning against the shelves were random stacks of unframed canvases, "a collection in search of a wall," as Werner called it. Two large armchairs with stuffing poking out flanked a large mattress, which was covered with a striped bedspread. Werner demonstrated a neon sign over the bed that, when plugged in, lit up with the word APPLAUSE. A small kitchen area was tagged onto the room as an afterthought, with a black gas stove taking most of its space. There was a musty smell, mixed with apple, and something exotic, like curry. Tibor sniffed.

"Indian restaurant right below me. Want some chicken vindaloo to blow off the top of your head?" Werner asked, unwrapped his scarf, and flung it onto the nearest unoccupied nail jutting from the shelves. He opened a cupboard above the stove, took two teacups, poured himself a brandy, and offered some to his guest.

"Nice place," Tibor said.

"Come on, now. It's a dump. I've only been a bachelor for a year, since Laura and I split, and I'm not much for keeping house."

"Were you married?"

"Past tense correct, yes, for, let me see, ten years. My college darling. She went on to be a doctor, and I went on to write, which was fine, since I could look after the baby while she was at school, and I could write after she came home to take over. Trouble was, we had no time for each other."

Werner drained his cup and poured himself more, his

smile uncurving to a flat line. "And your child?" Tibor asked.

"A son, Colin. He's five and a great lad. I miss him. But we're together on weekends. He loves to visit me here—he likes this dump."

"I do, too," said Tibor. "It's just the sort of place I always wanted for myself, a room, one huge room full of whatever you like, and no one to bother you."

"Don't you have your own room in Paris?"

"Yes, but it's all Louis Quinze."

"Elegant. What's wrong with it?"

"It belonged to Stephan Vlostid, my teacher. He died last year, and I can't stay there, in his shadow, forever."

"Where will you live?"

"I don't know. I've just started playing concerts. I'll be traveling a lot."

"But you'll need a place, a base of operations. Try London. It has life, energy, and it's civilized. You'll need a place to call home."

"I left home for good a long time ago."

"Hungary? Ah, yes. Well, don't be sentimental, my man. You can't go home again and all that. Don't dwell on it."

"I don't," Tibor said, put his cup down, and stuffed his hands deep into his pockets. Werner tipped his chair onto its back legs.

"You left five years ago when you were, let me get my math right, thirteen years old, a difficult age, a rough time to leave home, let alone your parents."

"I was ready for it," Tibor said with a swagger and thought of his apartment in Budapest, Szusza, their housekeeper, and the cakes she baked, poppyseed, apple, her rough hands and strong arms, and the folk songs from her village that she sang in a gentle voice as he sat on her lap, listened, ate cakes.

"And your parents, what were they like?"

Tibor hesitated, but it would be rude not to answer. He sat down opposite Werner, tried to tip his chair back too, but felt unstable, crossed his legs instead. "My father was a lawyer, quite successful," he began. "He studied piano himself, with a student of Schnabel's, but somehow he ended up in law. He was eager for me to have a career. In fact, sometimes I thought my progress was the only thing he cared about. Mother is a biologist and had a good research position. She worked very hard and we had a housekeeper named Szusza who came in a few days a week. She and my older sister, Maya, kept the house running, and—" He pushed his hair out of his face with his hands, having told enough, and looked at Werner. "Tell me about yours," he said.

"Mother, English. Father, German. I was born in Stuttgart and when the war broke out I was ten. Mother took me back to England with her and resumed her maiden name—for both of us. During the Blitz I was evacuated to the countryside. At school there I was bullied by the others because of my German first name."

"Why didn't your mother change it?" Tibor asked.

"I'm not sure. Maybe she wanted me to keep something of my father. He stayed in Germany to fight for the Führer. After he was killed Mother said he really worked for the resistance, but as far as I know, he was a Nazi."

"Do you care?"

"Do I care?" Werner's chair clumped onto four legs and he sat up straight. "I've spent my life caring, haven't you? Don't you question your parents, who they were, what they did, and then what that means about you? I've been struggling with it for years. But of course I'm thirty-two and you're just eighteen. You'll get to it. I'm somewhat obsessed with it. I've even written a novel about it, *Grave Doubts*."

"*Le Doute*, c'est ça?"

"Et voilà. Have you read it?"

"No. I want to, of course. But I remember Stephan talking about it. A young German who discovers that his wife's family were victims of his father during the war?"

"That's it, sort of. Speaking of which, aren't you Jewish?"

"Yes. Why do you ask?"

"I'm curious how your family survived Hitler. Not many Hungarian Jews did."

"I was a baby. But I've been told that a priest, a friend of the family, signed some documents for my parents saying we were Catholic. When it got dangerous, we went into the countryside and lived on a farm with some peasants."

"Then what?"

"Back to Budapest, where everything was OK, until fifty-six, that is. My father was violently anti-Russian. There were terrible arguments between him and his father, who lived with us. Grandpa Andras said, 'Let the Russians come, it will be good for the Jews.' My father would pound on the table and pull at his mustache and call him ignorant. Anyhow, in October fifty-six Mother sent me and my sister to Vienna. She and my father planned to join us later, but a bullet got in his way."

Tibor tossed his hair back and reached for the brandy. It was an old story, one he'd told before, but each time the telling made him flinch inside and he could see his father falling, and hear his mother whisper, "Follow Maya, be brave. Kiss me and go. Wait, first say good-bye to Papa." But he didn't, he couldn't, he did not want to leave and if he had to, it was Papa's fault. So he strode out into the long night of his escape without kissing his father good-bye.

"What about your mother?" Werner asked.

Eva Szabo reads to him, his head is in her lap, she strokes his forehead, she smells of lavender, his cheek rests against her warm belly. Tibor swallowed and said, "My mother lost her position at the Institute for Biological Research and couldn't get another job. Lucky for all of us Vlostid pulled strings and got her out of Hungary. But it took three years."

"Where is she now?"

"In Lausanne. She works in a laboratory there."

"Do you see her often?"

"Not really. She can't get much time off."

"Not even to come to her son's London debut? Pity, if you ask me," he said, his words beginning to slur together. "But I suppose, on the other hand, you may be lucky." Werner got up, went to a shelf, pulled out a recording. He knocked some books from a large pile and an old turntable emerged. He blew dust from it, carefully and with difficulty managed to put the record on, placed the needle in the first groove.

"Not that, please," Tibor said as he recognized the record from the first phrase.

"Why not?"

"He was a childhood idol of mine. It makes me too sad." Tibor took another gulp of brandy, stared at a rusting apple core. Werner pushed the stop button, turned to his guest, holding on to a shelf for support. "You ought to face up to that sadness," he said. "You ought to find out why Dinu Lipatti makes you cry."

"It's obvious. He died when he was only thirty-three, at the height of his career."

"We all die sometime. What better time than at your peak? Is it really the prematurity of his death that moves you, or is there something about his playing that goes beyond the person, beyond the illness, that says something else?"

"What do you mean?"

"Listen," Werner said, and put the needle back on the record. Tibor pictured Dinu Lipatti at the keyboard, small, swollen with cortisone, hunched over the keys, pain radiating through his body, music pouring from his hands. The recording was made in Besançon, at his last concert, two months before he died of leukemia. Filled with painkillers and drugs, he insisted on playing, and it was recorded. The program: a Bach partita, the Mozart A-minor Sonata, some Schubert impromptus, and the fourteen waltzes of Chopin. He never played the four-teenth waltz. Exhausted, he stopped, rested; then gather-ing all his remaining strength, he came back onto the stage and played a Bach chorale, like a final prayer.

Tibor listened. His throat tightened as the record ended with Lipatti playing the E-flat waltz, the Grande Valse Brillante—energetic, passionate, full of life.

After the last note, the whir of the record player, the click that shut it off—silence. Tibor's chest hurt with held air. He let it out slowly and watched Werner try to slide the record into its thin gray paper square, put it away.

"What made that man play?" Werner asked. "What made him go out there one more time?"

Tibor shrugged his shoulders and rubbed at an eye with the heel of his palm.

"It fascinates me—doesn't it you?" Werner went on. "Was it an attempt to achieve immortality? Was he paying the music a final homage, or was it the other way around?"

"It was a scheduled concert," Tibor said. "He promised to play. He had a commitment."

"But surely if he was so ill, it could easily have been canceled."

"You can't just cancel a concert. He probably felt it would be a betrayal not to play."

"Betrayal? Of whom? Of what?"

"Of his audience, and the music. I can't explain it very well, but I understand it. He had something left to say, and only one way to say it. Music is a mysterious language—it takes you out of yourself, and it gives you back strength. Music—in the end, it's all we have."

"We?"

"Those who play."

Werner pressed him to go on talking, but Tibor yawned and eyed the mattress on the floor.

"Have a sleep, if you like," Werner suggested. Tibor kicked off his shoes, hung his coat on a nail, then slumped in a heap onto the bed. Werner sat down at the table in a circle of yellow light, finished the bottle of brandy, put his head on his folded arms, and slept like a schoolboy at his desk.

The clamor of street vendors setting up shop woke them both at seven. They washed their faces, took their jackets, and went for a walk along the Camden High Street, the sun coming up, the buses beginning to roll, sleepy people queuing up for another day just the same as the day before. Werner stopped to ask a pretty young girl in a miniskirt how she was feeling. She smiled at him, and giggled, and then he asked her to come along and have tea. She accepted. Werner winked at Tibor and, linking arms with the girl, crowed a roosterlike good-bye and strutted into a restaurant, the Golden Egg.

"Please fasten your seat belts and extinguish all smoking materials as we make our final approach into the San Francisco area," Nancy announces.

Tibor closes his score, looks out of the window at the sapphire-blue crescent sparkling below, the beautiful white edge of beach, the calm cool blue, the bay drenched in sun. He presses his face against the small oval window like a child at a candy store and stares at Half Moon Bay, where William Kapell's plane crashed on its way from Australia. Kapell was a great pianist, thirty-one years old. He had not enjoyed his Australian tour. Before he boarded that plane, so the story goes, he told someone, "I'm never coming back here." He was right. Tibor collects Kapell recordings along with Lipatti's, listens to them with a devotion bordering on idolatry. He leans back now, closes his eyes, opens his mouth wide to clear his ears, and waits for the landing gear to lock into place. He hears the reassuring thump. It's these last few minutes of a flight that are crucial, it's now that things can go wrong, he knows it well. The plane banks to the left. Tibor grabs the chair arms and squeezes, wonders if the engines are on fire, if this is it, but the plane straightens out and glides in for a smooth touchdown.

"Who's Sally?" Harvey asks as he scampers down the jetway trying to keep up with Tibor.

"Why do you ask?"

"You said her name as we were landing, that's all."

"I did?" It's true—he saw her face, he thought of her, but could he really have?

"Well, don't look so worried. I'm not about to tell the press. Is she your wife?"

"Not yet," Tibor says, and likes the sound of it, the way it echoes with possibility.

Harvey peers up through thick glasses. He has short stubbly hair, wears a red bow tie and plaid jacket, and reminds Tibor of a fuzzy caterpillar. "I'm a toy inventor," Harvey tells him as they walk toward baggage claim. "Ever hear of Tommy Tuff?"

"No."

"I guess you don't have kids. It's a doll, my invention. We've sold forty million of them."

"What does it do?"

"Nothing. It's what you can do to it. Smash its face in, and it pops right back to normal, punch it in the belly, it falls down, says 'Ouch,' but gets right back up."

"Isn't that a bit sadistic?"

"It is, it is, but that's what sells. I'm a nonviolence man myself, and lately it's been worrying me, the stuff they want to sell the American kid. So I made a doll called Marvin. Plain face, freckles, glasses, doesn't do a thing, just sits there."

"Is it a success?"

"Are you kidding? The company fired me for it. That's why I'm in San Francisco. I've got interviews, I'm in demand, full of ideas. Here's one I got on the plane—a Tibor Szabo doll. You wind it up and it plays a Chopin mazurka."

Tibor laughs as his bag lumbers down the conveyor belt, rolls like a dead animal onto the moving circle of the carrousel.

Jim Hennings, the manager of the San Francisco Symphony, is waiting outside. They embrace, kiss on both cheeks, slap each other on the back. "Were you waiting long?" Tibor asks, then apologizes for being late.

"It's not your fault if Chicago is snowed in. Crazy weather for mid-April. Must mean we're in for a scorcher this summer."

"For me the heat is always on," says Tibor, straightening his tie. "What time is rehearsal?"

"Seven-thirty. You won't have much time to relax."

"Never mind. How is the orchestra?"

"Fine, fine. The orchestra has come a long way under Ozawa."

"So why can't I play with him? Why did you have to stick me with what's-his-name?"

"Adriano Delgado. He conducted in New York. They loved him."

"That's not what I heard. I heard he's an ex-Nazi who

fled to Argentina, changed his name, and disappeared into the jungle."

"Come on, Tibor, you've made it, you're box office, and so is Seiji. I have to count on you to bring in the public so we can give guys like Delgado a chance."

"Sure, support your local Nazi."

"He wasn't a Nazi! He was born in Argentina, for Christ's sake. You'll like him. He's about fifty-five, very personable, very knowledgeable."

"One of those conductors who love everything about music except the sounds it makes. There's got to be a reason he's never been heard of before."

"Some people are late bloomers. Will you stop worrying?" Jim says as they head up Nob Hill toward the Fairmont Hotel. After Tibor checks in, they take the glass lift up to his suite. Steep hills, cable cars, gabled housefronts, bright blossoms and vines fall away as they ascend in the crystal cage. The sun begins to drop like a fiery ball into the Pacific. The Golden Gate bridge is ablaze with light. Jim makes sure the bags arrive and that the rooms are in order before he leaves, saying he'll be back at seven to pick him up for rehearsal.

Tibor turns on the television set and glances at a basketball game while he unpacks, tossing rolled socks into one drawer, shirts and underwear into another. He shakes out his suits, hangs them up, drapes a handful of ties over a doorknob. His shoes, each in a cloth sack, are flung onto the closet floor where they pile up like a catch of fish. He strides across the crimson shag into the other room, checks his watch. Six o'clock. He panics. Swamped with work, inundated—the only cure is practice, and he doesn't have enough time. He hesitates, then opens the piano lid. He looks at the keys, plays a scale. Not bad, nice action, well-voiced. He tests the middle register with the opening of "Träumerei" from Schumann's *Kinderszenen*, then tries that new fingering for the octave trills in the

Brahms, then a few chords from the Adagio. He can't remember, do the triplets start now, or at the next entrance? He shakes his hands and stands up. He's dizzy, his head throbs, his ears are blocked from the flight. He must calm down, he must think of something, start somewhere, but where? Sally would know. She would glide quietly into the room, stand behind him; he would lean his head back against her breasts while she massaged his forehead. She'd talk to him. That's it—talk to her. He rushes to the desk, picks up the phone, and asks for overseas to London.

"What country, sir?"

"The United Kingdom. England!" he snarls, lights up a Disque Bleu and twists the phone chord. He taps his fingers on a guidebook, *San Francisco, Gateway to Adventure,* bites the skin around his thumbnail and waits.

"On the line, sir," the operator says. His heart pounds.

"Hello, Sally?"

"Tibor, is that you?"

"Darling, yes, I miss you."

"I miss you too, terribly. Where are you calling from?"

"I'm in San Francisco. I was delayed for four hours in Chicago, I've just arrived and I have to go straight to rehearsal. I'm in a state, totally unprepared. It's absurd and I have a headache. These damn airplanes, you spend the whole day sitting around and then you're expected to go play the Brahms D-minor, it's—"

"You sound frantic. Calm down. You could go out there and play the Brahms if you hadn't practiced for a week. You know it. You'll be fine, it's just a rehearsal, you have all day tomorrow to practice. Try to relax."

Tibor exhales. "You're right. I know all that, I just had to hear you tell me."

"I'm telling you something you know well. Are you all right? Is that what you're really worried about?"

"I don't know. It's all this work. And I can't stand being without you."

"It's not long now, just a few weeks."

"A few weeks. It's so much time."

"It will pass quickly. You have so many concerts anyhow."

"But it's agony without you."

"Please, Tibor, stop sounding so helpless. I know perfectly well what agony you have—adoring public, fabulous accommodations, all that glamour."

"Glamour? What the hell is glamorous about schlepping around from city to city, losing cuff links, forgetting toothpaste, being alone, alone!"

"Did you lose those cuff links I bought you?"

"Which?"

"The jade, jade and gold. Did you?"

"I don't remember. Sally, what difference does it make? I'm telling you I can't stand being without you. Get on a plane and come here. You can meet me in L.A. There is a direct flight from London straight over the Pole. Please."

"I can't."

"Stop saying you can't. You just don't want to. Admit it."

"OK. I'll admit it. I don't want to. I have a show in less than a month, and I have to be ready. You can understand that."

"There's someone else."

"Will you stop being ridiculous? Now you're making me angry. Darling, you know I want only you, you are all I think about, all I care about."

"Then why aren't we together?"

"We *are* together. You know I'm here, I'm yours. It should give you strength, make you happy. It shouldn't torture you."

"What tortures me is all this dead time between us, like

dead wood. It just gets chopped away, we'll never have it again."

"We'll have time, we'll be together. Just think how fresh it stays this way. Think of Alban Berg. Remember? When he was passionate about his mistress, his letters to her were extraordinary—poetic, yearning. They got married, and he started writing to her about the potatoes he was having for dinner."

"What's wrong with potatoes?"

"Nothing, I'm just saying—"

"I understand what you're saying, but I'm saying it must be a luxury to have enough of each other, to be content enough to talk about potatoes. It sounds calm to me, tranquil, it smells of evenings before the fire, of—"

"Of boredom."

"I would never be bored with you."

"How do you know? You haven't had the chance."

"Then give me a chance, get on a plane."

Silence. Empty space between them, and the crackle of the transatlantic wire.

"I can't, and I'm changing the subject," Sally says. "Tell me about New York."

"New York?"

"Last night, Carnegie Hall, remember?"

"That. It was OK, I guess. Schumann was pretty good, but the Liszt was abominable. I've never felt as miserable as I did in the middle of the sonata. I just wanted to stop, close the piano, and put my face in my hands."

"You didn't, did you?"

"Of course not."

"You scare me. You sound so depressed lately, I don't know when you mean what."

"I mean everything, always. I know I go up and down, I've just lately been more down than up. It all seems so ridiculous to me right now. I'm playing these concerts and for what?"

"You know perfectly well why you do it. You're just tired, you're feeling pressed, you've lost some perspective, that's all."

"Maybe. And what about you? Are you getting your work done?"

"Yes, more or less. I'm not doing anything spectacular."

"You sound depressed yourself."

"I am."

"About what?"

"Same thing you are. We're going around in circles. I miss you, you miss me."

"It's so hard, isn't it? I feel so terribly alone without you."

"I'm sure you're not alone. You play with entire orchestras, you meet lots of people, lots of women."

"None that interests me."

"Are you sure?"

"Now you're making me angry. Don't be ridiculous —and what about you?"

"I work at home, alone. You know it."

"And it's not good for you. You should go out a little, see a movie, go to a party. Call Werner, he'll be glad to take you somewhere."

"Werner makes me nervous."

"Why?"

"He's just so, well, intense."

"But he's interesting, he's fun."

"I'm not interested in fun."

"My little Calvinist, my little worker. What are you working on?"

"A portrait of you, if you must know."

"Uh-oh. I can see it now, scaly green monster, claws, fangs."

"Wrong. But it is a new departure for me. I don't want to describe it. You'll have to see it."

"Do I want to?"

"Sure, I've made you look just like Vittorio Gassman in *Rhapsody*."

"Is that the movie with Elizabeth Taylor where she loves a violinist and a pianist, and in the end . . . I forget which one gets her."

"I forget, too. We'll cuddle up together late one night in front of the telly and find out. Meanwhile you'd better hang up. This is costing a fortune."

"I make a fortune. What else am I going to spend my money on?"

"You could buy a house in the country."

"Would you live there with me?"

"Sure, one week a year, if you could take the time off."

"Now it's my fault we're not together."

"It's no one's fault."

"I love you. I'll call you from L.A."

"I hate the telephone."

"I know, but it's a thread, isn't it? It connects us even if it is unsatisfactory."

"I'm sorry for being so difficult, so awful."

"You're not. I am. We're both on edge, that's all."

"I love you so much."

"Me too you. I kiss you. Everywhere."

"Yes. Good-bye, my love."

"Bye."

"Bye."

Tibor rubs his ear, stretches. He feels better, he goes back to the piano and zips through difficult passages in the last movement of the Brahms. Then he stands at the window and watches the last light fade, tries to trap the exact moment of darkness, but he can't, one melts into the other, there is no division. He checks his watch. He has twenty minutes. He paces back and forth. The glow from his phone call ebbs, the last rays of Sally's light disappear, his mood darkens, and thoughts rumble in his head. She should be here with me . . . she should get on a goddam plane . . . she could come for two days . . . would two days kill her? . . . She could do that for me, for us . . . but she doesn't and what does it mean? . . . He clenches his fists, then thinks of Sally's hand, an angry, defiant, inflexible fist. He is fascinated by it, confused, sometimes even repelled.

"Why are you always talking about her hand?" Werner once asked.

"I just can't help being amazed by what she can do with it. I have two normal hands and most of the time they feel crippled. Sally's overcome a real disability."

"Sounds patronizing to me."

"Maybe it is, but we all need a little sympathy, don't we?"

"We need love. We don't need to be felt sorry for."

"Have you ever heard of compassion?"

"You've got compassion and pity mixed up."

"Have I?"

"Yes. And I'll tell you something else. You're jealous."

"Of what?"

"Of Sally's hand. She can't play the piano, can she?"

"God, you are perverse," Tibor had said angrily, but dreams of disaster no longer seem strange. He imagines accidents, he falls, he breaks an arm, he can no longer play, he buys a house and lives quietly with Sally while she paints and he does a bit of teaching. . . .

He takes a tie from the closet and, standing in front of a mirror, snakes it around his neck. Rehearsal, he thinks. Then what? Back here to this cell, tomorrow another rehearsal, a concert, back to this cell—a string of endless confinements. My life is booked solid, snatched away, drained from me, and Sally is the one person who seems to give it back to me. Sally. Damn her. I need her. I'll have to go alone to L.A., then Cleveland, Chicago . . . Chicago?

He thinks for a moment, then searches through his

briefcase for his red address book and heads for the phone.

"Hello, operator. Yes, it's me again. How are you? Good. I'd like to call Chicago, please, three-one-two . . ."

He hears the phone ring and imagines long legs poking out of a robe, blond hair cascading over shoulders as she runs to answer. "Hello?"

"Hello, may I please speak to Dolores?"

"This is Dolores."

"This is Tibor."

"Tibor Szabo?"

"Yes."

"You're kidding."

"I love that American phrase. You're kidding. I don't understand it at all, but it's charming. Kidding. I'm not kidding."

Silence. She's confused. What should she say? Apologize? Laugh? He likes the silence. He knows she's confused. He knows she never expected him to call, he knows her hands must be trembling, her head spinning.

"Dolores," he goes on, his voice a little more urgent. "Why should I kid you? Why shouldn't I call you and tell you how I can't get you out of my thoughts, how our meeting surprised me, how I almost couldn't get on that plane to San Francisco. I had to call you."

"How nice of you."

"Nice? Not nice. Necessary."

"You surprise me."

"Why is that?"

"Well, I mean, you're famous and sought after, and well, you meet so many women, and after all—"

"I meet many. So I know what I want." Silence. What a line, she thinks, it's so transparent. Still, the flattery of it is not entirely unwelcome. Not at all. "Dolores, are you there?"

78

"I am. Where are you?"

"I'm in San Francisco. Then I go to L.A., then Cleveland, then Chicago. Next Monday. Will you see me next Monday? I'm arriving at one p.m., American flight two-three-two from L.A. Can you meet me?"

"Of course. You might say I know that airport. I'll meet you."

"Fabulous. Then we can go to my hotel for dinner."

"Only dinner?"

"Whatever you like, Dolores. Dessert is included if you like."

"I like."

"Mnnn. Fabulous. I'll think of you until then. Take care of yourself."

"I always do."

"Monday I'll take care of you."

"Mnnn."

"I have a rehearsal right now, otherwise I'd love to talk. See you Monday."

"Yes, wonderful. Bye-bye."

"Good-bye."

Tibor hangs up, smiles, grabs his briefcase, races out the door and down the corridor, rings for the elevator, and floats down in the glass cage, free as a hawk.

"It is an honor, and a very great pleasure," Adriano Delgado says in the conductor's room backstage at the Opera House where the orchestra performs. He shakes Tibor's hand, and motions him to sit down next to him. Thin and nervous, with gold-rimmed glasses and wiry gray hair, Delgado makes a small grunting noise with each exhaled breath. He raises his eyebrows and lines print out on his forehead like a music staff. "I am so looking forward to working with you," he says, wringing his hands. "I have your recording, that one you made with Sir Malcolm."

"That was fifteen years ago, just after my London debut. In those days I knew how to play."

"Ha-ha. I like that. Now you tell me about tempi. First movement."

"About like this," Tibor says, and hums his opening solo at the speed he thinks is right.

"It is perhaps a little slow."

"I don't think so."

"But at your tempo I must beat in six."

"I think it works well in two. It lets the phrase move."

"I think in six is good," Delgado says firmly.

"As you like," Tibor says, not wanting to argue before the rehearsal. He's nervous enough, and besides, the musicians know him well; they'll follow him.

An electronically produced A is piped through the intercom system for the musicians to tune to, and then Jim's voice is heard: "Onstage, please, for the Brahms."

Onstage, removed from time or place, boxed in, curtained, Szabo is comfortable. With all the traveling, stage is the one place that, although different in every city, is the same for him, unifies disruptions, makes sense out of his travels. Szabo is onstage, greeted with cheers, slaps on the back, bear hugs. He plays with the San Francisco every season; he's an old friend. He tries the piano, the same one he used last year, finds it passable, and wipes at the keys with his handkerchief. Delgado signals the oboe to play another A. The orchestra tunes, and as the conductor raises his arms, Tibor exchanges a glance of solidarity with the concertmaster. A weak downbeat confirms suspicions. Tibor frowns. The long opening tutti is a mess. "No, no!" Delgado shouts. "No. Follow, gentlemen, please. Celli, basses, marcato, please, strong. I want to hear *va-va-va* not *pa-pa-pa*, more sustained. Measure twenty-three, celli, basses, alone."

Tibor leans back and folds his arms. He scans the

orchestra. A last-stand fiddle player crosses his legs, looks bored. The first oboe is shaving a reed, someone in the horns seems to be reading behind his stand, and the timpani player is hunched over his drums, turning knobs. The first-chair flute player nuzzles the silver rod of her instrument with her mouth, her pink tongue darting out to moisten her lips. She has large oval eyes and long black silky hair. She's probably bright and witty, with a fantastic tongue and a penchant for oral sex, like all flutists. Concentrate, Szabo tells himself, but Delgado stops every few measures, bellows, and the solo entrance is still miles away. The orchestra fidgets. Unless it's a genius on the podium, they don't want to be yelled at, and if it's a genius, he won't need to yell. Tibor's eyes wander, meet the flute player's, stare at her. She smiles. If he smiles back she might come to his dressing room, sit on his lap, show him some simply remarkable articulations in the slow hours between rehearsal and sleep. He smiles meaningfully, and returns his focus to the keyboard in time to ease into his entrance. The orchestra is with him, following every nuance. Stopping and starting with Delgado is no longer annoying. Szabo likes to rehearse, he likes to repeat, work out problems, even with a conductor he doesn't admire. The Brahms seems new to him again, he concentrates, he is in a small airless space, no windows, blinding lights, but again he feels free.

His last ascending arpeggio, the orchestra's final D-major chord, and then cheers, the shuffle of approving feet, and voices yell, "Bravo!" Tibor shakes hands with Delgado, claps him on the back. It isn't so bad after all, and with another rehearsal tomorrow, the concert might even be OK. Tibor throws his jacket around his shoulders and walks to his dressing room, passing musicians as they pack up instruments. A poker game has picked up where it was interrupted before rehearsal began, coins jingle in

Coke machines, hands wave, eyes wink, bravos echo as Szabo heads down the hall. The flutist is leaning against the door to his dressing room, an oblong flute case resting on her arm.

"Are you waiting for me?" Tibor asks.

"Yes, just to say how marvelous you sound."

"And you, what a glorious tone, so round, full. I love it."

"You loved it last year, too," she says, sarcastically enough for him to take another look and realize he stroked that silky hair, gazed into those oval eyes the last time he played in San Francisco. Yes, of course, and how much easier it will be this time. He takes her into his dressing room, kisses her hand, tells her how wonderful it is to see her again while he fishes for her name. She's fine, thank you very much, and married now to the first clarinetist.

"Congratulations," Tibor says, curiously relieved. "I wish you every happiness."

Jim takes him back to the hotel and invites him to dinner. He says he's tired and declines. There is another rehearsal in the morning, and he needs some sleep.

In the lobby, heading for the elevators, he hears a piano being played in the Wayfarer's Lounge. On the display board, a glossy photo with the name Bobby Bontempo shines at him. Tibor stands at the door to listen for a minute. A man with a red toupee, diamond rings on his fingers, sits at the keyboard of a white upright piano. He puckers his lips and says into a microphone, "And now, from my last motion picture, for which I won an Academy Award and sold twenty-five million copies, here's the song you've all been waiting for, 'You Are My Lunch.'" Folks at the bar chuckle. Bobby turns on the mellotrone, the electronic rhythm machine, and selects a disco beat. He cracks his knuckles, adjusts a sleeve of his silk blouse, takes a sip of his drink, and tickles the ivories. Mid-number he leans over to talk to a customer. He smiles, he laughs. Imagine, Tibor thinks, being able to do that, play the piano and live at the same time. Bobby arpeggios up and down, ends his selection with a thumbnail sweep of the keys.

Tibor goes up to his room, automatically switches on the television but turns the sound off. He watches Arabs dash across the desert, camels rear onto hind legs, blood in the sand. Obviously a love story. He switches the set off. Opening his briefcase, he takes out a manila file, looks for his itinerary.

Artist: Szabo. Date: April 17, 1976. San Francisco. Is it still April 17? He checks his watch. Yes, but with the three-hour time change it's been a long day.

April 18, April 19. Concerts: San Francisco Opera House. Fee, $12,000. He'll have to talk to Michael. If he gets ten for a single, then a pair should surely be fourteen.

April 20. Recital: Los Angeles. Dorothy Chandler Pavilion. Program I. Program I? It must be a mistake. He thought the L.A. program was the same as the one for Carnegie Hall. He looks through the file for Program I. *Gaspard de la nuit?* It can't be. He flings the file across the bed and rushes into the next room to the piano. His heart is racing. He rubs his chin, puts his fingers on the keyboard, and sails through the entire piece, spraying the notes of "Ondine" into delicate mists, steadily tolling the B-flats of "Le Gibet," and negotiating the intricate hand-crossings and waves of staccatos in "Scarbo" with ease. It's solidly in his head and his hands. What is he panicking about?

What's the big deal, Szabo? Pull yourself together, he thinks in adopted American phrases. He takes on the coloration around him, soaks up language and dialect like a sponge. "Cool it," he tells himself, sighs, stretches, and ambles across the room to the window. The city is lit up, the hills outlined with thousands of lights, the water rippling in the distance. He's hungry. There's always room service. He could order a steak and watch the late movie, but he hates the idea of eating alone in his room like a rabbit in its hutch. Some hutch. If Stephan could see it, this luxury, this extravagance, he'd narrow his eyes. "When I was your age," he would say, looking like an eagle with his long nose, his white hair like feathers around his neck, his thin fingers like talons, "I was on tour in Prussia. There were no cars, only slow trains, and the hotels were freezing. . . ."

Tibor remembers those long nostalgic stories his teacher told, filled with perils and rewards, evoking an elegant era—Paris at the turn of the century, the gloire of prewar Europe. Tibor would sit for hours watching him and listening. . . .

"I was playing a recital. It had taken me two days by train to get to that town. I was exhausted. The snow was very deep, and I had to wear snowshoes to get to the concert hall. I arrived frozen, and the piano was impossible, and the hall was half empty for the concert. After I played, no one came backstage, no one greeted me, congratulated me. Nothing. I went back to the hotel thoroughly depressed. You know, in those days in Prussia there were no closets in the hotels. One hung one's clothing on a peg outside the door to one's room. I came back from the concert, cold and lonely, and I dragged myself up the stairs to my room, and on the peg on the door to the room next to mine was hanging a skirt, a long woman's skirt. It had a tiny waist, so small, and delicate embroidery, and on the floor in the corridor were a pair of satin shoes, completely wet, drenched from the snow. I was excited, thrilled by the sight of that skirt, those shoes. Can you imagine what I did? Yes, I knocked on the door. A young woman opened the door, but what a woman, what a beauty, and such a smile when she greeted me, and she was wearing a long white robe trimmed with fur. She smiled at me. I began to stammer and mumbled something about seeing her wet shoes and wondering if she had caught a chill in the snow and if she was all right.

" 'Come in,' she said to me—in such a voice, like little bells. She had a suite of rooms, and flowers everywhere, roses, roses, it was like a garden. She was an actress, she told me. 'I am a pianist,' I told her. 'I know,' she said. 'I have just been to your recital. You are a magnificent artist. You moved me deeply.' I was in heaven, as you can imagine, my heart raced. I fell to my knees and kissed the hem of her robe. She began to stroke my hair. Then she made love to me. My first experience. It was beautiful beyond description."

Tibor's stomach growls. He'll have to eat something, and since it's still early, he'll go out. He takes a cable car to Fisherman's Wharf. He listens to the motorman ring a bell in rhythms, watches people hop on, hop off, and he holds on to a pole, leans out of the car as it heaves up and down the steep hills. The air is cold against his face, refreshing, and at the end of the line he stays on while the car turns around for the trip back, tons of steel moving gracefully, effortlessly, and the motorman ringing his ring. He jumps down, walks around. He looks in an antique shop, at rusted clocks, old shoes, diamond pins, and finds a silver butter knife with the ornate letters *SFS*. He thinks about his first breakfast back in London and how surprised Sally will be when he tells her to look closely at the knife she's buttering her toast with. He can see the cerulean blue of her clear eyes looking back at him, he can feel her buttery kiss. He buys the knife for five dollars, then walks to the end of the pier, looks into the black water. His body reflected in the surface seems to break apart, magically come together, disintegrate again. He is dizzy and decides it must be hunger. There is fresh fish for sale even at ten p.m., shrimps to eat right there on the docks, mussels, clams, but he can't eat standing up. He picks a restaurant, the Silver Fish, sits down, orders wine, and chats with the waitress. She's a college student named June, working nights, with hazel eyes and freckles.

"What do you do?" she asks, watching him butter his sourdough bread.

"I play the piano."

"Oh, yeah? You have a group?"

"Not really."

"Oh, I get it, you play at a bar someplace around here?"

"I'm a classical pianist."

"Oh," she says, "Beethoven, heavy stuff?"

"Yes," he says, smiling at her, watching her hips sway under her white nylon uniform as she balances a tray that looks so heavy he wants to carry it for her. "You're awfully delicate to be carrying such a load," he says.

She smiles as she serves him broiled bluefish. "Would you like it off the bone?" she asks.

"Always," he says, "I'm very particular."

She likes the way he talks, his foreign accent, and his tweed jacket, and his long clean hair, very artistic. He asks her to join him for a drink. She'll be free at eleven-thirty, and he waits for her, watching her bend over tables, wipe crumbs away.

June goes into the kitchen, comes back changed into tight blue jeans and a green sweater.

"What is it about California that makes you girls so golden?" Tibor asks as June sips a brandy opposite him.

"The sun just loves us," she says, a dimple on either side of her mouth, her long hair falling over her shoulders like sheaves of wheat.

"You're lovely," Tibor says, "you should be in films."

"I've made a few," she says and opens her eyes innocently wide, "just porns."

"Pornographic films?"

"Just for money. It's one way to pay for textbooks. I

remember one film you would have loved. It was about this girl who falls in love with a violinist, but he loves only his art, and in the end she commits suicide to the slow movement of *Death and the Maiden* by Schumann."

"Schubert."

"Is it?"

Tibor hums the melody of the slow movement.

"That's it," she says, and Tibor imagines her naked, expiring on a pink silk chaise, looking into the camera sad as Camille.

"What are you studying?" he asks.

"Anthropology."

"Maybe you're the next Margaret Mead."

"Maybe I am." June giggles.

"Tell me, then, what is it that separates man from the other animals?"

June beams like an eager student with the right answer. "Cognition," she says.

"Right. But monkeys perceive, so do dolphins. What else makes us truly different?"

"Our complex social structures, our advanced civilization—"

"Do you really think it's so advanced? I don't know. Sometimes I get the feeling we should have stayed in the trees."

June wrinkles her nose. "You're a cynic."

"I am and I'm not."

"How can you be both?"

"How can you not be both? How can you look at what's going on in the world—repression, starvation, torture, depravity—and feel anything but contempt? But, on the other hand, how can you hear a Beethoven symphony, a Bach prelude, and not be elated?"

"If you feel that way about music, it must be a wonderful profession."

"It's not a profession. It's a way of life."

"I wish I had that kind of devotion to my studies," June says, pouting.

"You can," Tibor tells her, touches her sleeve. "You can."

June tips her glass back, runs her tongue along the edge to catch a last drop of brandy, the way Tibor as a child licked the last of his málnaszörp, the raspberry syrup mixed with soda that was his favorite treat. He looks at June and thinks of his sister. He'll see her in Cleveland in a few days, his yearly visit to her home; she'll have raspberry syrup waiting, and they'll talk. He feels tired now and says he'd better be going, he has to get up early. He pays his check and leaves some money on the table.

"Hey, are you crazy, you gave me a two-hundred-dollar tip," June says.

"I know."

"I can't possibly accept it."

"Buy yourself some textbooks," Tibor instructs, kisses her hand, and rushes out the door.

He rides the cable car back to the hotel, takes a hot bath, asks the operator not to put through any calls, yes, even out-of-town, even overseas, thank you, and a wake-up call for eight a.m. Willy Kapell surfaces in his sleep. They are face to face underwater, treading water, beautiful colored fish swim past, seaweed brushes against them. Kapell opens his mouth to talk. Only bubbles come out. He looks at Willy's face. His face is calm. He is at peace.

"Maya, you're an artist," Tibor says as he stands near the kitchen table in her house in Cleveland, copper pots gleaming on a wrought-iron rack, plants hanging above, children's collages pasted to the fridge next to him. His sister slaps the dough, rolls it, eases it out like thrown clay. Black curls dangle into her eyes and she tosses them back with a shake of her head.

"You're not the only genius in the family," Maya says, waving a floured hand, "and get your paws out of the poppy seed."

Tibor grabs a clump of seeds mixed with sugar, the filling for her mákosrétes, and pops it into his mouth before she can stop him. Maya looks annoyed, but he throws his arms around her, tells her not to be angry, rocks her back and forth, then pinches her bottom. "You still have a nice ass," he whispers into her ear, and ducks from anticipated revenge.

"And you are still the baby brother. When are you planning to grow up, for God's sake, going around goosing your sister in the kitchen."

"In the ass. Be precise, Maya, be precise."

She throws a sponge at him. He catches it and heaves himself up onto a counter top, sits swinging his legs, looking at her defiantly, just as he did when he was a child and she'd tell him to wear his galoshes, or to remember to buy milk, pick up bread, or come home early. And Maya looks back with the same penetrating eyes, the eyes of someone always watching, always on guard, looking out for everyone. Their mother, Eva, was involved in her work, and as her position at the Institute for Biological Research kept improving, it meant more hours away from home. There was Szusza, the housekeeper, who came in from her village twice a week, but Maya had the apartment in order anyhow, doing much of the tidying, baking, cleaning herself, making sure the groceries were brought in, Katya the parakeet fed, her brother well behaved. Five years older than he, she was "so grown up," as her parents proudly said, that responsibilities were handed to her like candies to other children. She was competent and sensitive, and when Tibor was five, and one day sat down at the piano, picked out the melody of a Beethoven bagatelle by himself, Maya listened and said, "Papa, you must teach him." She was the one who made sure he practiced, who sent him off to his music lessons on time, who hugged him if he came home sad, who shared his secrets. And it was Maya who told him secrets, especially the secret of the Szabo household—that the divine theories of communism taught at school were not worshipped by their parents. It was a dangerous thing to know. A child could send his parents to prison if he betrayed any knowledge of their disillusionment with The System. The State Protecting Group, the AVO, watched everyone everywhere. Their cousins' father spent two years in prison camp for forgetting to go to a meeting. A colleague of Eva's had been arrested for writing an article disputing Lysenko's unscientific genetics, which Stalin favored. It was a dangerous time, it became more dangerous, and before they knew it, it was 1956 and Maya and her brother were crossing a swamp at night, leaving their country, their home, their family.

"Have you heard from Mama?" Tibor asks, and leans back against a cherrywood cabinet.

"I had a letter last week," Maya says and goes back to kneading dough.

"And what did she say?"

"The usual, she's working hard, her research is coming along, her apartment is cozy and cheerful."

"Sounds like she's having an affair."

Maya laughs. "You fool," she says. "Always inventing what people should do, should be like, never understanding what they are."

"That's not true."

"Ah, he's defensive."

"I'm not. I'm just instinctive. I know when Mother is happy in her little nest, she's happy for personal reasons, emotional reasons. There must be a man involved."

"Wishful thinking. I don't think she's had anyone since Papa died."

"What about Gustav?"

"That old Czech painter? No. I'm sure they're just friends."

"I suppose we'll never know."

"Why do you care?"

"What kind of question is that? I care, of course I care, because it's natural. She's my mother. *Our* mother."

"Yes, *our* mother," Maya says, her tone acid.

"What's that supposed to mean?"

She looks away. "I don't know."

"Come on," Tibor says, annoyed. "Stop being coy. Talk."

Maya wipes her hands on her apron, picks at small bits of dough that stick between her fingers.

"I've never quite figured Mama out, that's all. She seemed fine until you started playing the piano. Maybe then she got frightened that Papa's attention would focus on you, that you'd become the most important thing in his life. And you did. And Mama started working, harder and harder. I don't think she wanted to spend so much time at her lab, but she took refuge there—she became an exile, a stranger in her own house, an occasional visitor. Remember how in the summer, when she'd manage to take time off to join us at Lake Balaton, her enjoyment seemed qualified. I could see that she was sad underneath, knowing we'd go back to the city and she'd be pushed away again."

,"Then she must have resented me, and I never felt resented. Maya, you've got it all wrong."

"Have I? There was resentment in our house, all right. But not toward you. *I* was the one she resented, because *I* took her place."

"Nonsense. She adored you, you were the perfect daughter."

Maya rolls a tiny chunk of dough between two fingers, speaking softly. "I'll never forget her eyes, the night she sent us away—cold gray eyes, hard as steel, and the rough way she buttoned my coat over those layers of clothes, and—"

"Maya!" Tibor stops her. "I don't believe it's you talking like this. It nearly killed Mama to send us away. *She* was the brave one."

"She could have come with us," Maya insists. "If she had, then Papa would have come too, instead of staying behind to be a hero. A dead hero."

Tibor bites at his thumbnail, spits out a sharp piece. "Maya," he says, "let old wounds heal."

"Some hurts never heal."

"Not if you keep picking at them."

Maya turns abruptly away.

"Forget it, just forget it," he says. She lights a match to turn on the oven, wipes her hands on a striped dish towel, and tugs at her blouse. Tibor can't help noticing her still-firm breasts, her still-slim waist. He can't help wondering if Walter, her husband, a diligent surgeon who is nice but humorless, successful but self-effacing, can possibly satisfy this voluptuous, energetic, vivacious woman.

"Sometimes I wonder," Tibor says, "what would have become of you if you'd stayed with me in Paris."

"I wanted to come to the States."

"I know, but still. I can't help seeing you in a spruced-up garret on the rue Jacob, a free independent woman."

"There you go again, inventing instead of seeing. It's a good thing you can play the piano—otherwise you'd be a total fool."

"Flattery will get you nowhere, my dear bourgeois suburban sister."

Maya clicks her tongue, steps toward him belligerently, hands on hips. "Listen, having these children, Walter, this wonderful house, being free to enjoy them, and what's more, *enjoying* them, is this a crime?"

"I just wonder if you're happy."

"Who has time to think about being happy? What about you? You should be the happy one in the family—you're famous, you're on top of the world."

"I thought I was in Cleveland."

"Clever. You use that clever, charming voice of yours like a ventriloquist. Only you're the dummy."

"Why is that?"

Maya puts her hands on her brother's knees. She's hurt him, somehow, she knows it, sees it in his eyes, dark as a covered sea. "I care so much about you, Tibor, that's all. I just hope you have what you want."

He hops off the counter and hugs her, the clean soapy smell of her hair mixing with the sweet smell of cooking pastries. The kitchen clock ticks loudly, the stove pings like acorns dropping, as they did in Buda, on the hilltops in autumn, fog rolling in as he and Maya raced from oak to oak, baskets on their arms, collecting acorns to take home and paint, make people with matchsticks and acorn heads, while Szusza cooked a chestnut puree and sang a song about the wind.

He feels suddenly tired and says he should have a nap, after all, there is a performance to play that night. "Wake me up when the kids get home, OK?" he says, kissing Maya on the head.

"OK," she says and watches her brother slowly climb the stairs.

He dreams: he is with Maya in a swamp, holding her hand; silver light from the moon hurts his eyes, and cattails shake like rattles in the wind. He squeezes Maya's hand so hard she nearly cries out and flashes him a warning look. Her eyes are full of silver and she pulls him to keep moving. Water and mud suck at his feet, the earth becomes a giant mouth sucking at him, and birch trees close around them with branches sharp as knives. He looks up and sees stars sprinkled like broken bits of glass in the sky. Laszlo, their guide, makes the signal to stop, and he crouches low with Laszlo, Maya, the lady with the baby strapped to her, the baby that has been drugged so it will not cry, and Josef, the old man who clutches at his heart. Tibor feels pain somewhere, he cannot seem to locate it, pain in the center of his body, somewhere in his chest. He has stopped breathing, he is suffocating. You must inhale, he tells himself, but do it slowly, for God's sake, slow, easy, otherwise you will make noise. Slowly he fills his nostrils with cold air, slowly the air enters like a thin sharp pipe up his nose, down into his throat. It must be torture. Is it? Is it he who is being tortured or is it his father? He sees his father, reaches out to touch him, but his father falls, disappears. Laszlo is gone, and the mother with her baby is helping the old man across the swamp. He and Maya are left behind. The earth sucks at them, the sky explodes with grenades, and eyes are everywhere, everywhere. He tries to scream, he tries and tries, but there is no air no breath no voice.

"Uncle Tibor!" Kitty yells, jumping on the bed. "Uncle Tibor, you're all wet."

Tibor opens his eyes. He blinks and looks at the small dark-haired child wrinkling her nose at him.

"You're wet," she repeats.

"So I am," he answers, looking at her eyes, so like Maya's. He kisses her forehead.

"Yuck," she says. "Why are you all wet?"

"I must have been sweating in my sleep, dreaming."

"What did you dream about?"

"About a forest, an enchanted forest."

Kitty chews a cookie thoughtfully and drops crumbs onto the sheets. "And what happened there?" she asks.

"There were lovely silver trees and birds that sang all night and the moon was beautiful."

"It sounds stupid."

"Does it?" Tibor asks, pulling back the covers and getting up.

"My daddy wears baggy panties, but you don't," she observes and watches him dress. Her brother, Lenny, comes into the room, glass of milk in hand.

"Lenny," Tibor says, patting him on the back, "how are you, how's school?"

Lenny groans. "How's school? Can't you be more original? I'm ten, you know. You can talk to me like I'm a person now."

"Sorry, person," Tibor says, takes the glass of milk out of his hands, puts it on the bureau, grabs him, and they fall onto the floor, wrestling, tickling. Lenny pins Tibor down, Kitty hops onto his stomach, and he pleads defeat, begs to surrender. Reluctantly they get up, and Tibor hoists them both into his arms, clatters down the stairs, making Maya rush into the front hall. They fall into a heap at the foot of the stairs, laughing.

"Come on," Maya says, clapping her hands, "time for homework. Time for Uncle Tibor to practice."

"I forgot about that," Tibor says, smoothing his hair, his eyes narrowing.

"What's the matter?" Maya asks.

Tibor leans on the banister. "I had such a frightful dream."

"About the piano?"

"Worse."

"About what?"

Tibor wants to tell her, but thinks of the children and wants to tell her how he adores them, and thinks of Sally and wants to tell her he's in love. Thoughts swirl in his head, but his performance in a few hours of the Beethoven

Second Piano Concerto with the Cleveland Orchestra rises through, holds steady, sound replaces thought, and he heads for the piano. He closes himself into the sun porch to practice on the Steinway Maya keeps tuned just for his yearly visit. She listens from the kitchen, remembering when he was twelve and just discovering this concerto. "Listen, Maya," he said to her then. "It's so happy, it is an unhappy man's happiness, listen." Tibor practices the last movement, the Rondo, so ebullient and full of joy. So why am I crying? Maya wonders, wipes her eyes, and continues making the salad.

Ten weeks later, Maya Szabo Rothman hung up the phone, brushed some strands of black hair out of her eyes as the corners of her mouth pushed down and her chin dimpled, began to tremble. She firmly placed one open palm against her mouth to steady it but felt tears welling up anyhow, blurring her vision of an avocado plant that, she noticed, badly needed water. She reached for a Kleenex and called, "Walter!"

Her husband rushed into the kitchen, put his arms around her and felt his shirt get wet where her eyes pressed against him. He cradled her head against his long neck. Nicknamed "the Giraffe" by his children, he was tall, redheaded, and freckled, with an endless neck, and he didn't talk much, stood quietly and thoughtfully, his lips moving slightly as if nibbling at leaves in high branches. Maya provided all the voice needed in the house. She was quick and volatile, and after fifteen years of marriage, it was still hard for Walter to know when to take her frequent outbursts seriously.

"Sit down," Walter told her and kissed her on the head. Maya sank into a white plastic chair and sobbed. Tears poured down her cheeks, her mouth and nose pinched together, and her hair began to droop like wet feathers. Walter sat next to her, patted her arm, looking at her with his large brown eyes.

"I just spoke to Mother," Maya said, hiccoughed, and blew her nose. "She knows he's disappeared. She's already been contacted by his managers, even the police.

She sounds distressed, but in control, as always. I wonder if she even cares."

"That's unkind," Walter said.

"Is it? Was she ever there when we needed her?"

Walter sighed. "You know," he said, his voice careful but firm, "there comes a time in your life when you have to give up your grudges against your parents."

"Grudges? I have no grudges. I simply know the woman well."

"Do you? Maya, you're upset."

"Of course I'm upset. My brother, my baby brother, is in trouble. I've been afraid of this for years. I knew it would happen. He had to explode, it was inevitable, and it's my fault."

"How can it be your fault?"

"There were signs, I saw them when he was here in April."

"Like what?"

"He was secretive, repressed, vacillating between childishness and seriousness. He said he had a bad dream, he—"

"In other words, he was himself."

"He was troubled. I knew it but I couldn't help him."

"Was he in love?"

"He's always in love—it's never serious."

"Maybe it is now."

"I'll tell you what is serious—if Tibor Szabo didn't show up for a recital in Berlin and no one knows where he is, there is something wrong, something serious and complicated. He's never canceled a concert, he's played with pneumonia, he's walked through blizzards to perform, played on broken-down pianos, he's always played."

"Well, maybe there just comes a point when it's simply too much, too tiring, too much travel, all that endless practicing, endless adulation, no time for reflection."

Maya shrugged her shoulders, stood up and reached for a pitcher, filled it at the sink, and watered the avocado plant. She watched the water spill into the cracked and grooved flesh of the exposed pit, reminding her of the wrinkled animal brains she saw as a child in her mother's laboratory.

"Why do you work so hard," Maya asked her mother then, "and with dead things?"

Eva Szabo patted her chignon into place. "It's from the dead that we will learn the secrets of life," she said, a strand of golden hair falling across her high forehead, her mouth in a serious pout that could at any moment turn into a smile. Maya looked up into her mother's pale gray eyes and wondered how she could smell of flowers when she worked all day with formaldehyde, and how she could be so pretty and so smart, so busy, and yet even when she came home late at night she still seemed fresh and full of stories. Maya had a favorite and begged her mother to tell it over and over again, the story of the Kecskeköröm, the little shell that is found only at Lake Balaton, the resort where the family took its yearly vacation in August. Long ago there was a goatherd who had a beautiful flock, but when he did something wrong—it was never quite clear what—the goats were all swallowed up by the lake. That is why, at the bottom of Lake Balaton, under the blue water, there are tiny crescent-shaped shells like the hooves of the lost goats. Once, when they went swimming, Eva helped the children collect the shells and they sat up late that night pasting them onto cardboard, then drawing goats to go with the hooves.

"Why is he drawing goats when he should be practicing?" their father, Imre, asked, wiping at his stiff mustache with an embroidered handkerchief, his deep-set dark eyes looking straight at Tibor, who smiled and gave his sister's ankle a conspiratorial kick under the table. Eva kicked her other leg, and Maya said, without flinching, "He practiced today, Papa, two hours. I even heard him practice the Chopin B-minor Étude slowly."

"Really? Fine, fine," Imre said, nodding at his wife and children with pleasure, as if Tibor's progress was the source of their communal well-being. "I'd like to hear it before you go to bed," he added, and went into the living room to smoke his meerschaum pipe and wait for his son to play for him on the little Pleyel upright they rented for the month of August.

"You see how musical I am," he would say while playing a tentative *secondo* to his little son's assured *primo* in Schubert's Divertissement à la Hongroise for four hands. "But I haven't the equipment, I didn't work hard enough."

Maya watched their hands, Papa's like large bears marching proudly next to Tibor's two small cubs.

"Maya?" Walter asked.

"What?" she murmured distantly.

"I don't know what to make of this supposed disappearance, and I don't want you to think I'm taking it lightly, but I'm sure he'll turn up somewhere. He'll probably even call you. He always does. Didn't he talk to you last week from Vienna?"

"Yes."

"How did he sound?"

"Fine, same as ever."

"You see?"

"I see nothing. He always sounds fine. He wears a camouflage of good spirits."

"Sometimes people *are* in good spirits, they *are* cheerful, they *are* happy. Tibor always struck me as happy. He's certainly got more to be happy about than most people."

"He's not most people."

"Oh, come on, Maya," he said, reaching out to pat her arm, "he's fine, just fine. Don't worry. It's all a big exaggeration, the phone will ring any minute." Walter picked out the *New England Journal of Medicine* from the basket of magazines next to the table and began to read, his lips moving slightly. Maya gazed beyond her husband's head at the green push-button phone that clung to the daisied wallpaper, trailing its long green twisted cord like patient ivy.

≽ *Artist: Szabo. Date: April 26, 1976. Chicago.*
O'Hare International Airport, American flight 232 from
L.A. is on time. Dolores is there to meet him, and as they
wait for his bags, they chat about this and that, his concert
in L.A., did he play any French music, was it wonderful.
She looks around wondering if there will be any photogra-
phers.

"Doesn't the press meet you?" Dolores asks.

"I'm just a pianist, not a movie star, not a politician,"
Tibor says. "Besides, the press can stuff it."

"Did you get a bad review somewhere?"

"How can you tell? Yes, in fact, in today's *Cleveland Plain
Dealer*, courtesy of Marvin Schaden, and he should know,
since he's a failed pianist himself."

"What did he say?"

"Nothing important, just that I can't play Beethoven."

"Well, you know you can, so why get annoyed?"

"It's hard not to. The trouble with reviews is that when
you get a bad one, you know it's wrong, but when you get
a good one you also know it's wrong, because the
reviewers are basically deaf—the ears have walls."

In the taxi Dolores leans close, looks intent, tries to make
conversation. Tibor frowns and says he has a muscle
spasm in his right shoulder. "I am being a terrible bore,
please forgive me," he says, and touches her hand, lovely
but lifeless as a sun-warmed autumn leaf, not like the lotus
of Sally's hand, curled, succulent, delicious. He closes his
eyes.

"You're in pain," Dolores says. "I'm very good at massage." After he checks in at the Drake, they enter his suite and Dolores tells him to take off his coat, jacket, tie, and shirt. He strips obediently and collapses face down on the bed, groaning appropriately. Dolores massages his shoulder, talking softly. He is aware of her voice, but drifts off, answers in grunts as her hands press and knead, like Maya shaping dough. Her perfume is sweet as pastry; he sighs and falls asleep.

Dolores wonders if she should leave. She decides instead to make herself useful, so she quietly opens a suitcase, hangs up his suits, pairs up his shoes, placing them neatly on the closet floor, slides drawers open and arranges his shirts and socks, gliding around the room like a soft breeze. When Tibor opens his eyes an hour later, she is sitting near the bed in a wing chair, the Gideon Bible on her lap.

"Keeping vigil, are you?" Tibor asks, and reaches out his hand for her. She moves to the bed, sits on the edge, caresses his shoulder and asks if it's any better.

"Much," he says, rolls over on his back and looks at her eyes carefully outlined in black, her lips pulled back into a tight smile, her porcelain skin like a prize Sèvres plate, more pleasing to admire than to touch. "Sorry I fell asleep," he says casually. "What did you do while I slept?"

"I unpacked for you," she proudly announces, which sends a weak flurry of annoyance to Tibor's head, but he's too groggy to take exception. Besides, the invasion of privacy involves only suits and shoes, nothing important.

"Well, what did you find to read?" he asks.

"The Song of Solomon."

Tibor has looked into eyes as dovelike as hers, touched breasts as like twin roes, and although she is fair—she *is* fair—it's a song he strangely feels no desire to sing. "Look, Dolores," he says, stroking her hand, "I have this recital tonight, so please forgive me if I seem distracted. I think I'd better go over to Orchestra Hall to practice."

"May I come and listen?"

You called her from San Francisco, Tibor tells himself, you said you wanted her. Be nice.

"Of course," he says.

Dolores comes along, a solitary audience sitting in the middle of an empty gray hall, while Tibor ignores her entirely for two hours. First he stretches his hands—left, reaching for tenths, elevenths, then the right. He stops, cracks his knuckles and plays scales in thirds, pushing to make them clean and even. Next, Chopin's Étude opus 10, no. 4, left hand only, twice. And because he feels strong, the Schumann Toccata. Now he can practice. The last movement of Beethoven opus 57 has been bothering him, and he tackles the passages with left-hand leaps, playing them slow, fast, faster, repeating them over and over. Then he goes through the entire sonata, concentrating on levels of dynamics, rebuilding like a fastidious architect.

He shakes his hands, moves his head side to side, and without resting, thinks of *Gaspard*—the opening, the monster opening. He spends time on the right-hand triads, tries a counting trick of Stephan's, rejects it. The action of the piano isn't even. How can he be expected to play on an unmade bed? He'll have to ask for the tuner to come back. Meanwhile he moves to a passage at the end of "Ondine," then plays all of "Scarbo," under tempo, making sure it's clean before whipping through it once like a demon. When he stops for a moment, Dolores's voice, asking if he'd like coffee, startles him.

"Was that Beethoven, that piece you were playing in the middle?" she asks, standing below the lip of the stage, looking up.

"Yes," he says and sits down on the edge of the stage, takes a sip of coffee that's too sweet, too weak, and tastes of paper, and thanks her for being so thoughtful. She smiles, pleased to help, pleased to guess the composer. "That reviewer is an idiot," she says.

"Which?" he asks, forgetting, remembering. "Oh, Cleveland. Well, it was a different piece. If he heard me play the 'Appassionata' he'd probably hate it, too."

"I doubt it. It's so exciting, so dramatic, the way you play it. When you waited, just before that last fast part, and then played again, it really sent chills through me."

"I think you mean the cadence into the third movement, when you're expecting the tonic, a perfect resolution, and suddenly he hits you with a diminished seventh, then jolts you out of that peaceful hymn with those violent figurations—"

Tibor stops abruptly, splattering coffee on the stage. It's Dolores he's talking to, not Werner, not Zev, not someone with whom he can discuss Beethoven's use of Neapolitan harmonies, his fixation on D-flat. He is alone, without his friends.

"Is it your shoulder?" Dolores asks, concerned.

"I guess so," Tibor says and winces.

"You really should rest again before the concert."

"I should," he agrees. But he worries that she'll want to rest with him, and he feels no warm surge of blood to his thighs, no pressing need. He's relieved when Dolores wants to go home to get ready for the evening, glad to sleep alone, crisp sheets cool against his skin, a soft pillow to put on top of his head to block out noise, thoughts, everything but sleep.

Tibor is wide awake for the concert. Strong and expansive in two Brahms rhapsodies, relentless in the "Appassionata," gracious at intermission, sensuous in Ravel's *Gaspard de la nuit*, elegant in the Chopin impromptus, and after ovations and encores, he's backstage with flowers and handshakes, smiling at Dolores, who waits patiently, glowing with the excitement of a Szabo recital played for her, her alone.

At Maxim's de Paris, Tibor orders a sumptuous meal, entertains Dolores with stories, imitations. He's funny and charming, delighted with himself for playing well, winding down like a top spun hard. When it's midnight, when Dolores nuzzles beside him, waits for his next move, he feels suddenly exhausted, motionless. It's hard to breathe, his arms ache, his head hurts, his shoulder is acting up.

"Maybe it's the flu," he tells Dolores.

"I'm not afraid of catching it," she says.

"I'd feel terrible if you did."

"Don't worry about me," she says, but he does, she worries him, he doesn't want to hurt her feelings, but in less than a week, three concerts, and a stop in New York, he'll be home with Sally, and for the first time in his life, he decides to skip dessert.

"I'll take you home now," Tibor announces.

Dolores tries to be a good sport, smiles at him as she would for a passenger who's made one request too many, and goes home thinking Szabo's performance is restricted exclusively to the stage.

At the hotel, Tibor takes a long hot bath with bubbles smelling like a pine forest. It seems an absolute luxury to get into bed with a book. It doesn't move and it lets him fall asleep. Pages flutter past his eyes and his hand rests on page 40 of Schumann's *Music and Musicians*, a fine edition, in German, presented to him by an admirer. "Music resembles chess," the aphorism his index finger touches begins. "The queen (melody) has the greatest power, but the king (harmony) decides the game."

Artist: Szabo. Date: April 27, 1976. West Lafayette, Indiana.

A daisy pokes through the tarmac and the air feels soft, the sun warm on his shoulders as Tibor leaves the plane on shaky legs. "Looking forward to tonight," the pilot of the six-seater jet-prop Indiana Airways plane shouts to Tibor, waves, and runs toward the parking lot to get to his class on time. "I'm a psychology professor at Purdue," he told Tibor, who, last to the plane, got the only seat available, next to the pilot. "I just fly in my spare time," he had said as he checked the gyroscope and leveled off at 15,000 feet. White numbers on the black instrument panel jumped at Tibor like smashed piano keys. He closed his eyes and tried to breathe. Michael had warned him that the only way to fly to West Lafayette, Indiana, was by commuter aircraft, but he hadn't told him he'd be flying in a mosquito with a Jungian at the controls.

A bearded, heavy-set student named Brian, wearing a red flannel shirt and hiking boots, meets him, pumps his hand, and says, "Looks like summer."

"Doesn't it, though," Tibor agrees as they heap his bags into the back of a Pinto. Warm air after the chill wind of Chicago is a relief, his mood, nascent with high spirits, lifts like spring mist and he whistles, watches green leaves flash by.

Brian drives and recites the history of the school: "When Abe Lincoln signed the Morrill Act the federal government turned over public lands to any state which would use them to establish colleges devoted to the study of agriculture, which is why we're mostly aggies here and technical types, but we still like the arts. There are thirty thousand students and we have several performance series during the—"

"What's the hall like?" Tibor interrupts as they bump over flat roads potholed from snow and ice.

"Elliott Hall is one of the largest in the country; seats six thousand."

"I've heard," Tibor says, having reluctantly agreed to this concert after arguing with Michael about the loss of intimacy in such a gargantuan place. "But all those kids out there dying to hear you," Michael had pleaded. "Besides, you can't only play in the major cities, it's bad for your career. It's the smaller cities that keep an artist alive."

"Are the acoustics decent?" Tibor asks Brian.

"There's some echo. I mean, it's a big place. We don't have many solo recitals there, only when it's someone like you, a real superstar who can sell out for us."

The superstar stops in front of the massive stone Memorial Union. He turns, squints at the sun, longs to drop his briefcase and run down the street, gambol in the grass, but he looks at his watch, sighs, and climbs long marble steps to check in.

Brian shows Tibor to his room in the Union, the only place to stay in town. Tibor wants to see the hall, try the piano, and they walk together, through the Memorial Union into the Stewart Center, a vast complex connected by intricate passageways and tunnels to other buildings on campus. The day is shut out, gone, as they walk down stairs, up stairs, through dim subterranean passages painted sky-blue to get to Elliott Hall. "There are passageways like this connecting the whole university," Brian tells Tibor, "catacombs with treacherous turns. Once they found a student dead in one of these mazes. He had eaten most of his senior thesis in a desperate attempt to stay alive. All they found were a few scraps and the title page, 'Paradise Lost: A Modern Dilemma.' "

Tibor laughs and walks close to Brian, the click of his leather soles in counterpoint with the squeak of Brian's boots. Crowds of students pass, wearing jeans and holding books, laughing, joking. "It must be fun to go to school here, to have a real college life," Tibor says.

"It's pretty nice. Didn't you go to college?"

"No. I studied at the Paris Conservatoire, that's all," he

says, remembering the serious faces, young people burdened with the motivation toward one obsessive goal—to be a great musician. "What's this?" Tibor asks, stopping at glass windows to look down into a huge game room with dozens of tables for pool and snooker. "Fantastic. How about a match?" he asks Brian.

"I thought you wanted to practice," Brian answers.

It presses at him like a firm hand against his back, the need to practice. It pushes Tibor away from games, and they turn another corner, take another ramp up to Elliott Hall.

The hall is so vast Tibor can't see the last rows in the audience. "That's OK," Brian tells him, "they won't be able to see you, either."

The stage crew, all students, gather around, move the piano, fix the lights, watch and listen as Tibor tries a few scales, plays a Joplin rag, lets them lean against the piano before he announces that he's sorry, but he'd better work, could they please allow him some privacy.

"I'll wait for you," Brian announces. "You could get lost trying to find your way back."

Tibor pictures himself wandering aimlessly through labyrinthine passages, losing his way, lying down in a low tunnel, listless, waiting to be rescued. He smiles and finds his way easily, effortlessly, into the intricate passages of the Liszt sonata, which, even though it will be the eighth time he's played it on this tour, he practices as if it will be the first.

At five-thirty Brian leads him back to his room, stop-first at a deli, where Tibor wolfs down Bavarian cream pie and a cup of tea. In his room, he pulls back dusty curtains, watches the quadrangle below, where couples walk hand in hand, some embrace, a girl skips off coltlike in the sunshine. He'd like a walk with Sally just now. He'd hold her hand and watch her cape billow in the wind; he'd embrace her, her long hair twining into his, twisting around him like a vine. Only a few days, but she's thousands of miles away, an entire ocean separating them. He closes the curtains, undresses mechanically. He naps, he wakes, he watches the nightly news, and he dresses for the concert.

Wearing tails, he is stared at as Brian leads him through the clusters of students back to the hall.

"I feel like a stranger from another century, a walking anachronism," Tibor half jokes, cracking his knuckles. He's nervous, more nervous than he was in Chicago. His nerves are unpredictable as wild horses; they will not be tamed.

In the dressing room, Brian wishes him luck, promises him a game of pool after the concert, and leaves Tibor to pace back and forth, trying to calm himself. He chants through his schedule: "Tomorrow, Evansville, next day Boston, then New York, then home to Sally, home to Sally. . . ."

Thoughts of her should calm him down, but they make him even more frantic, a drowning man fighting the rescuer. He flails, he panics, he opens the door to the toilet, raises the seat, and vomits into the bowl. There is still no relief. At eight forty-five a stagehand announces they can wait no longer, and Szabo marches out onto the stage like a prisoner to the gallows, into the merciless spotlight. Six thousand fans applaud, a few whistle, some scream. He's a cult figure, known to old and young in America, a pet of the press—he makes such good copy that at colleges they treat him like a pop star. He is a titan, but he feels minuscule, a dot on the stage, isolated from the crowd, alone. He bows like a toy penguin bobbing up and down, and sits at the keyboard. Wound up, his fingers move as if independent of his will. He watches them curiously as they scatter across the keys; then with fierce determination he snaps his head back, his hair flies, and Szabo races after himself, catches up.

"I had to force myself to play tonight," he confides to Brian as they chalk their cues and rack the balls.
"I couldn't tell. I thought it was terrific."
"Did you?"
"Yeah," Brian says, knocking in the ten-ball. He tries to sink the five into the top left-hand pocket, misses, and leans back against the wall. "I don't know a lot about music, but when you play, it's not like it's just sounds, it's like you're saying something."
"Thanks, Brian," Tibor says, and sinks the four-ball into the right-hand pocket, shoots the nine straight down the middle. It hovers on the edge, drops into the pocket.
"Son of a bitch," Brian sighs, "can't you do anything wrong?"

Artist: Szabo. Date: April 28, 1976. Evansville, Indiana.
"Dear Zev," he writes on the Executive Inn stationery. "When the most exciting building in town is the post office, you know you're in trouble."
He puts down the pen to open a window, finds that the windows do not open, and returns to the desk. "I am a prisoner in Evansville, Indiana, hermetically sealed into an hotel room. If you do not see me by the end of May, send the Israeli Air Force."
He chews on the end of the pen, crumples the paper, throws it into a tin wastebasket. Why do I always wait until the end of a tour to write? he asks himself, and takes another piece of paper anyway.
"My darling mother," he writes in Hungarian. "This tour has been exhausting. Last night I was so sick with nerves, I could hardly make myself go onstage, and when I did and sat down at the piano, it was as if my head was

111

not connected to my body, my hands seemed to move on their own. I was outside of my flesh, an out-of-body experience, as if close to death. I managed to revive myself but . . ."

He sees his mother, Eva, crouched beneath the piano as he found her late one night, pawing at the yellow fringe of the Spanish shawl, weeping. "Mama," he had said, falling to his knees, "what is it?" He had crawled beneath the piano and hugged himself tight against her thighs as she rocked back and forth and cried and said, "It's nothing, my love, don't be afraid, it's nothing," and still she cried.

He taps the pen against the paper and listens to distant voices on the television in the room next to his. He rips up the paper, and decides to take a walk.

He passes the most exciting building in town and walks down an empty street in the center of Evansville, which, like so many centers of so many cities he's seen in the States, is now dying, the population preferring to drive to shopping malls outside city boundaries. He passes turn-of-the-century wooden buildings, some boarded up, some with signs saying FOR SALE, and a large empty Woolworth's. He is the only pedestrian, and his footsteps echo as he walks. He turns back toward the hotel and feels tired, too tired to practice. He drags himself back to his room, lies down fully clothed on the bed, and takes a long dreamless nap.

That night, he plays the best recital of the entire tour.

Artist: Szabo. Date: April 29, 1976. Boston, Massachusetts.

After the recital, his last, he makes excuses to friends and fans and returns to his room at the Ritz Carlton, dines alone at a round table with wheels, eating gravlax and toast, a telephone cradled between ear and shoulder.

"And nobody knew," he says to Michael between crunches. "I play like a god in Evansville, the hall is half empty, and no one cares. Then I come to Boston, the place is sold out, stage seats too, all those smart university people come, and Szabo plays like a pig, a real swine."

"You're exaggerating. I'm sure it was marvelous."

"I'm telling you, it was abominable. Never mind, the tour's over, done with."

"It was a good tour, you did fine, masterful, in fact. Listen, don't waste energy worrying about Boston."

"It's a major city, and Symphony Hall is magnificent. They may never invite me back."

"You're playing with Boston next season. What's the matter with you?"

"I forgot. I must be tired."

"You should be tired, twenty concerts in six weeks. Listen, get some sleep, take an early shuttle to New York, and I'll see you after your meeting with CBS. Don't let them push you into anything you don't want to do."

"No one pushes me; I can handle them. See you tomorrow."

Tibor hangs up and stands at the window, looking out over the Common. The pond is still as a mirror, and a woman stops at the edge, pulls up her collar, turns and looks up at the hotel. Tibor waves, but the woman has already turned and vanished into the darkened streets. What would he want with her, anyhow? He's totally Sally's now, he admits it to himself, and a decision creeps up on him, quietly, persistently, stalks him, holds him— he'll go to London, he'll tell Sally it is no longer acceptable to be apart, he cannot go on without her. She will feel the same, she will agree, she will come everywhere with him. She will.

"I want a plan, P-L-A-N," he says. "It's an English word. Do you know what it means?"

Johnston T. Midford tightens his tie, unbuttons his

brown twill jacket, then scratches his head. Taken off guard, he picks up a paperweight, shakes it, tries to get a plastic ring to float over the head of the smiling dolphin inside. "Tibor," John says, leaning forward, nostrils flared, "why are you so hostile today?"

"Hostility has nothing to do with it," Tibor says, smiling. "I'm just disappointed in you and in your record company."

"We're the top sellers in the classical field."

"So why are my Chopin impromptus in the icebox, my Brahms concerti selling a lousy sixteen thousand copies? I'd like better promotion. And I want a copy of my royalty statement sent to my hotel this afternoon. If you expect me to sign an exclusive contract with you, don't you think you should give me some solid reasons for being with your label?"

John loops a ring over the dolphin's nose, grins proudly, hands the paperweight to Tibor.

"Ever been there?"

"Where?" Tibor asks, and looks at the plastic letters behind the dolphin. "Yes, I've been to Miami."

"It's nice, isn't it, warm, relaxing, just the sort of place you could use right now, to rest, think a little. You're very tense."

"I'm touched that you're concerned, but as a matter of fact, I have a holiday coming up, six days, and I'm going somewhere a bit nicer than Miami—Maspalomas, in the Canaries. Do you know it?"

"I do indeed."

"You do?"

"I know a lovely little church near the sea in Maspalomas. It's got a dragon tree in its courtyard that some say is more than a thousand years old. And it's got fabulous acoustics inside, perfect for recording."

Cornered, Szabo rears back. "If you're thinking of asking me to record, you can forget it."

"You asked me about your Chopin impromptus. The reason they're not released yet is that the record isn't finished. You owe us the Chopin Fantasy, remember?"

"I'll do the Fantasy, but not in Maspalomas."

"It's a shame, really. We wanted to release that record in time for the big convention on the West Coast in August, but according to Michael, you won't have a minute to record before next November. But if no is no, I'll understand. Do go see that church—it's called San Mateo de la Playa. It's a perfect little gem."

Tibor is silent, shaking the paperweight. He could probably do the Fantasy in one session, one morning. Sally will want to sketch, anyhow, won't she? She'll go off into the mountains, or down to the beach and want to be alone for a few hours. He should finish that record. He hates leaving things undone.

"How much time do you think it will take?"

John rubs his bald pate and tilts back in his chair. "Depends on you, Tibor. Probably one session, one morning. Tell me what day you'd like to do it, and I'll send the equipment, the engineer and producer, and let me know where you're staying. I'll send a car, of course. What do you say?"

Tibor puts the paperweight on the desk and stands up, holding out his hand to shake. "I say, get me those statements, John, and if they look right, I'll do it."

"You're kidding. You agreed?" Michael asks at his hotel later that day.

Tibor nods and tears open a large envelope containing yet another new score sent by some hopeful young composer.

"But when am I going to have time to look at this?" he asks, passing it over to Michael.

"The question is, do you want to?"

Tibor pushes hair out of his eyes with a puff of breath.

"It's ludicrous. Here I am zipping around the world on jet planes to play the music of composers who traveled by horse and carriage."

"Well, it's not your fault. Audiences like what they know. By the way, Palm Beach doesn't want the Webern Variations next season. Too contemporary."

"It was written fifty years ago, for Christ's sake!"

"I know, but—"

"No buts, and I'm not changing the program. Fuck Palm Beach. Here." He hands Michael piles of letters, photographs, records that have accumulated during his tour.

"Memorabilia," Michael says. "I'll save this stuff and get it published and make a fortune."

Tibor doesn't answer. Now he's concentrating on packing, folding jackets, fast, one-two-three, suitcase-lids down, combinations locked.

"You're so neat, so precise," Michael says. "You're so driven. I suppose that's what makes you so great. You've got such endless energy. You ought to slow down, you know. You just might explode someday."

Michael thumbs through snapshots. "Who's this?" he asks, holding up a picture of a blonde dressed in a sarong next to a palm tree.

Tibor looks and says her name is Dolores, she's an air hostess.

"You're a phenomenon, a fucking phenomenon," Michael says, laughing, and pops a seedless grape, courtesy of CBS, into his mouth. "You juggle all these women. How can you keep them straight?"

Silent, Tibor glares at Michael, then feels remiss. How should Michael know about Sally, his total devotion to her, unless he tells him, and he can't tell him, not yet, not before he goes to London, not until Sally says yes, because—and the possibility, vague but ominous, makes him shiver—she could say no.

"Is something bothering you?" Michael asks.

"I've never felt better," Tibor says.

Michael opens his mouth to say something about overextending oneself and the dire consequences thereof, but he eats another grape instead and shuffles through more papers. "Look at this," he says, waving a letter, "from Mrs. Isaac Cohen, Cincinnati. 'Dear Maestro Tibor Szabo, would you do us the great honor of extending your personal congratulatory message to our son, David Akiva Cohen, on the occasion of his milestone thirteenth birthday, his Bar Mitzvah? He would be doubly appreciative if you would add an anecdote of your own thirteenth year. His hobbies are model airplanes, CB radios . . .' Can you believe the chutzpah of some people?" Michael asks, laughing.

"I'd like a piece of paper," Tibor says.

"What for?"

"I'm going to answer. It's important."

"It's important? Do you know this boy?"

"No. May I borrow your pen?"

Tibor sits at the desk, thinks of his own thirteenth year, in 1956, the household growing tense, and the arguments between Grandpa Andras and his father, who refused to make a ceremony for his son. Michael mutters behind him, "It's important, is it? So write already, Reb Szabo, will you? We have lots to talk about, you know, your fee, for instance, if I should raise it from ten to twelve for a recital . . ."

Grandpa Andras, red in the face, beating at his chest, shouting at his father, "Thief, thief!" as Tibor hides beneath the piano, playing with the yellow fringe of the Spanish shawl, feeling sad and confused, wondering if it's true, if his father has really stolen his manhood from him. . . .

"Dear David," he writes. "Congratulations on your Bar Mitzvah. I wish you health, happiness, and courage in your life as a man. Sincerely, Tibor Szabo."

He addresses the envelope, hands it to Michael, and

117

they map out a plan for the 1980 season, discussing recordings, recital requests, and whether or not he should go to Japan in December of that year. His life is being snatched away from him, his freedom taken away yet again. Tibor balks.

"Wait a minute," he says. "How do I know if I'll want to go to the Orient in December 1980? It's only April 1976 now."

"What kind of a question is that? You have to go to Japan. You're popular there, thousands of people are waiting to hear you play again."

December 1980, more than four years in the future, and he may not be alone in 1980, he may have Sally's needs and wishes to consider, and what if they have children by then? Ashkenazy travels with his four children, or is it five, and what about Perlman and his? The thought of a caravan of kids, Sally beside him as they clatter onto planes with bottles and bibs, holding small bundles in their arms, delights him. He'd like a girl first, blond ringlets and eyes like her mother's and then a boy.

"So what shall I tell Yokida?"

Tibor sighs. "Tell him I'll have to let him know."

"It's not like you to be indecisive."

"Isn't it?" Tibor asks, smiles mysteriously, and calls for the bellhop. He tips the maids, shakes hands with the clerks at the front desk of the Navarro. Everyone wishes him a good trip and they all look forward to his next visit to New York.

"Take care of yourself," Michael says, concerned, "and try to get some rest." He kisses Tibor on both cheeks, slaps his back.

He waits until Tibor is in the limousine, watches it glide east on Central Park South, and then walks back to his office on Fifty-seventh Street.

Estelle Stillman powdered her nose, clicked her compact shut, rubbed its smooth surface like a worry bead as she watched Michael Klein make himself another double martini, straight up. The bags under his eyes had stretched to pouches, his complexion was pasty.

"It's been a week," Michael said, "a whole week, and no one knows anything."

"People disappear for months. Years," Estelle added.

They looked despairingly at each other. Michael poked at his drink with a silver swizzle and sank into the armchair next to Estelle. He unfastened his top shirt button, pulled at the knot of his tie, and stared at the three baskets in the corner of the Stillman den, a poodle sleeping in each.

"This whole miserable business is so bizarre, so strange, so unlike Tibor," Michael said, took a sip. "I forgot to ask, what did you think of that story in the *Daily Mail* his London agent sent?"

Estelle thought of the front-page photograph of an attractive woman, not beautiful, with a wide mouth, high cheekbones, and long, rather disheveled hair. The headline, SZABO'S LAST WOMAN, was tasteless, and so was the text: "Sally Fraser, one of England's foremost painters, has been linked with disappeared pianist Tibor Szabo. . . . For the last several weeks sources here and abroad say they have traveled together . . . now admits to having been with him before he disappeared . . . begin to suspect foul play. . . ."

"Sensationalism," Estelle said to Michael. "Fraser doesn't look his type."

"Exactly why, my dear Watson, she should be suspect."

"It makes you wonder—" Estelle's voice choked and Michael turned, saw her swat at her eye, brush off a tear like an annoying fly. "I thought I knew him, understood him. I thought he could come to me with any problem, anything, anytime."

Michael reached over and patted her shoulder. "People's lives take unexpected turns, that's all."

"True," she sniffed, "and how well can you ever know someone? I remember a little girl, a violin prodigy, Ben and I drove all the way to Hartford to hear her play. She wore a white lace dress, patent leather shoes, and bounced onto the stage, smiled so happily, played the Mendelssohn Concerto wonderfully. Soon after, she committed suicide. She left a note, 'Good-bye, Mama, I love you.'"

"Penny Ambrose. I remember her well. It was tragic, scary. But Szabo is a grown man, and he loves to perform, and no one pushed him to do it."

"But maybe there were inner demons, maybe he felt tortured, secretly. Come to think of it, he seemed more secretive than ever this spring, more covered, inward."

"He's saddled with success, that's all, and he's a guy with a lot of defenses, impenetrable defenses. Hell, they're laminated to him. If playing tortured Szabo, you'd have heard it in his playing, and you didn't, did you?"

"No," Estelle agreed.

"Then let's stop analyzing, let's just stick to facts. Did you call his bankers in Liechtenstein today?"

"Yes. Tibor has not contacted them."

"Good. That means he doesn't need funds. He must be with someone who's taking care of him."

"Not necessarily. It could mean that he's dead." She looked at Michael with wide, terrified eyes, the thought no longer hidden even from herself.

"Estelle, if you don't cut it out . . ." Michael said, but couldn't finish the sentence, finished his drink instead, and chewed on an olive.

"Did you call Rawlings today?" Estelle asked.

"Yes."

"And?"

"No answer."

"Maybe he's on to something."

"I doubt it. What about that gypsy fiddler in Munich? Rawlings said he had sources in Hungary."

"Gyorgy Votor. We checked out all the possibilities in Budapest. Nothing."

"How well does he play?"

"Votor? How should I know? He's supposed to be the best in Europe. What's the difference?"

Michael squirmed in his chair, reproaching himself for the thought, one he could not suppress, that if Votor is that good, maybe he could get him to come to the States for a tour.

Estelle sat up stiffly, opened her handbag, dropped her compact in, took out her keys from the zipped side compartment where she always kept them, and stood up.

"Well," she said, dismissing Michael, her fears, her worries, "it's late. Come on, children." She whistled, clapped her hands, and hooked her three poodles to their three leashes.

"I'll go with you," Michael said, put his glass on a silver coaster on the marble coffee table, and followed Estelle into the elevator, tripping over Mimi, stifling the urge to kick her in the woolly head. He could feel blood rise to his face as the elevator descended, and he followed Estelle out onto Park Avenue. The air was hot and humid, smelled rancid. "They say it's worse than this in London," Michael said, wiping his forehead.

"Poor Tibor," Estelle said and stood on the curb while the three furry dogs turned circles in the street, crouched low. Estelle looked the other way, watched a drunk lean against a NO PARKING sign. "Happy birthday, America!" he shouted.

"Hey, that's right," Michael said, waiting with her. "It's the Bicentennial. Passed me right by."

"Me, too. Well, let's hope we'll have something to celebrate soon. We'll send up Roman candles."

"At least," Michael said, waved good-bye, and headed toward his office to check the Telex machine for possible news before going home to his one-bedroom apartment on West Fifty-fifth Street.

On the corner of Fifty-seventh and Sixth Avenue, a man with matted gray hair sat in the haze of a streetlight, playing an approximate version of a Bach partita on an electric portable keyboard. Passersby stopped to listen, smirked with amusement, some with contempt, and tossed coins into a tin cup. The player, sweat running down his cheeks like tears, closed his eyes, swayed back and forth, oblivious of them all, aware only of his music. Poor slob, Michael thought, he might once have been a talented student, who knows, even a Szabo. He threw a quarter, and hurried past.

The hatch door of Pan Am flight 100 from New York opens. Tibor thanks the crew and, first passenger to disembark, rushes up the jetway, follows bright yellow ARRIVALS signs, like Jason in search of the golden fleece. *His* treasure is here, waiting for him at Heathrow. He's battled his way across a continent, crossed the ocean, and he dashes down glassed-in corridors to claim his prize —his Sally, his own. At the entrance to the immigration hall his pace is slowed as arriving hordes stampede toward passport queues. Women in colored saris swirl past, turbaned men follow, a lady in sable crashes her baggage trolley into the heels of a caftaned Arab, a baby wails, voices rise, but Szabo surges ahead, breezes past the FOREIGN line, thanking God and Queen Elizabeth, straight on to BRITAIN AND COMMONWEALTH, home free.

He fidgets while one of the regulars at Desk Five looks at his passport. "How long have you been away?"

"Six weeks," Tibor answers, thinking how long it sounds, how long it felt, six weeks without Sally and he'll never leave her for so long again.

"How did the concerts go?" he is asked. They know him well at Heathrow, he passes in and out so often, he's on television so much. A few are fans, some even critics, like the customs man who once told him, "I loved your Rachmaninoff Three at the Albert Hall, even if the last movement was a bit too slow."

"Welcome home," immigration says, and as he races down the stairs to collect his luggage he can hear Sally's voice saying the same, her head tipped back, her eyes misted. He'll see her now, almost now, any minute, as soon as the bags arrive, if they ever do, and if he isn't stopped at customs, he'll reach the automatic sliding door, and like magic the last barrier will part and she'll be there, leaning against a railing, reaching through the crowd for him, her face luminous, golden. His Sally, his own.

"Tibor!" she calls and Tibor forgets the forty-five minutes he's had to wait for the bags, he forgives the customs man his search, and he sees only Sally, Sally wearing blue, a blue cape, blue scarf, a clear blue perfect sea of woman. He dives toward her, crushes her to him as a surge of delight swamps him and he can hardly stand up. He kisses her and wants to weep, feels his knees buckle. "Darling," he whispers, stroking her hair, smelling the sweet grass-like smell of her, touching her face. She tilts her head back and he looks into her eyes, clear, deep pools of blue ringed with long pale lashes. No, he will never leave her again, he will take her everywhere with him, everywhere. She cannot refuse him, can she?

"You look sad," Sally says.

"No," he says, circles his arms around her waist, lifts her up against him, buries his head in her neck. People stare, a small boy points, and his mother smacks at his hand.

The driver of the hired limousine clears his throat, removes his cap, and says, "I'll take the bags then, sir, and bring the car around, shall I?"

"Yes, thank you," Tibor manages to say, and Sally holds his hand, leads him to the door. The room spins around him, he is weightless and disoriented, as if underwater, not knowing which way to surface. Outside, a sharp intake of wet spring air, acrid with the smell of jet fuel, revives him, and with his arms around Sally he is on solid ground at last.

They nuzzle together as the car zips down the M4, past the house where Hogarth lived, which Sally usually points out but this time forgets, into Shepherd's Bush roundabout, toward Hampstead. Dazed with emotion, Tibor kisses Sally's hands, keeps asking if she's all right. "Yes, my love, yes," she assures him, touches his cheek, rests her head against his chest. Downy hairs on her forehead glow like a halo in the half-light. He brushes his lips against her forehead, tries to speak but can't, while Sally, nervous about what waits for them in Willow Road and overwhelmed by the immensity of what she plans to tell Tibor, sticks to small words about small objects.

"Did you lose those jade-and-gold cuff links?"

"Which?"

"You know, the ones I bought you."

"Those? Yes, I think so. Are you angry?"

"Very," Sally says, scowls at him, but even scrunched up, her face is exquisite, radiant, perfect. ". . . and Gorky shredded the new armchair, the one you said is so comfortable. Maybe I should have him de-clawed, although, I don't know, I think it's cruel, don't you, and besides . . ."

Tibor nods and grunts as Sally talks, her voice a gentle purr. He cannot think about anything, he wants only to reach her house, her bed, feel her flesh against his. He slides one hand inside her cape, presses his palm against her breast, feels the nipple rise toward him under the cloth of her dress. The breath of her sigh sets him in motion like lyre strings in a breeze. He trembles, feels reverberations through his flesh, rumbling his veins. He burrows his face into the blue wool covering her breast to muffle a groan.

"Here we are, then," the driver announces, slowing down to stop in front of 37 Willow Road.

"We're home," Sally whispers, and Tibor lifts his head,

looks out the window at the familiar wooden gate opening onto a stone walk leading up to three steps to Sally's front door. With a sudden burst of energy, he opens the door, hops out of the car, helps Sally out and scoops her into his arms, kicks open the gate and charges toward the front door. Sally clings to his neck and yells, "Wait a minute, Lancelot, the key is in my bag in the car." Tibor stops short, puts her down ceremonially and, bowing like a chevalier, clicks his heels and runs back to the car, giving Sally a chance to reach the door first and ring the bell three times. She's whistling when Tibor hands her the bag, and she fishes for keys, taking her time.

"Hey," Tibor says, realizing how strange it is that she hasn't key in hand as usual, wondering why the house is completely dark, when the door flies open, voices roar, and bright lights blind him, hands grab and pull him in. He stumbles into a room full of friends, who shout, "Surprise!" sing "Happy Birthday," toot plastic horns, throw colored streamers at him. Tibor blinks and splutters, his arms flapping at his sides.

Sally flings her arms around him, kisses him, and says, "Happy birthday, I love you." He is rigid and pulls away. "What's wrong?" she asks, and looks up at his frowning face. "You look positively stricken. It's a party, darling, for you, for your birthday."

"I know," he says, taking her hands. "It's just . . ." but she looks wounded and upset and he can't say, You should have waited. Do I have to get off a goddam transatlantic jet which was delayed who remembers how many hours to be surrounded by everyone I know in London when all I want to do is be with you, alone? Why would she do a thing like this anyhow? She hates parties. It must mean she doesn't want to be alone with him or she's stopped loving him. Is it possible? No. But she's made a party, and if she wants him to be thrilled, he'll be thrilled. "It's just that I'm so touched," Tibor says, hugging her. "I've never been quite so surprised."

"I have another surprise, too," she whispers.

"What?" Tibor asks, worried again.

"I'll tell you later," she says softly. "But I think you'll really be pleased."

"Tell me now," Tibor says, desperate to know, but Zev Barzlil whirls him around, claps him so hard on the back that he coughs.

"Emphysema?" asks Zev.

"Worse," Tibor says and accepts the glass of schnapps Zev pours for him, gulps it down, hot liquid burning his throat but easing his mood.

"Do you know the one about the lady who coughed every time she—" Zev begins, but Werner interrupts, kisses Tibor on both cheeks, squeezes his shoulders.

"How are you?" Tibor asks. When he sees a petite brunette at Werner's side who dotes on his every move, he doesn't need an answer. Werner introduces him to Mirèse. Tibor turns to greet his English manager, Nigel Smythe, and the violinist Miles Wilson. He chats with Sally's friend Asquith Dart, a writer who lives down the street, then obeys Sally's order to come into the sitting room to open presents. Guests sit on large oriental pillows around a low glass table piled high with packages. They drink wine, eat cheese, and wait for him to begin. A recent landscape of Sally's, dark figures disappearing into a gray background, covers most of one wall. Etchings and prints fill the other three, and a large oak hutch displaying plates her mother had collected stands like a sentry beside the French doors leading down to her garden. Tibor would like to take Sally outside, walk with her beside the just-budding tulips, the ones he watched her plant last fall, on her knees in dirt, digging with a trowel. He remembers the surge of love that washed through him when she deftly patted the earth

127

down around the bulbs, using the side of her fisted hand, and he feels it again. But the pile of presents waits for him and he knows he must open them, perform, delight his friends. Sally sits by his side, eager as a little girl at a carnival. He's never known her to be comfortable with a crowd, but here she is, center of attention in the middle of a party she's arranged, smiling up at him, waiting for the first ribbon to be pulled. How can he possibly disappoint her?

"Just what I needed," he announces, putting on the first gift, a red mohair sweater from Zev. He leaves his head inside and imitates a gorilla, then flings a striped tie from Nigel around his neck, borrows someone's glasses, and says through his nose, "Today, class, we shall discuss the music of Ockeghem and diseases of the recorder." With a Havana cigar from the box of forty Montecristos Werner has given him, he sits at the piano he bought for Sally, or rather, himself, chomps on the cigar and plays "Malagueña." Applause. And finally the last gift—jade-and-gold cuff links from Sally. "I won't lose these," he promises, "for at least a week."

Boxes lie scattered like carnage on the floor. Tibor is exhausted but wine is abundant, the mood is festive, and after all, he is the host. Stories are requested, and when Tibor refuses to tell the Hofmann-Fischer story, someone asks Zev to do his Abba-Yma routine. Zev demurs, but preens himself, pulling at his vest, smiling coyly. While company pleads, he drains his glass, bangs it on the table and begins.

"Abba Eban is the first guest to arrive at a party, followed by Yma Sumac. The host introduces them, 'Abba-Yma, Yma-Abba.' Then in walks Oona O'Neill and the host introduces her, 'Oona-Abba, Abba-Oona; Oona-Yma, Yma-Oona. . . .'"

Though he's heard it many times before, Tibor listens eagerly, still dazzled by Zev's virtuosity, but Sally gets up quietly, goes to the kitchen to prepare the cake. Zev's voice trails behind her ". . . when in walks Ina Claire. 'Ina-Abba, Abba-Ina; Ina-Oona, Oona-Ina; Ina-Yma, Yma-Ina. . . .'"

Instead of amusing her, the joke grates. A giddy evening with endless musicians' stories is not quite what she had in mind, although she did intend the party to be a celebration, not only of Tibor's birthday but also of her decision, her special surprise. But as she slides the cake out of the red-and-white box marked "Louie's," she wonders why she felt compelled to make a party at all. Perhaps she's less certain of her feelings than she can admit, perhaps she was afraid to face Tibor alone.

Werner comes into the kitchen wanting to help, and opens a package of blue candles, spikes them into the chocolate frosting.

"Not in the rose," Sally scolds.

"Why not?" Werner asks and meets her eyes, holds her gaze. In Tibor's absence and at his urging they've spent some time together, but Werner's presence still makes her jumpy. It's not just the envy she knows she feels at the tight friendship between him and Tibor, or the fact that Tibor seems to rely on Werner for a kind of support she cannot give him. It has more to do with attitude, stance, the way Werner observes and then devours, his distance and his voraciousness. And then there is his somewhat suspect youthful look. At the age of forty-seven, his hair is still fair, his face is unmarked with years except for a few lines sketched lightly around the eyes, and he is lithe as a tiger, with the same hungry look. He's a man to mistrust, Sally thinks, and to avoid, unless one could surrender to him totally, give oneself absolutely.

Werner's eyes are sharp, unblinking; he pins her motionless like a moth beneath glass. She squirms, troubled by her thoughts and by the sudden heat that fans out from her pelvis to her thighs. Zev's pretend party in the other room has grown to include Ava Gardner, Uta Hagen, Anna Russell, the Aga Khan, and Ugo Betti, and the introductions beat like a jungle chant in her ears: " 'Ugo-Abba, Abba-Ugo; Ugo-Yma, Yma-Ugo; Ugo-Ina, Ina-Ugo; Ugo-Oona, Oona-Ugo; Ugo-Ava, Ava-Ugo; Ugo-Uta, Uta-Ugo; Ugo-Anna, Anna-Ugo; Ugo-Aga, Aga-Ugo . . .' "

"What's the matter?" Werner whispers. She stares at his full mouth, then looks away, focuses on the cake, but on the wooden counter next to it is his hand, smeared with chocolate. She follows the fingers as they leave the counter, reach his mouth, and she watches, holding her breath, as his tongue slowly licks frosting off his thumb. She quickly turns away and fumbles for matches in a drawer, hands them to Werner and dashes back into the sitting room just as Zev gets to the punch line, ". . . when in walks Mstislav Rostropovich, Stanislaw Skrowaczewski, Mieczyslaw Horzowski, and Gennady Rozhdestvensky."

Hooting laughter and applause ring in her ears as she squeezes a place for herself next to Tibor. Someone dims the light, voices are quiet, and Werner enters holding the cake, triumphant, his face incandescent above the blazing candles, and a rousing chorus of "Happy Birthday," remarkably out of tune, fills the room.

"How old are you, anyhow?" Asquith asks Tibor as he blows out candles and cuts straight through the rose.

"Let me see, thirty-three, I think."

"I shall simply have to stop booking you as a child prodigy," says Nigel.

A champagne cork pops and glasses are passed, cake is eaten, and Zev announces that he's brought music—the Schubert E-flat Trio, opus 100—and his cello, Miles Wilson has his violin, how about it, Tibor? Tired as he is, the prospect of reading through something delicious with those two—at home, relaxed, for friends—excites Tibor.

He looks at Sally to see if she objects, and when she nods happily, he lurches toward the piano, plays a scale while Zev and Miles take out their instruments and tune up. Pillows are arranged for everyone except Asquith, who needs a more substantial perch. Sally points to an armchair, apologizes for the cat-scratches in it, and helps Asquith turn it around, watches him sink slowly into it like a ship going under. He wheezes and Sally pats his shoulder, wonders if she should invite him to come to the Canaries—it would help his asthma. But the trip is for her and Tibor, the two alone, no interferences, nothing to dilute them. She sits down at Asquith's side, rests her arm on his knee, feels his hand pat her head. She snuggles closer, and thinks about her visit to him only a few days before, on a cold bleak afternoon, when she felt alone, at odds with herself, her life. Since their meeting at the greengrocer some years before when they discovered they lived only a few doors apart, Asquith has provided an anchor for Sally whenever she has felt at sea. That afternoon she sat with Asquith in his library, patting his cat, Attila. An orange glow from the electric heater lit up the bust of Winston Churchill and the collection of painted porcelain cows, and while she sipped her tea and ate a scone with clotted cream and Tiptree blackberry jam, she listened to Asquith talk about his asthma. He thought he might go away for a cure, but ever since he and Donald split up he couldn't bear the idea of traveling alone.

"Why did it end?" Sally asked.

"No particular reason, no large issues in dispute. I guess it was just the little things. It usually is, isn't it, the little things that get to us, annoy us, drive us away? One of the things I absolutely hated about Donald was his habit of taking scalding hot baths, then marching around in his underwear, his skin splotched bright red and his glasses fogged up. Toward the end it drove me so mad I used to race out of the house the minute I heard the bath water running."

"I suppose I'd find that annoying, too," Sally agreed.

"And Tibor doesn't annoy you?"

"Come to think of it, no, he doesn't, he doesn't have any habits that displease, no gestures or twitches that irritate me."

"Probably because you haven't spent enough time together."

"It's been nearly three years."

"Ah, yes, but, Sally," Asquith said, adjusting himself in his chair, causing a chapter on Coventry he was busy editing for a new book on cathedrals to fall to the floor. Sally bent down to collect pages, and Asquith went on, "Three years, but not of constantly living together. You ought to be with him more, in my opinion, and then you'd know."

"What would I know?"

"Whether or not you plan to share your lives forever."

Was that an issue, Sally wondered, was it necessary to know their future? But lying awake that night, curled into a corner of her large bed, she realized that much of her recent dissatisfaction centered on the incompleteness of her life. After all, she thought, I'm in my thirties, still driven to work, but there is more to life than making art, and I'm in love. She got out of bed and wandered around the house, thinking of Tibor, filled with a longing that was shapeless yet overpowering. With her left hand on her belly, she wondered what it might be like to feel stirrings inside, flutterings of life. But she looked at her right hand, gnarled as a stillborn fetus, and she felt afraid. She had hidden behind her work for so many years that the thought of emerging to take chances, to expose herself to the risks of a real day-to-day life with Tibor and the inevitable possibility of progeny, terrified her. And yet it was time to take those chances, she knew it. By morning, pleased with the conclusions she had reached, the canvas of her thoughts was completed and she hung it in her mind: She would be with the man she loved, she would make the necessary compromises.

Zev closes his eyes, wraps himself around the cello, and listens to the funereal chords of the piano at the opening of the Andante. He starts upbow with a burnished sound, plays a long line, eloquent yet grieving, and when Tibor takes over the melody from him, it seems to Sally he is speaking of pain and beauty, torment and acceptance, in a language so pure, so direct, so intimate it makes her want to weep. And yet she is aware of the distance between player and listener, how absorbed Tibor is in the music, how very far away from her. She sits quietly, listens resolutely, as the second theme rises after the darkness of the first, promising light.

At the end of the Allegro moderato, someone suggests that they play the Mendelssohn D-minor Trio. Miles has the music, and Tibor, warmed up now, eager to play, consults Sally with a glance. It's late and she'd like everyone to leave, but Tibor is riding full tilt and she will not be the one to pull the reins. She consents with a kiss on his forehead, and picking up a full ashtray, she tiptoes into the kitchen.

"Need someone to dry?" a voice whispers. Werner steps toward her and she backs up against the sink as the haunting melody in D minor swells and fades.

"I'm not washing dishes," she says.

"I can see that," he answers, listening with her. Sally dumps cigarette stumps into the trashbin and stands, feeling awkward, wondering what to do with the empty ashtray. Werner stares at her, reaches forward and removes the object from her hand, placing it on the counter.

They stand close to each other, listening, separated by the music, brought together by it. Neither makes a move.

"That large dark landscape," Werner asks during the tranquil Andante, "in the sitting room—when did you paint it?"

"I finished it a few weeks ago. Why?"

"I thought so. The way you used color—something experimental?"

"Yes. How do you know?"

"It's unlike anything of yours I've seen before. Reminds me of Jacopo Bassano—you know, twilight, the illusion of luminosity."

"I've always admired the Venetians, the way they managed to find fugitive colors even in deep shadow, the way they . . ."

"Heightened reality?" Werner asks, watching the crimson flush of her wakening cheeks.

"Yes," she says. "I guess I'm drawn more toward the elusive quality of things these days, or maybe I'm just becoming resigned to ephemerality. Must be intimations of mortality."

Werner smiles. "Or fear of permanence?"

The suggestion intimidates her. She picks up a cloth and wipes at a spot on the counter.

"Sally, I don't mean to sound glib. I think you're reaching a new level in your work."

"Do you?" she asks, folding the cloth, unfolding it.

"Yes. Don't you sense it?"

"I don't know. I sense change perhaps, but most of the time I feel that what I paint is useless."

" 'The most beautiful things in the world are the most useless. . . .' "

" 'Peacocks and lilies, for instance,' " she says, "I've read Ruskin, too." She blushes despite a resolve not to and looks away as the cello continues a line begun by the violin; then both strings murmur together over the piano's final statement.

"Sally?" Werner asks, but she will not look up.

"You know," his voice continues, closer now, his breath ruffling her hair, "I would like to see you paint the dawn—the dark petticoats of night lift, and soon the pink thighs of day . . ."

Sally laughs, raising her eyes to meet his amused, probing glance as the players leap joyfully into the Scherzo.

"And now the C minor," Asquith demands over applause, but one Mendelssohn in minor is enough, and the pianist is, finally, tired.

Guests depart, except Asquith, who finds it hard to rise from the chair, let alone leave. He announces that he simply must tell Sally and Tibor about the dinner party where he met the man who owns Liszt's piano.

"Asquith," Tibor says, "there are as many of Liszt's pianos in the world as there are pieces of the true cross."

"Ah, yes, but Dr. Cyril Ramsey, a coroner, has the real one, he assured me. Anyhow, halfway through the soup—Lady Curzon, by the way, and quite tasty—his beeper went off. He made a phone call and came dashing back. 'Must leave,' he whispered to me. 'An old woman's been bashed on the head with a vase. Probably murder. Shouldn't take long.'"

Asquith coughs, and Tibor and Sally sit wide-eyed as two children listening to a bedtime story, waiting patiently for him to go on.

"Well," Asquith continues, "when he came back he told me the lurid details. He said she'd been dead for over a week, and when I asked him how he could tell, he said, 'By the size of the maggots,' and then he devoured an entire plate of shrimps."

The three exchange amazed glances.

"But what about Liszt's piano?" Tibor asks, fully recovered.

"Ah, yes, the piano. He told me that sometimes, late at night, he hears the old man himself improvising."

"Liszt's ghost?"

"Of course."

Tibor laughs but stops abruptly. "What a chilling idea," he says, "if, even after death, one must go on playing, condemned to eternal practice."

"Is that condemnation?" Asquith asks, yawns and stretches, his jowls quivering. "I would have thought eternal grace myself."

Tibor looks at his watch.

"I suppose you want me to leave," Asquith says. "What time is it?"

"One-thirty."

"In the morning, I assume. Well, it's late and I must stop rattling on like an old nanny. Help me up."

Empty plates are scattered about, the smell of cigarettes is strong, and the silence is oppressive. Sally hurries to the garden doors to air out the room, and feels Tibor's eyes follow. She is uncertain as a cornered doe and he keeps still, afraid to make a move, afraid that she will flee. She clutches a brass doorknob to steady herself and says, "Shall we go upstairs?"

Tibor sits down on a pillow and plays with a tassel, looks back up at her, and asks, "Are you sure you want to?"

"Darling, I—"

"Come here," Tibor half commands, half begs, and his frantic eyes, looking up at her through a stray lock of hair, make her rush across the room into his arms. She sits on his lap, sighing with relief, no longer feeling trapped, convinced that this is where she belongs. A long kiss, like a drink after unbearable thirst, satisfies them for a mo-

136

ment. Tibor rocks her back and forth in his lap, then pushes her dress above her knees, strokes her legs, her thighs, and asks her if she loves him, darling, do you, and she says yes, oh yes, as she leans back against pillows and he frees her from shoes and tights. She feels his tongue trace the curve of her belly, touch her soft secret shell and part it, press against the small pearl inside as her legs rise above his head and she moans like a distant gull. He drifts deep into the dream-blue sea of her until a wave of pleasure crests, hovers, and breaks and she lies by his side limp as a fish washed to shore. Sally smiles and wipes at Tibor's face and laughs.

"What's funny?" Tibor asks, her moods confusing him.

"It's funny. I'm sorry, darling, it's just funny, the way that happens, limbs in the air, everything."

He looks somber. "It's not funny, it's beautiful. I love giving you pleasure."

"I know, and I love it." She can't stop laughing. "I'm sorry."

But he is stern, looking at her, waiting for her to stop. "I don't understand anything tonight," he says. "This party, it's so unlike you. You worry me. Is there something you want to tell me?"

Laughter evaporates and she is serious. "I'm sorry about tonight. I'm sorry for making this silly party. I was nervous, afraid to face you alone."

"But why?" Tibor wants to know. His stomach is in knots, but he steadies himself for an admission of loss of love, the possible rejection he's suspected all evening.

"I've made a decision, just in the last few days, and it seems so monumental to me, I suppose I'm frightened by it. I meant to tell you before the party, but I couldn't."

"Why? What is it?" he asks. Blood drains from his head.

"It's that I love you, and I think it's time to be with you, I mean I think I ought to travel more with you." She swallows and adds, "I want to."

137

"You do?" Tibor asks. The combustible mixture of amazement, relief, and elation shakes inside him and he sits staring at her for a few seconds, then collapses against her, his head in her lap. She touches his face, feels tears. He kisses her hands and cries, convulsed with sobs, and mumbles incoherently about needing her, wanting her only, only her.

She has not seen a man weep for love since her father cried at her mother's grave, and those were tears shed for love lost. "I'm here, I'm yours," Sally tells him, wipes at his cheeks with her dress, wanting him to stop.

He stops, sighs deeply, and rises to his feet, pulling her up with him, and they walk silently through rooms, turning off lights, checking doors. Stairs creak under their slow footsteps, and near the top, Tibor whispers, "I want to have a child with you."

Those words, more thrilling than declarations of love, more terrifying, immolate her with desire, and she is suddenly wild, primitive, fumbling with Tibor's belt, wanting him now, there, immediately, she cannot wait. He bends down, lifts her skirts and thrusts himself into her like a knife in a ritual sacrifice and they writhe together at the top of the stairs, precarious, frenzied. On his knees, clutching at the banister for support, Tibor has the sensation of falling anyhow, fast, faster than he would like, but he lets go without a struggle, knowing now that there is not only the bed at the top of the stairs, but endless promised beds to come.

"Did I hurt you?" he asks, and pushes back wet hair from Sally's forehead.

"No," she says, feeling suddenly shy, embarrassed at her abandon. She sits up and rubs at her back and pointing to the bottom of the uncarpeted steps says, "We could have gotten killed."

"Never," Tibor promises, and untangling his legs from a nest of trousers, shorts, and socks, he picks Sally up, carries her off like the sun-god himself to a sleepless night on the altar of her bed.

On her knees in the garden a few mornings later, Sally digs with a trowel at the mulch she put down for the winter, flings it into a basket, then carries it to the compost heap near the tool shed and dumps it. Weeks behind in her gardening, she hurries to catch up before they leave. Her garden is small, fifty feet along two high stone walls and thirty feet wide, but it is her turf, her own ground. She marches back to the flower bed and digs some more, stopping for a moment to scratch her chin. She notices the violets doing well, the tulips, the brilliant butterfly wings of blue irises next to golden ranunculuses. The smell of earth thick with growth, pullulating with the moisture of an entire winter, invades her. She grabs a shovel and turns over the soil, preparing it for pungent marigolds, delicate portulacas, graceful petunias, which must be planted within the next few weeks. I suppose I'll have to call Asquith and have him ask his gardener to do it for me this year, she thinks, and spray the roses against mildew and . . . She digs quicker, plunging the hard edge of the trowel deep as she can, beads of sweat beginning to glisten on her forehead.

"You should have done all that in March," a voice says. "It's May, for God's sake." Sally spins around on her knees to find Werner leaning over the back fence, a maroon scarf around his neck, an unlit cigar in his mouth. Sally says nothing, but turns back around and digs furiously. Werner watches her on her knees, hair caught back by a gold ribbon from one of Tibor's gifts, an oversized shetland sweater rolled up to her elbows. Two spots of red spread on her cheeks and she sniffs, wiping at her nose. Werner reaches over the fence and opens the latch, walks past a flowering quince dotted with shocking-pink buds, and squats on his heels next to Sally. She jerks

139

her head sharp as a blue jay and says, "You might ask permission to enter." Her eyes are bloodshot.

"Have you been crying?" Werner asks, ignoring her outrage.

The tenderness in his voice annoys her and she does not trust his look of concern. His lashes curl away from the bodies of his eyes like spider's legs, rest ominously still against the finely webbed lines around them. She sniffs and says, "I suppose Maestro Szabo sent you. I assume he rang you up and said we've had a tiff. I wouldn't be surprised if you knew all the intimate details."

Werner's smile broadens, infuriating her. "You're uninvited," she says. "You can leave now."

"I'll make you a cup of tea first," he announces and before she can object, he disappears up the back steps and through the doors into her house. She wipes her hands on a cloth, scrapes mud off her shoes, and hurries after him. If he has tracked mud all over her house she will make him clean it up himself, but when she sees his shoes left neatly on the mat next to the door, she enters the kitchen, disarmed.

Werner stands at her sink, filling her kettle, and asks why she's so upset. Then he turns on a burner and reaches into just the right cupboard for the teapot and cups.

"How do you know where I keep the cups?" Sally asks, sitting down at the small wooden table in the middle of the room.

"Observation," Werner says. "Since you use your left hand more than your right, you would put those objects most often used in the left-hand cupboard near the sink." He sits opposite her at the table, waiting for the kettle to boil. She is uneasy, pulls at a loose thread on her sweater. She looks at his feet and notes that his socks do not match.

"Are you angry because Tibor is going to record during your holiday?" Werner asks.

Sally pounds her permanent fist on the table. "Why the

140

hell does he have to tell you everything? Why can't he manage his life himself?"

Werner traps her hand with his, holds it still on the table-top. Sally struggles to free it, but he is strong and his long, thin fingers feel warm, enfolding her fist like a nest.

"Sally," Werner says, and like a scolded child, she slowly raises her eyes to meet his. "There is nothing wrong with asking a friend for help. Tibor is desperately in love with you, you're angry with him, he doesn't know what to do."

"No, he doesn't, does he," Sally says, slipping her hand slowly out of Werner's grasp. She stands up to turn off the kettle. "He's so upset he's gone straight home to practice. I couldn't paint right now if I tried. But Mr. Piano has no problem, does he."

"I wonder if you understand the nature of his commit-ment," Werner says.

"Oh, come off it," Sally says and pours boiling water into the teapot.

"You forgot the tea," Werner says, reaches for the jar marked Orange Pekoe, and hands it to her. When two cups are poured, sugar and milk added, biscuits offered, Werner says, "I'm not insulting you, Sally. It's taken me fifteen years of knowing the man to realize this about him—for Tibor nothing, I mean *nothing*, can come close to the satisfaction he gets from making music. There is no good cigar, no glass of wine, no beautiful sunset, no relationship with any superb woman which can mean as much to Tibor as playing the piano."

Sally takes a sip of tea and steam curls around her lips. "That's nonsense," she says.

"Is it? If Tibor had to choose between you or playing the piano, which would he choose?"

"That's ridiculous—the choice doesn't have to present itself."

"Maybe not, but you do want to be central to Tibor's life,

141

the very core of his existence. You'd never ask him to do it, but you need to feel he would give up everything for you. But he won't. He can't."

"Nor could I or would I give up my work for him."

"Wouldn't you?"

Sally huffs impatiently, but wonders if he is right. Doesn't her decision to travel with Tibor compromise a total commitment to her work, and didn't she willingly make that compromise? "You're angry that Tibor decided to record during your holiday," Werner says. "Why? It's only going to take him one morning, only a few hours, and you'll probably want some time to yourself, anyhow. To Tibor your anger is excessive, but to me it's completely understandable. It's not the recording that's upset you, it's what it means that he agreed to do it during time saved for you, you alone."

Sally is quiet, tries to balance her spoon on the edge of her cup. She looks into the dark circle of tea, thinking about Werner's words, accurate about her anger, but doubtful about Tibor and his music. To care so ruthlessly about what he does would make Tibor inhuman, and perhaps Werner has some reason to want her to see Tibor that way. Perhaps he hopes she will back away, leaving Tibor to him. Although he seems to like women and they certainly, as she well knows, respond to him, Werner could be in love with Tibor. It's not impossible. She has no grounds for accusation, only the anxiety she sometimes feels when she sees them together, only a vague suspicion.

"Sometimes," she says, clears her throat and raises her eyes to meet his, "I wonder what it is that binds you and Tibor so tightly together, what attracts you to him."

She blushes, but Werner is not embarrassed or unprepared. "We met when Tibor was a kid," he says. "I had just divorced—I was emotionally dried out, devoid of motivation—and here was this spunky kid, spilling over with drive, fresh, full of enthusiasm. At first we were inseparable. I couldn't get enough of his life. I traveled with him, I soaked up those rehearsals and performances as if they were mine. His enthusiasm and devotion to music inspired me to reconsider mine to writing. I felt rejuvenated through him and through the music he made. When he played—I don't know, I felt such a bond with him, I identified so totally with him, it was as if we were playing together. Call it love, if you like. Yes, OK, I was in love with him. But a spiritual love. What I was hungry for was his dedication, his talent, perhaps his genius." Werner reaches for a sweetmeal biscuit, bites, then brushes at small crumbs that tumble onto his sweater. "Each concert was an affirmation of his strength," he says, "and because we seemed the same person, that meant it was an affirmation of mine. I regained confidence and I started to write again. I put my life in order—moved to Chelsea. I was, and still am, in awe of the absolute uniqueness of what Tibor does. His gift is so singular it defies statistics."

Sally leans her chin on her hand and asks, "Are you jealous of him?"

"I admire him. You might say I envy his satisfactions, his self-sufficiency. He doesn't need me or you or anyone, and what he does is everything to him."

Sally frowns. "You are everything to me, everything," Tibor always tells her. And he means it. He must. "I refuse to accept that," she says.

"Suit yourself. But since you are about to ride off into the sunset with him, don't say you weren't warned."

"I didn't ask for your advice," Sally says, bristling.

"No, you didn't. And maybe I'm wrong to give it. It's true I was sent to patch things up, and instead I seem to be tearing at the fabric. I'm sorry."

"Are you?" Sally asks.

"Yes," Werner says and stares at her with his spider eyes, filling her with revulsion. But when he tells her she has some dirt smudged on her cheek and reaches across the table, gently touches the spot, his eyes change and she is looking into blue crystals, clear as a cloudless sky. He is being honest with her, she thinks, and direct, and she has greeted him with anger, suspicions, accusation. It's ungracious, unattractive of her. She should be pleased with his openness, grateful for his concern. He is Tibor's close friend, trying to help, and she is turning him away. She feels a sudden need to bring him back.

"I've been thinking," she says, the thought taking shape as the words come out, "maybe you'd like to come with us to the Canaries."

Werner stares at her. "Thank you very much, but I wouldn't dream of it."

"Why not? It could be fun. You could bring what's-her-name, that French girl."

"Mirèse. I'm afraid she's gone back to her husband in Toulouse."

"Ah," Sally sighs, wondering what to say now, wishing she had censored her impetuous invitation.

Werner rolls his cigar between thumb and index finger and takes advantage of the silence. "Mirèse was, well, diverting. It lasted a few months, but I couldn't see the point of continuing. As I get older I seem to have less patience, and I'm less willing to compromise. I'm very demanding, so I've been told, and very possessive, and maybe even too intense. When I'm in love I need so much of the other. Mirèse told me she felt devoured, just as I felt there wasn't enough there to sink my teeth into."

Sally pulls at the thread on her sweater, twists it. "Did you hurt her?" she asks.

"A bit, I suppose."

"Have you ever hurt anyone badly?"

"Yes," Werner says, "my son, Colin. I left his mother,

144

but there was something I had to have—my freedom, and a chance to find a perfect love."

"And has your freedom been worth it, and have you found the perfect love?"

Werner laughs. "I sound a right old fool, talking like a teen-ager at the age of, what am I, forty bloody seven. Yes, freedom has been good, useful, productive, but love has been partial, satisfying, frustrating, and ultimately elusive. I struggle, I flounder, I fall, but I get up again and keep going."

"I like your courage," Sally says.

"Courage? Now there's a quality I'd really like to have. You're confusing it with stubbornness."

"No. I think you are courageous, with your life, with your writing."

"My writing." Werner sighs. "I'm in a terrible state with that. I'm in the middle of a new book." He scratches his head, then attempts a synopsis. "The setting is Munich and the time is now. Widower father and son in love with the same woman, she in love with both. Son has recent information about what his father was up to during the war, sordid, of course, and is torn about whether or not to divulge this to their mutual love. Meanwhile the father finds out that his son has sired a child and acted badly toward its mother. Should he tell all? The tension builds. And here I am, stuck."

"Maybe you need some time away from it," Sally suggests. She thinks of Tibor and imagines his pleasure when she announces that Werner will join them. After all, he's been complaining that he has no time to see Werner these days, and if Tibor knows Sally has company, he'll feel less guilty about going off to practice. It was an impulsive invitation, but the more she considers it, the more it makes sense.

"You simply must come with us, Werner, even without Mirèse. It will be good for you, and Tibor was saying how

145

little of you he sees, and after all, he and I will have the rest of our lives to be alone together."

"I don't want to interfere. I might get in the way."

"You wouldn't, really. It would be nice if you came."

"Nice is rather an apologetic choice of word."

"Words are your territory. You find one."

Werner smiles, takes her hand and kisses it. "Suppose we leave it blank," he says, turning her hand over, brushing his lips against the inside of her wrist, "until after the trip."

"Then you will come?"

"Yes."

Sally interprets the kiss on her wrist as gallantry, and as her pulse quickens, she decides it must be pretrip nerves. "Do you suppose it will be very hot where we're going?" she asks.

"Very," Werner answers.

"Then I shall leave my woollies at home," she says cheerfully. "I'd better start packing. And you'd better go home to collect your things, too. I'll call the travel agent and get your ticket. We're leaving at eight tomorrow morning. Don't forget a bathing costume. And, oh yes, our host is German. You'd better be polite."

"I shall be the very model of propriety."

"Comme toujours," Sally says, and blows him a friendly kiss as she trots off toward the stairs.

They drive south, parallel to the sea, following the coastal road that curves away from the port of Las Palmas, past white stucco buildings with wooden balconies, Coca-Cola signs, rows of palm trees, and brilliant bougainvillea, tracing the cockleshell shape of the island. In the distance cultivated fields and groves alternate with patches of sand, abrupt cliffs, and craters. Steady rivers of volcanic ash crawl like serpents down the hillsides, and above them, volcanic cones raise truncated heads—deformed reminders of the telluric rage that created this island, four degrees north of the Tropic of Cancer, off the coast of Africa. Sunlight spangles the calm water and boats hoot in the distance as Karl Arnheim's open jeep zooms along the hot black asphalt. Condominiums are scattered among the dunes.

"In a few more years there will be no more beach left, only luxury villas and hotels, but what can we do?" Karl shouts above the noise of the engine. A heavy-set man with large powerful arms, he holds the wheel securely with one hand, pointing with the other.

Tired from a five-hour flight and the sudden heat, his guests murmur agreement. Sally sits in the back next to Tibor, a white scarf tied under her chin, and pulls at his arm to show him a gull hovering in the wind.

"It looks like a mordent," Tibor says.

"A what?"

"You know, a marking over a note, an embellishment. If you see it over a G you play G-A-G. Never mind." He closes his eyes. Sally sinks into her seat and looks at the back of Werner's head. His blond curls dance, he turns to say something, but the wind in the open jeep covers his words and his mouth opens and closes, teeth white as a shark's.

"There's San Mateo de la Playa, over there," Karl shouts, pointing left, and surrounded by palms and olive trees, topped with a silver cross, is the stone church where Tibor will record. Without an invitation, the Chopin Fantasy opus 49 marches into his head and Tibor puts his hands over his ears.

"What's wrong?" Sally asks.

"Nothing. Just a headache. The flight."

"And down there," Karl yells, "see that dirt road, is the stable where I keep my Arabians. I ride bareback on the dunes every morning. This is something fantastic, riding on such·a perfect animal, the sea spray in your face, the wind, a rimless view. I will take with me tomorrow whoever wants to come."

Tibor remembers Maya on horseback, racing through the lavender-covered hills near Lake Balaton, clouds like lace doilies above her head. He remembers her taking the ride forbidden to him. "You might hurt your arms, and then what?" his father had said, and so he stood on top of the hill and watched his sister gallop while his heart pounded like angry surf.

"I'll ride your fastest," Tibor yells to Karl, but Sally and Werner turn, look questioningly at him, and he knows he won't. He'll stay at Karl's house. He'll practice.

Like a sudden oasis in the desert landscape, foliage surrounds them and they drive into the town of Maspalomas, dense with shrubs and flowers, first-class hotels, spas, and sparkling beaches. They stop for gas, drink Cokes, and Werner buys four hats from a little boy, passes them around. Back on the highway, there is a mile or two more of desert drive and then Karl turns sharply to the right, toward Fataga, a village high in the mountains. Cutting through jagged rock formations, a road twists and turns, climbing into arid hills. Karl points to a lintel-shaped plateau in the distance, and, squinting, they can just make out a few buildings sitting on top, Karl's realm. "I bought it ten years ago from one of the local landed families. 'You are crazy,' they told me. 'There is nothing in those hills.' But I built a road, I built my house, and now, look, there on the hillsides, you see more houses." Dotting the bleak landscape are a few green areas, and Karl points out vineyards on terraced hillsides, and talks about irrigation and the rich volcanic earth, which, once watered, flowers like Eden. In a valley they see a flock of sheep being led by a small boy; bells around their necks tinkle. Dust flies, the road gets steeper, narrower, twists and turns, and finally they arrive at the top of the plateau. Karl honks his horn, and a servant in dark pants, white shirt, and a straw hat comes running barefoot down the driveway, opens heavy iron gates, and they drive into a tropical paradise, flowers everywhere, olive trees, tomato fields. They hop out of the jeep, the man in the straw hat appears and disappears with luggage, and Karl leads them down a flagstone path to the main house, a large square stucco building with an open inner courtyard filled with passionflowers, roses, orchids, vines. Intoxicated by the scents, they glide through rooms looking at antiques, paintings, and furniture brought here from Germany, heavy Bavarian sofas, dark wood everywhere. A Hamburg Steinway catches Tibor's eye and he feels himself slip onto the piano stool, open the lid. The Chopin Fantasy marches from his fingers onto the keys, lugubrious but serene. Sally stands behind him. He thinks of Chopin, weak with consumption, sitting at a similar keyboard on the island of Majorca, George Sand by his side. He feels feverish. Arpeggios race upward, poco a poco doppio movimento, faster, more intense, agitated, lead him to the heroic climax, the march that disappears again into hymnlike reflection. Then, breaking like a storm, the agitation returns. In an eerie moment, just before the end, a single line of notes climbs upward, to another summit, the calm after volcanic tumult, and he hovers there, in a celestial pause. Tibor stops, his hands in the air. He cannot play the last twelve bars, he cannot break that silence. He holds his breath, closes the lid, and rushes away from the piano out onto a patio overlooking the sea.

"What is it?" Sally asks, catching up.

He puts an arm around her, stares off past the long marble pool, the beds of roses, the edge of the plateau, where long plumed grasses sway, seem to sweep the surface of the distant blue water.

"I'm so sorry." His voice is hollow as the bones of gulls.

"For what?"

"For being what I am—selfish. I should never have agreed to record the Fantasy here."

"Why not? You should finish that record, you said so yourself. I'm the one who is sorry for objecting, especially when I hear you play it like that."

"That's the problem. What you just heard—*that* was playing for keeps. I don't know why. That moment, this setting—but I can't play it better than I just did. That should have been recorded, kept for all time. Who knows if I'll feel like playing it at all at the recording session?"

"You'll rise to the occasion," Sally says, slipping her arms around his neck, "you always do."

Karl and Werner inspect the grounds. There are cages near the pool with a cockatoo in each. The birds take seeds from Werner's fingers with long dry tongues, crack them with sharp beaks, tilting their white crowns.

"So you were born in Frankfurt," Werner repeats, urging his host to go on.

"Yes. I went to university in Leipzig, then into the family business. But of course it was interrupted by the war."

"And what is the family business, if I may ask?" Werner smiles, moving in for the kill. He's caught another one, Nazi bastard, probably a steel manufacturer, maybe even a Krupp. How can Tibor be friends with these people, how can he be so naive? Karl is stocky with a ruddy face, and despite his monk's circle of white hair, he could be brutal, capable of a monstrous past.

"We were art collectors," Karl says. Werner blinks. "For over one hundred years. But because my wife was Jewish, everything was confiscated. My wife was exterminated and our two sons. I managed to get to Switzerland. It is a sad story, but unfortunately not a unique one."

150

"Yes," Werner says softly.

"So in Switzerland I learned a little about investment banking. It has been a useful education," he says.

"I can see that," Werner says, surveying the pool, the grounds, the breathtaking view of dry lunar hills splashed with occasional color.

"Perhaps you would like to wash before dinner?" Karl suggests and walks him to the smaller of two guest houses near the front gate, stopping on the way to pick a rose. He smells it, and with his eyes closed, his white head bowed, he looks like a priest. Father, forgive me, Werner wants to say. People are never what they seem. We deceive and we are deceived. But he clears his throat and says, "It's awfully kind of you to let me come like this at the last minute. I feel a bit of an interloper."

"Quatsch," Karl says, "nonsense. You are Tibor's friend, you are my friend. And you are the author of books I admire."

"You've read my work?"

"All of it, unless you've written more than eleven."

"I'm halfway to twelve, but I'm stuck."

"You'll get there," Karl says, clapping him on the back. "Writers like you always do."

"The cook must be having a fight with her husband," Karl says at dinner.

"How can you tell?" Tibor asks.

"Someone has been crying into the soup. It's too salty."

"It's not. It's delicious," Sally says and accepts more from the servant in a starched white uniform. "Cold cucumber soup on a hot night is my idea of perfection," she says.

"Is it too hot? Shall I open the doors?" Karl asks.

"You're sounding more apologetic than an Englishman," Tibor says. "Please stop." He winks at Karl.

Karl smiles and leans back in his chair, his sherry-brown

eyes glowing. A Flemish tapestry hangs behind his head, depicting a hunting scene, deer impaled on spears. The table is laid with Belgian lace and Danish silver. Miniature yellow roses float in a central crystal bowl, and brass candlesticks gleam.

"Karl has been trying to get me to come here for years, since we met in Zurich," Tibor says. "I never had time, I was always too busy. But now that I'm here, I may never leave."

"You're welcome to stay," Karl says, "but the world would be sad."

Tibor laughs and raises his crystal glass, drains a goblet of local wine.

"Is it true that Saint-Saëns lived in Gran Canaria?" Werner asks.

"Yes," Karl explains, "in the town of Guía. In the days when all the ships in the world stopped in the Canaries, Las Palmas was a cultural center. Saint-Saëns was music director of the Philharmonic here for two years, and after the turn of the century, all the great artists played here when their ships stopped to get supplies on their way to the States. In fact—I haven't told Tibor yet—the piano you will record on was played by Rachmaninoff, Schnabel, Rubinstein, and by your teacher, Vlostid."

Tibor swallows hard. "Stephan was here?"

"I looked it up for you. In 1907. He was twenty-six years old."

"My God," Tibor sighs, and imagines Stephan, young and debonair, in a top hat and tails, walking down a ship's gangway, stepping into a coach with four horses, driving slowly to a concert hall, playing like a god. "I'll have some ghosts to contend with," he says.

"You always do," Werner says.

"Do you remember the time—you were with me, Werner—in, where was it?" Tibor asks, "do you remember the ghost of Sir John?"

152

"And Mrs. Winterbottom?" Werner asks. He looks at Tibor and the two of them roar at the memory.

"Do you mind telling us about it?" Sally asks.

"Sorry, darling, yes, of course. We were put up by this lady in, I can't remember, someplace in the north of England. She was a very proper, prim matron, very serious, and in the morning at a very serious breakfast I simply mentioned I'd had a hard time getting to sleep in that top room. I said that little noises had kept me up all night. 'Well, of course,' Mrs. Winterbottom said, 'that must have been the ghost of Sir John. He died in that room in 1902.' Werner and I got such a fit of giggles, it was terrible."

"Impossible. We were rolling on the floor," Werner hoots. He and Tibor laugh wildly. Karl smiles.

"Excuse us," Tibor says, noticing that Sally isn't amused. "You had to be there." He can't stop laughing. Sally crunches on a sprig of watercress and watches.

"Mrs. Winterbottom," Werner squeaks, wiping his eyes, "was she the same one who came up to you after an all-Schubert recital and said, 'That was lovely, but how *do* you pronounce it, is it Schu*bert* or is it Schu*mann*?'"

"No," Tibor says, red with laughing. "that was in Philadelphia. Karl, you know what Stokowski said about Philadelphia, don't you—"

The three men laugh raucously. Sally is angry at herself for feeling annoyed. After all, one story sparks another, she should sit back and enjoy the display of fireworks, but somehow she can't.

"Why was Werner with you, and when was that?" Sally asks.

"When was what?" Tibor asks. His mood darkens as a fresh fruit salad is served—bright berries, papaya, and cream.

"When you traveled together, you two. You've not told me about it before."

"It must have been ten, twelve, maybe thirteen years ago. In those days, when he was in the mood for it, Werner tagged along on tour."

"God, it was fun," Werner says. "Do you remember the lady in Düsseldorf . . ."

Dinner over, cigars being lit, and stories still flowing, Sally excuses herself and wanders into the inner courtyard, lit by hanging lanterns. Cool air floats around her and she pulls her knitted shawl closer to her body, shivers under her cotton dress. She moves slowly from flower to flower, peering at each like a solitary moth looking for a place to land. She is swept up into dangerous drafts, agitated, and wishes she'd stayed on Willow Road. It's natural to feel regret, she tells herself. Give things a chance, don't be so quick to anger, quick to be disappointed. Calm down. She stops to examine a large bright blossom with intricate threadlike outgrowths, layers of yellow petals.

"That is a passionflower," her host says, joining her in the garden. "Some see in it the last hours of Christ's life. You see there, the corona is the crown of thorns; those armlike structures, the styles, are the nails of the crucifixion; the stamens in that cup are the five wounds; and there, the five sepals and those five petals are ten of the apostles, excluding Peter and, of course, Judas."

"Who betrayed Him," Werner offers, reaching them as a Chopin nocturne wafts from the living room. Tibor is at the keyboard. "Flowers," Werner says, cupping a rose in his hand. "They rise through dirt, radiant, triumphant. We can only buzz around their textured surfaces, never taste their hidden centers."

Sally stares at Werner; his golden ringlets frame an angelic face. Sensitive bastard, she thinks, and he stares back, the corners of his mouth curved up.

"Goethe said that when he looked at a flower he could

experience the entire cycle of existence," Karl says.
"And Maeterlinck on the rapture of flowers?" Werner asks and begins pacing slowly, like a novice, next to Karl around the periphery of the courtyard.

"Yes, flowers as the key to mystical experience," Karl says, "the source of spiritual awakening . . ."

Sally thinks of Monet's garden in Giverny, transformed by the artist into a vision of intense, endless continuity.

"Look at her," Werner says, stopping, pointing at Sally, pensive in the half-light. "Like a madonna walled into a flowered courtyard. You are a Renaissance vision."

"I'd rather be a flower," she says curtly, "perfectly self-sufficient."

"Like our friend in there?" Werner asks, nodding toward the doors, through which scales and arpeggios can be heard.

"He's digging in for a long practice," Sally says, "I can tell." She paws at the grass with a sandaled foot.

"Shall we go for a walk?" Werner asks. "The moon is bright. Will you come, Karl?"

"I think I will stay here and listen," he says. "I don't have the opportunity to hear him very often, even in practice. But you can walk along the road as far as you like. It is perfectly safe and very lovely."

Sally walks silently beside Werner, through the front gate, past a tomato field. The road is still warm from the sun, and she feels the heat rise against her bare legs. Hills are outlined sharply against the sky and the stars are adamantine. In white pants and a thin white shirt Werner glows beside her, walking at her pace, sharing her silence. They follow the road up over a hill and down, turn a corner and find themselves at the foot of a steep cliff.

"There must be caves in there," Werner says, "las cuevas. The island is famous for them. They say the original inhabitants, the guanches, lived in them. They maintain a uniform temperature all year, and I suppose you could still live in them. It's not such a bad idea, is it, living inside the earth, protected by it?"

Sally says nothing as she turns to face Werner. He seems to hover over her, pale but voracious. She will not be cowed. "Shall we go look?" she whispers.

"Come on," Werner says, and leads her slowly off the road toward the shiny dark surface of the cliff, edging through brambles and boulders. Putting hands against the still-warm rock face, they feel for openings, squint for crevices.

"What if there are snakes, or scorpions?" Sally asks.

"You're right," Werner says, stopping, leaning back against a rock. "We should do this in the daytime. It's foolish now. But sometimes you can't help being foolish, can you?"

Sally finds a spot near him and leans against the rock while looking up into the sky, feels cool air against her face, the warm rock underneath.

"There's the Dipper," she says, "and Leo."

"Hydra and Hercules," Werner adds.

"It's so clear," Sally says.

"Yes."

Sally feels Werner's eyes turn toward her, follow her silhouette along the rock. She presses her body hard against the stone, wanting to melt into it so he will stop looking.

"You're breathing so hard," Werner whispers. "Why?"

"I don't know," she says, rolls to her side, facing him. His eyes burn into hers and she is afraid yet fascinated. The white of his clothing vibrates against the dark rock, blurring contours. He seems to float before her, a vapor in the night, his presence flowing out, surrounding her.

"Let's go back," she says, her voice strained, and she runs quickly to the road, waits for him to catch up. He moves slowly, like a panther stalking, and she is afraid again. She dashes off down the road, calling out, "I just feel like running. See you back there."

"You're out of breath," Tibor says when she arrives at the house. Sitting in a wicker chair on the patio with Karl, looking out over the sea, Tibor pulls Sally onto his lap, wipes her sweaty forehead with a handkerchief, and she nestles in, content as a cat. Tibor and Karl continue their conversation . . . the quality of pianos . . . plastic keys instead of ivory . . . and she listens to the voices weave in and out of her head as she did when company stayed late at her parents' house and she dozed off in her father's arms.

"Ah, there he is," Tibor calls, and Sally is jolted awake as he strains forward beneath her.

Werner strides toward them.

"How was your walk?" Tibor asks.

"Lovely. And did you work well?"

"Fair."

"He is never pleased," Karl says. "I listen and I hear perfection. But Tibor, he is never satisfied."

"If I were satisfied I should stop practicing, and if I stopped practicing I'd no longer be satisfied, so it's best to keep things as they are, don't you think?"

Karl offers brandy, and as he pours the amber liquid, he says that Felipe, the gardener who took their luggage when they arrived, would be honored to sing for them.

"They still speak of honor on this island," Karl says. "You will like the natives. They are straightforward, loyal. The men seem to have a kind of spiritual elegance, but they do tend to dream and to be melancholy."

"Sure, they're oppressed, exploited, the—" Werner begins, but a warning look from Tibor quiets him as Felipe comes forward, a small guitar in his hand, a shy smile on his face. He speaks in Spanish and Karl translates. "He says his instrument is called a timple, and he will play a seguidilla for you."

Felipe puts one leg up on a chair, leans over his instrument and strums it, playing chords lightly, rhythmically, making a gentle sound. He smiles as he plays, his eyes shining under half-closed lids. When he plays an arrorró and sings about maternal love, his voice is pure and bright and tears glisten on his cheeks. Sally listens to the lullaby, sips her brandy, and strokes Tibor's arm, longing to take him to bed, embrace him, but he sits forward in his chair, absorbed. Felipe bows and thanks them for listening, refuses the money they offer, and backs away into the night.

"That natural rubato, the nuances of phrasing," Tibor bubbles, "it's fabulous. You can never learn it, it's there, or it's not. And did you hear the folía he played with those intricate variations? The one in F minor, didn't it sound like Corelli's, and his technique!"

Sally pecks Tibor on the cheek and says she's tired, she'll get ready for bed.

"I'll be with you in a few minutes, darling," Tibor says. Sally walks alone down the flagstone path, knowing if the subject is music the few minutes will stretch into many, and by the time Tibor climbs into bed beside her she will be asleep. Will it be like this every night? she wonders and undresses slowly, limbs heavy. She lies on the brocaded coverlet on the guest-house bed and looks around the room at porcelain lamps, antique bedstands, a dour portrait of a cardinal by some quattrocento hand. Looking up, she sees a gecko, a small lizard, on the ceiling, its tiny legs clinging to the nubbly white surface, its transparent body somehow fetal, unformed. In a spurt of disgust Sally flings a pillow at the ceiling, barely misses. The lizard scuttles away and Sally heaves herself under the covers, pulls them tight and lies awake, terrified that the lizard might squirm under the sheets, scratch at her with small, pointed claws, cling to her as to the ceiling. She listens for the comforting sound of Tibor's footsteps, but she falls asleep long before he arrives. When he does, he tiptoes toward the form bulging under the covers, strokes the locks of her hair, which pour like honey across the pillow. He undresses quickly and slips into bed next to Sally, presses himself against her back, wraps around her, and she wakes with a start.

"Ma chatte, c'est moi, calme-toi. . . ."

She sighs with relief and turns toward him, buries her face in the warm fuzz of his chest. He takes her fisted hand, covers it with kisses, but Sally pulls it away whispering, "It will not open out like a flower." Tibor's attention is on other textured surfaces and he cannot hear her.

He drinks the wind. Nostrils flared, Inshalla pounds the sand, arching his long chestnut neck, impatient to run. Karl straddles him like a king, one hand holding the reins, the other waving as he turns the horse, clicks his tongue, and they race across white sand, a streak of brown against the violet sea.

"Imagine naming your horse God's Will," Sally says.

"It's better than Max."

"It terrifies me."

"The name?"

"The horse. All that power, muscle, sinew, and the eyes—so dark and enormous."

"Look at him!" Werner shouts as Karl heads back toward them, the horse galloping, its small tapered head elegantly poised, its movements graceful, sand spraying from its feet like diamond dust.

"Karl says they're bred to withstand extreme temperatures, sandstorms, hunger, thirst. They're perfect animals, aren't they?" Sally asks.

"Not exactly. They have huge hearts, but not much brain."

"Exactly—they're perfect," Sally says, smiling up at him, her hair whipping in the wind. Werner laughs and grabs Sally's hand, pulls her after him onto the beach, making her run.

Barefoot at water's edge, Sally stoops to look at shells, as the sea swirls around her toes. Werner rolls up his white pants.

"Their bones are dense as ivory," he says.

"Whose?"

"Arabian stallions."

"Oh," she says, concerned with a snail.

"And their origin is unclear—central Asia, maybe Mongolia, no one knows. When I was a boy I was mad to know all about them. I wrote a story about some Saracen horsemen. . . . 'Prince Muftiwana fled into the night on his swift Arabian steed, leaving the Princess Chandru weeping on her bed, draped in silks like a dragonfly. . . .'"

"You hopeless romantic," Sally says as she draws with a stick in hard wet sand, sighs as the tide erases her lines.

"That was nice," Werner says.

"But it's gone."

"Just like making music. Now you know how it feels."

"What time is it?" A moment of guilt, like the fin of a fish, flashes into Sally's thoughts. Tibor is recording, working hard, and she is playing in the sun. But Karl races past again, Inshalla's tail unfurls, the sun begins to warm, the morning waits to be conquered.

"Want to swim?" Sally asks, and pulls her caftan off over her head, stands before Werner, innocent yet knowing, nude except for white cotton underpants, half schoolgirl, half siren.

"Catch!" she yells, throws her dress at him and dives into a cresting wave.

"Raise the mike track one db," Jack Tischman, the producer, says to his sound engineer, Harley Blackston. A heavy wooden door squeaks and Harley ambles into the sanctuary of San Mateo de la Playa, where Tibor sits slumped over piano keys. Wires and microphones hook into the piano like a life-support system.

Pull the plug, Tibor thinks, shaking his icy hands. I want to die with dignity.

"Let me hear something, just once more," Jack's voice orders, and Tibor takes a breath, smiles, and plays the opening lines of Liszt's "Bénédiction de Dieu dans la solitude."

"Terrific," Jack says, "but now there's a hiss on the tape. Hang in there."

"I'm hanging, I'm hanging," Tibor says, stands up and wants to walk away, but won't; it's bad luck. He has to get something recorded, something in the can, before he'll change position. His eyes wander around the church. Sunlight streams through arched windows, madonnas watch, saints wait. Jack's voice echoes again from the vestry—there's no glass partition, as in a studio, through which Tibor could at least see a face, even the pallid round visage of Jack Tischman, himself a pianist years back.

"OK, we're ready," Jack announces, "Chopin Fantasy in F minor, opus forty-nine, take one."

"Wait!" Tibor yells, sits down again, feeling dizzy, unprepared. He looks straight ahead at a large bronze crucifix. The compassionate eyes of Christ are upon him. He begins. Yes, the march, as to Calvary, grave, tempered with resolution, yes, Tibor thinks, good—

"Hold it." Jack's voice interrupts like a nail driving into his side. "Terrific, great, but we're still having a problem."

Tibor cracks his knuckles, gnashes his teeth, tries to bear

this pain, tries not to groan. He imagines Sally beside him, her patient hand on his shoulder.

"Take two," Jack announces, and Tibor begins again, shutting out thought, starting the march again, but it is ponderous now, contrived.

"Sorry," Tibor says, stopping and, after a pause, announces himself, "Take three."

Now the first octaves are well placed, heavy but not lumbering. He moves on, slowly, to the A-flat chord at measure 46, holds firm, prepared to move forward with the triplets, thinking ahead to the B-flat octaves, the next resting place—

"What's that noise?" Jack again.

"Christ!" Tibor shouts, pounds his fists on the keyboard, and stands up. "What the hell is going on here?"

"We have a problem."

"You always have a problem," Tibor growls. "And when you don't, I do. I hate recording!"

Sweating now, wiping at his forehead, Tibor paces back and forth, his footsteps echoing through the church. He stops at a mahogany confession booth, peeks inside. "I have sinned, I have agreed to record in this holy place," he whispers through the iron grate and moves on to Pietàs hanging in gold frames, gilt halos, angels' wings. He reaches the west door. Maybe he should go outside, sit in the shade of that thousand-year-old dragon tree. No, he'd better wait, wait until it's finished, over, done with. He leans against a marble pillar, looks up at a gargoyle, who smirks back down at him. Jack is walking toward him, wants to chat to pass the time, says Harley has the problem nearly fixed.

"I thought CBS had good portable equipment," Tibor says.

"We do. The remote is great. The problem seems to be in the electric generator. But we'll fix it, don't worry." Jack moves on to music. "By the way, do you really mean to take so much time on the last sixteenth before measure seven? You're spreading that beat a lot, you know."

"I know."

"I guess you like it like that."

Tibor clenches his fists. "You make the record, I make the music, OK?"

Jack's smile shrinks to a small thin line. When Szabo gets nasty, he thinks, remembering the time they were recording "Papillons" and he made the mistake of suggesting less rubato, Tischman takes off.

"I'll see if Harley is ready," Jack says and slinks away toward the sacristy, where Harley, sweating profusely, crouches next to the mixing console, turning the spool of an Ampex recording machine, muttering to himself.

"How are we doing?" Jack asks.

"You can give your royal we a wipe," Harley says. "The generator's dead."

"You're kidding."

"Would that I were."

"What are we going to do?"

"*We*, meaning *I*, will have to rush around Las Palmas to locate another. You'd better tell the maestro he'll have to wait until tomorrow morning."

Jack Tischman pales, flushes, pales again, starts to swear, but remembers where he is. He looks helplessly at Harley, who shrugs his shoulders. Then Jack turns on his heels, marches through the door, between carved wooden pews, toward the piano, toward the tall, thin figure standing stiff as a martyr beside it.

Close to noon. Werner on Inshalla, shirtless, dashing past Sally. She, covered again, shaded by a sunhat, watches his torso rise like a centaur from the body of the horse. His curls dance. He turns the horse around and rushes toward

163

her, leaning to one side, arm out as if to snatch her up, carry her off. She thinks of the Sabine women and backs into the foaming surf, mimicking fright. Werner tosses his head; his laughter echoes across the dunes as he slows to a trot, posting up and down. Sally's eyes follow his spine to his buttocks, to the warm smooth-gaited horse moving between his thighs, as the sea curls around her ankles, decorating her feet with soft green weeds.

"It's noon," Karl says, squinting at the sky as they leave the stable and pile into his jeep. "Perfect. We'll be back the same time as Tibor."

"Good," Sally says, "and he'll be done with his work." She is sleepy, flops like a rag doll as the jeep bumps along, looking forward to a long nap with Tibor after lunch, cool sheets against her sun-baked skin, Tibor, pleased with his session, cares gone, rolling across her like a wave.

"Tomorrow morning?" Sally asks.

Tibor's eyes glow like coals behind narrowed lids as he recites the morning's catastrophe, the session's postponement. Then, excusing himself from lunch, he steams across the lawn toward the guest house, leaving Sally, Karl, and Werner holding wineglasses, silent as sand.

"I'd better go," Sally says, and hands her glass to Werner.

"I'm sorry, darling," she says, sitting gently on the bed next to Tibor, who lies on his back, staring at the ceiling. "Karl says they have lots of generators in Las Palmas. They'll have no trouble finding one for the morning."

He says nothing.

"If you're worried that I object to your being gone another morning, I don't. I understand. Of course I do. Tibor?"

He rolls onto his side, curling up like a touched worm.

"Tibor, what is it?"

"Go have lunch." His voice, muffled by his knees,

164

strains with anger. His head throbs, the thwarted session sickens him. He just needs to be alone. He just needs silence.

"Is it me?" she asks.

"It's not you. Just go," he says, and when she hesitates, he adds a tense "please."

Werner eats cherries. His ease annoys Sally and so does the way he looks at her—cool and distant, yet ravenous. A line of cherry juice trickles from his lower lip, tumbles down his chin toward his white shirt. If Sally reaches out her hand she can catch it before it stains, but she watches with some satisfaction as the drop splashes onto white cloth, spreads like a small wound. His neck, she notices, is bronzed with sun, but under his chin the flesh is still pale, vulnerable. She would like to sink her teeth into the flesh just there, or would she rather caress it? She turns her head quickly, pained with confusion.

"Stop worrying about Tibor," Werner says.

"I'm not even thinking about him," she says, angry at Werner, wanting to hit him, pound him again and again with her fisted hand.

Werner sucks on a cherry pit, then asks her why she's so angry.

"I'm not."

"Of course you are. You're upset with your lover and you're taking it out on me."

"I am not."

"And you're petulant." He taunts her with a smile, tips his chair onto its back legs and rocks, pressing his bare toes against the patio stones. Sally feels her cheeks flame with chagrin and fury. She leaves her chair without looking at him and walks past the pool toward the edge of land, where her view is unimpeded, only valley below, sea beyond, stretching, unconstrained. She watches a gull bank against the wind, ride the current of air. She listens to its cry.

"Here," a voice says, and she turns to find Werner beside her, handing her a sketchbook and some pencils. She turns away.

"Come on," he says. "It's surprising to see how well you can work when you're angry."

Sally laughs and takes the pad, touching his fingers. "I guess you're not the enemy," she says.

"No, I'm not," he answers, his voice soft, his eyes trapping hers.

"I don't really feel like sketching," Sally says. Her mood is restored, her energy is renewed. She wants to fly like a gull. "Do you want to look for those caves?" she asks.

"Now?"

"Now is the only time."

They take the main road, padding silently in tennis shoes, side by side. Sally wipes at her forehead and puts on a straw hat, tells Werner he should do the same. He squints back at her and fastens his loosely under his chin. They find the same rock wall they saw at night, but it is sheer, no openings at all, and Werner suggests they follow a path just up ahead, leading down into a valley. Sally follows behind him, watching little puffs of dust where he steps. She trips on a stone, and when Werner catches her by the arm, she feels faint and refreshed at once. Werner stops to examine the earth.

"Must be a path where lava flowed," he says, and points out volcanic ash, shows her a small brown grasshopper. Sally looks into the distance, the sea no longer visible. Angular dry hills rise above them, and sun filters through the dust, hazy and hot.

"We should have brought some water," Sally says. "I'm parched."

"We'll find some," Werner says, "Columbus did," and

166

leads her down into the valley, confidently turns right. Balls of dried brush scuttle along the ground, and the color of the earth changes to gray, orange, deeper rust. They start up a northern slope, follow it until tufts of green spring up around them, promising oasis, and a few yards farther at the top of the hill the land rolls away like a green carpet before them, grass, bushes, an occasional red poppy. Small bells tinkle, and ambling slowly into the grassy valley below is a herd of sheep followed by a young boy carrying a stick.

"Hola! Qué hay!" Werner yells down at him, waves, and taking Sally's hand he rushes down the slope toward the child. The boy looks frightened, but Werner calls, "Amigo!" waves his hat, and the boy laughs.

"Cómo está usted?" Werner asks in stilted Spanish.

"Bien," answers the boy, with a shy smile. His face is streaked with dirt and his pants, tied around his waist with a piece of rope, are torn at one knee. He removes his hat, scratches at his head, and plays with his walking stick.

"Por favor," Werner asks, "dónde está agua?" The boy points beyond them to the rise of a hill.

"Y las cuevas?"

The boy points to the same place, nodding his head up and down, then runs off toward his flock.

"Gracias, muchas gracias," Werner calls after him and the boy turns to wave.

"Poor little thing," Sally says, "he can't be more than ten. He should be at school."

"Maybe it's his holiday," Werner says, seeing her frown. "Don't let it make you sad. Please." But as Sally follows behind him she feels heavy inside; each foot drags a weight. It is an effort to move. She stops.

"What is it?" Werner asks, turning, and the angle of his head, the light on his face, the balance of his body makes her want to weep.

"I don't know. I just don't know," she says, and begins to cry, rubbing at her eyes with her fists. He reaches out his hand, but she flinches at the touch of his fingers on her arm.

"Am I hurting you?" he asks.

"Yes."

"How?"

"I don't know."

"You do," he whispers. "You know perfectly what it's about and why it's happening."

"Why what is happening?" she asks, and even as his arms close around her, his breath is on her cheek, his lips move toward hers, she denies knowing.

"I want you so badly," he whispers, his body shaking. "I have since I met you, but I've stayed away, I've stayed away." He moans the last word and Sally is faint with desire and dread of it.

"What are we doing?" she asks, terrified, wanting him.

Werner's mouth covers hers and she sinks with him slowly into a nest of long grass. He rolls on top of her, his hands move under her jersey and she tugs at his shirt, pushes it up. His bare chest against her breasts makes her gasp with pleasure, a sharp sensation, almost pain.

"Stop," she says weakly, and buries her hands in the lamb's wool of his hair as he kisses one breast, the other, and unzips her jeans. As she wriggles out of the denim, Werner sits back on his haunches to look at her, but she turns her face away.

"Don't," he says, leaning over her, bringing her back, brushing a stalk of grass away from her cheek. "This is right, it is inevitable. . . ."

"And Tibor?"

"This has nothing to do with him."

"It has everything to do with him."

"And if it does?" he asks, standing up to remove his

clothes. He is thin as a boy and firm, the only hint of his age a slight thickening above the waist. He towers above her with muscular legs and thighs, aroused, eager as a faun. She reaches out both arms for him as he falls to his knees and the sky spreads over them like a thin blue tent.

They climb through thick grass, arms around each other, stumbling, kissing, unable to let go. A white shirt trails from Werner's hand, flutters in the soft breeze. Sally chews on a stem of grass and chatters about hill-walking with her father in the Highlands.

"There's a ruined cottage at the foot of Coire Dubh and we started out in the early morning, climbing north to what looked like smooth white slopes, but as we got nearer we saw there was a lot of quartz and scree and the ridge-walking was perilous and once we nearly—"

Werner stops her with a kiss, twisting around her, reaching beneath her shirt. "I'm afraid I want to hold you again," he says, and she says, "Yes," and she sees her father scrambling up a quartz scree, feels the same exhilaration as on that high walk, breath knocked away, chest bursting with the beauty of it, wanting to explode, climbing, climbing, finally there, on top, the world spread out around her, bountiful, exquisite—hers.

"You two are very quiet," Tibor says after dinner. "It must have been quite a hike."

Sally hides behind a sip of wine while Werner tells about the shepherd and the drastic change in vegetation and how thirsty they got.

"And did you find any caves?"

"No. We found something better."

Sally chokes on her drink and watches Werner, chair tilted back, bare toes pushing at the patio, as he describes the stream they came to late in the afternoon, with thick succulent weeds trailing into cool clear water, wild roses growing nearby, bees humming. He omits the part about lying beside her on the soft bank, dropping rose petals onto her naked breasts, cupping his hands for water, taking a sip and sharing it with her mouth to mouth. His warm lips, cool water passing into her mouth—the pleasure of it, pure as that stream, so easily given, so willingly taken, seemed so natural at the moment. But now, with a night chill blowing in from the sea, with Tibor to her left, Werner to her right, she is wedged between, unable to move. She looks at Werner's face, then Tibor's, like a negative and its photo. Without both there is neither. She closes her eyes, listens to men's voices and smells cigars, and wishes they would both disappear.

"How is Colin?" she hears. The name is familiar.

"He's reading English at Cambridge," Werner says. "Can you imagine, my son, interested in the same things as I?"

"What's so strange about that?" Sally asks, testily.

Werner pushes against the stone, rocking faster, and says, "Normally, nothing. But in my case, I assumed my antipathy toward my own father would pass, like a dominant gene, to my son."

"It's the sins of the father that get handed down, not always the sensibilities," she says.

"Then maybe Colin has both."

"Maybe. But what I can't imagine is you having a grown son at all," she says.

Tibor laughs and joins in. "It's true. You look and act such a kid yourself."

"Why are you two ganging up on Werner?" Karl's voice asks from a green canvas lounge chair. He shifts his position and turns toward his three guests. "Werner, tell me, what was so terrible about your father?"

"He lacked courage, he had no spine."

"Are you certain?"

Werner hesitates.

"I remember what you have written about your father," Karl says. " 'I writhe like a frenzied snake, for yours is the skin I cannot shed.' "

"I'm flattered to be quoted," Werner says, "but why do you remember that particular phrase?"

Karl sighs and rolls onto his back, stares up at a dimming sky. "Because I was a father. Because my sons were killed. Because, when I read that passage, I asked myself, had they lived, would they have thought such a thing about me?"

"I think not," Werner says.

"I'll never know. But I'll tell you one thing. A man who cannot forgive his father is a man who cannot forgive himself."

"Maybe," Werner says, his voice clipped, "and maybe not."

"And maybe we're all a bit tired," Karl says with a beneficent smile. "I certainly am. And so I'll say good night." He rises to his feet, excusing himself, and leaves the trio alone on the patio, Sally in the middle, flanked by the two men. As if a vein were bulging beneath the surface, the roseate sky thickens with blue, holds back for a moment, and seems to light up once more before sinking into darkness.

"I wonder," Sally says, drifting with the fading light, "what one can ever know about anyone else."

"Everything," Tibor says, "and nothing. It's what you know about yourself that counts."

Werner has stopped rocking, turns his chair to look at Sally and Tibor in sharp profile against the opaque sky. "I just realized something. The three of us share a similar loss—a parent at an early age. Maybe that's what makes us so close to each other."

"We may be semi-orphans," Tibor says, "but we're three complete fools." His laughter rings, shrill and manic.

171

"What makes you say that?" Sally asks, guilt catching at her throat like a sudden hand in the dark.

"Well, look at us. Me thinking only of Chopin, Werner unearthing parents yet again, and Sally wondering why we know nothing about each other. We're not linked by loss, we three. What creates our bond is mutual self-obsession. I'm a prisoner of the piano, Werner is a slave to his typewriter, and Sally is chained to her brushes, and none of us makes a move toward freedom. What we share is a kind of willful slavery."

"But wait a minute," Werner says. "Obsession is necessary to making art."

"And what's so bloody important about art?"

Werner chuckles. "What's so funny?" Tibor asks, looking at Werner's head outlined in the dark, his mound of hair an obstructive, craggy shape.

"It's just funny coming from you, only the most gifted musician of the century—an artist disdaining his art."

"I'm a pianist," Tibor snaps. "I work hard. I make music. If you want to call that art, talk about it in pretty little phrases, that's your business. As far as I'm concerned, it's work like any other."

"It's different and you know it," Werner says, his chair firmly on the ground, his legs crossed. "I can't figure you out, Szabo. You've been given this gift and you carry it around as if it's a ball and chain. You're afraid to take responsibility for it. You kick it around because it frightens you. You pretend it's a burden because oppression gives you an excuse to be irresponsible."

Tibor scratches a match against stones. The flame sizzles. He lights a Disque Bleu, blows smoke at the sky, wisps of white curling into the air. "Go on, Rawlings," he says, "now that you're warmed up. Tell me how I'm irresponsible. I only practice all the time."

"It's not your work. It's your attitude. Look, you're the

one who's always talking about losing yourself in music, as if that complete intimacy comes from some magical source. It's *you* who makes the music, it's *you* who creates that intimacy. And I've watched how you do it—practicing like a madman, working on a piece, struggling to take possession of it, to make the music yours. And then when you perform it, all that effort falls away and the piece soars. The listener's response is immediate. Hell, it takes me two years and hundreds of thousands of words to say what you can in a two-hour concert. I hope for your sake, one day, you learn to value what you have."

"I value it all right," Tibor says, the edge on his voice sharpening, "I just don't need to glorify it."

"I'm not trying to—" Werner tries to say, but Tibor is on his feet, grinding his heel into the cigarette.

"It's all a matter of survival. If I'm going to face the microphones tomorrow, I'd better get to the keyboard tonight. So if you don't mind, I'll leave you two to get on with the meaning of art."

Silence for a minute, until Sally says, "How well you know yourself."

"And how bitter you sound," Tibor says, his eyes searching for hers in the dark. "Why?" Sally doesn't answer, and Tibor stands before them, brushing his hair out of his eyes. "I'm sorry, Sally. I have to practice. I thought you understood."

"I do," she says.

"Well, then," he says, and wanting suddenly to make up for his lunchtime sulk and his nighttime outburst, he says, "Why don't you and Werner look for those caves again in the morning?"

"I'd rather come with you to the recording session," Sally says.

"Why should you be inside a damp old church when the weather is so glorious? Besides, Karl is coming." Tibor bends down to kiss Sally, but she turns her head away.

"You're angry."

"I'm not," she says. "Just tired."

"I understand," Tibor says, patting her head, "my hiker, my little explorer."

Scales rise through the still air, descend again, twist into patterns and designs in Sally's mind.

"What are you thinking about?" Werner asks, reaching out with his foot to cover hers with his bare toes. Sally shivers and scrunches down in her chair.

"I was seeing the sounds Tibor makes, that's all," she says, ignoring the foot.

"You are linked to him, you know. Inextricably."

"Please, Werner, let's not talk about it. Not about today, not about tomorrow. Please."

"We have to. It was wonderful with you today—exquisite. I'm not willing to let it sink into memory. I've told you I'm possessive. Sally?"

"I'm here," she says faintly. "I'm listening."

"When you asked me in London to come to the Canaries with you and Tibor, I thought you were admitting that you felt something for me. But now—I don't know, I'm confused. Maybe it was just an innocent whim, a way to deflect your problems with Tibor, your ambivalence."

"I am *not* ambivalent," Sally blurts.

"Aren't you?" Werner asks, forcing her to look at him, forcing her to feel his foot, which presses firmly on top of hers.

"I don't know," she says, on the verge of tears, "I don't know anything. How this happened, what it means, why—"

"Some things aren't meant to be understood. Only felt. And you felt a lot today, didn't you?"

He leans toward her, but Sally closes her eyes, slides even deeper into her chair.

"Hiding from it won't help. Sally, listen to me. I want you. I want to be with you. I realize what's at stake here, and if you think it's easy for me, you're wrong. Tibor is a brother to me, even more." His voice trails off. He touches Sally's knee, caresses it. "What I feel for you is so strong," he whispers, "and after today I know it's right. For you, for me, for all of us."

"How can you presume to—"

"Shh, keep your voice down."

"Why should I? The damage has already been done."

"What damage? We made love. And well, at that. What damage did it do?"

"I'm just beginning to find out. And I've made a decision," she says, making one as she speaks, "to consider what happened today an isolated incident, the result of circumstance. It won't happen again."

Werner pulls his chair closer to Sally's, leans toward her. The pupils of his eyes seem to dilate, try to capture her, fix her as she is, hair streaming across her shoulders, eyes wide with fear and longing, lips slightly parted.

"I don't accept," he says.

"You must." Sally gets up and walks over to the birdcages, places some seeds on the side of her hand, feels Robespierre, the largest cockatoo, nibble at her with his dry beak. He tilts his head, gurgles contentment, looks for more.

"What if," Werner says, leaning across wire netting toward her, "what if it was not just circumstance? What if the feelings you had today were real, for me alone?"

"I have to find out," Sally says, safe, a cage distance away, "for my sake, and for Tibor's."

"Yes, the great genius. Your responsibility to him is greater than your own needs. He'd fall apart without you, I'm sure."

"Sarcasm doesn't suit you."

"Sally, I can't help it. Trust me, please. Trust what

happened today, how good it was, how equal. I accept you as you are. I have no need to see you as some sort of goddess, like our friend in there. Sally, we could have such a good life together, I know it, a real life. Sally?"

He strains toward her, his hands reach over the cold wire of the cage. Light from the pool throws blue shadows across his face and he looks tired, pained, an older man. Sally wants to fling her arms around him, make him young again, lead him to the long grasses at the edge of the cliff and cling to him there once more. But she hears herself speak of commitment, and announces her plan to go on to Spain, with Tibor.

Werner is silent, looks out toward the sea. A memory sails into his head. Stresa, Italy, standing beside Tibor on a boat, an island looming in the distance. "Che bella!" Tibor had exclaimed and, throwing his arms around Werner, had hugged him hard. There, chest to chest, a sensation of contentment, of complete serenity—Werner remembers it. He speaks, pausing between each phrase, unable to connect thoughts. "Yes . . . if you want to make it work with Tibor, try . . . perhaps you should try. . . . I think I'll go back to London . . . yes, tomorrow. . . . I'll be there for you, if you want me. . . . Sally?"

Sally reaches out to touch his cheek, and as his hand closes over hers, he bends his head and kisses her fingers and she can smell grass and wild roses in his hair. She pulls her hand away and runs back toward the guest house without saying good night.

"I think you're covered," Jack says the next morning at church, after two solid hours of recording.

"Are you sure?" Tibor asks. "Have you got those double octaves in the recapitulation?"

"Come and listen for yourself."

Tibor stands and stretches, smiling at Karl, who rises from a pew, a satisfied congregant.

"Thanks," Tibor says, throwing an arm around Karl as they walk together toward the vestry.

"Whatever for?"

"For being my audience. It helped to play for a friend."

"You know it's my great pleasure, and privilege."

"Are you sure you don't mean penance?" Tibor asks and leans with all his weight on the heavy wooden door leading into the room where the mixing console has been installed.

At the whirring high-pitched backward spin of tapes Tibor covers his ears. Jack offers him a Disque Bleu, from a pack bought for the occasion. He inhales, combs his fingers through his hair, sighs, and waits to listen.

"Let's hear take four," Jack tells Harley. "Then move to take six, insert three for the recap and ending."

Tibor settles into an armchair placed between two speakers to listen to the playback. Cut off from physical contact with the piano, he is isolated, withdrawn. It seems a strange soliloquy, those sounds, those glittering passages he hears coming through two cloth-covered squares, and yet he just made that music himself, pushing keys, pressing pedals.

"What was that?" he asks, sitting up at a wrong note.

"Rewind a bit, Harley," Jack orders, and sure enough, when they listen again, at measure eighty-seven the last high F is muffed.

"Don't worry, we have that on another take, I'm positive," Jack says, pointing to his score, where he had marked a plus after another take number.

"I want to hear it. I want to be sure," Tibor says, and spends the rest of the morning sorting through takes, being objective and critical, suggesting just the right inserts for editing, demanding more presence in the bass, less in the treble, crafting the disc himself.

"You know so much about it," Karl says, impressed, on the way home.

"I've had a lot of experience, that's all."

"And do you enjoy it?"

"Recording? Are you kidding? I hate it. Except for one thing. After a concert, all I can do is an autopsy; but after a recording, I have a chance at my own resurrection."

"What do you mean he's gone back to London?" Tibor asks.

Sally rubs Bain de Soleil onto her neck and says, "Just what I said. He packed his bag, called the airport, and took off. He said he's had a sudden inspiration and wanted to get back to his typewriter. He hopes you understand and apologizes for rushing off."

Tibor looks at Karl, then back at Sally.

"I hope he didn't feel unwanted," Karl says.

"Or ignored by me, I—"

"Karl, I know he felt wanted and very much at home, really," Sally says assuringly. "He has a project he's obsessed with. It's understandable, and has nothing to do with any of us." She wipes an oily hand on her leg and looks up at Tibor. "How did it go?"

"What?" he asks, still stunned.

"The session."

"Finished, over, done," Tibor says, and flops down onto the grass next to her at poolside.

"He was brilliant," Karl says.

"For eleven minutes fifty-six seconds of recorded music it only took me two days and the alienation of my closest friend to achieve."

"Come on," Sally says, rubbing at Tibor's shoulder where she knows it always knots up. "Werner left because he had to. It had nothing to do with you. Darling, now we can really relax. Why don't you put on your bathing costume? The water is lovely."

"I will," he says, "in a minute." He rolls over, takes her

hand and holds it, and she feels weak, listless, as if recovering from a long illness.

"God, am I glad it's over," Tibor says. But he spends the slow afternoon at the pool, still thinking over every phrase he played, unable to stop the tapes in his head, while he splashes and clowns for her.

By evening, clouds have gathered out at sea, start to move inland. At supper, during the roast duck, a clap of thunder rattles the silver, and Karl, Sally, and Tibor rush out to the patio, watch the sea churn through rain, wait for the first drop to splatter on stone, listen to leaves thrash in the wind. Felipe enters the living room with logs and lights a fire. Brandy is poured, and a chess set with ivory pieces appears.

Tibor snatches up a black pawn and a white pawn, one in each of his large hands. Karl lightly taps the left. Tibor smiles and uncurls his hand triumphantly to display black.

"I'll clobber you with my opening," Tibor announces to Karl, and moves his white king's pawn. Karl quickly counters in kind, and when, after some deliberation, Tibor makes his second move, his knight, Sally curls up on the sofa, her head resting on Tibor's thigh. She thinks of all the rainy evenings she has spent in London, alone, waiting for Tibor to come back from his tours, her knight-errant. She lies quietly, wondering which she prefers, the anticipation or the actuality.

"Aha!" Tibor says with glee when Karl moves his queen's pawn. "Philidor's Defense. It won't do you any good. Look—you're cramping your bishop."

Karl holds up the brandy snifter, studying the board through the amber liquor.

"Did you know Philidor wrote operas when he wasn't playing chess?" Tibor asks. "Lucky bugger. There was something else he could do besides making music."

"Some of us," Karl says, rubbing his hands together,

179

"would give anything to be able to make music."

Tibor moves a pawn and strokes Sally's hair, golden strands twining around his long, thin fingers. "Isn't she lovely?" he whispers to Karl, thinking she has dozed off. "She is everything to me, everything. Did you feel that way about your wife?"

"Yes," Karl answers while moving his queen's pawn again, "at first."

"Dearest Father," Sally writes on the postcard of a town square filled with red geraniums, tall baroque buildings rising behind it. "This is Bilbao, Spain, Basque country. . . ."

She puts down her pen, takes a sip of espresso from a white china cup, sits back in her white metal chair at a white metal table under an umbrella, and looks at the buildings thrusting themselves pompously into the air, people moving past, a little too quickly, a little too angrily. There is unrest here, she senses it. She should rent a car, drive out of the city, find some farmers, real Basques, and talk with them, find out what's going on. But Tibor is practicing and expects her back at the hotel in an hour for lunch and a nap, so there is time only to walk down the street for a quick look at the Museo de las Bellas Artes. She finishes the card. ". . . It's exciting to travel like this. It really does expand one's vision. I miss you. . . . Love, Sal."

In the hotel dining room there are white linen table-cloths, a surgical lineup of silverware, an aging clientele, and a red rose on every table. Tibor orders angulas for them both, baby eels in garlic, the local delicacy. A plate of worms, Sally thinks when it arrives, and bravely tries a mouthful, imagines the eels growing, becoming snakes as they slip down her throat.

"Do you like it, darling?" Tibor asks.

"Delicious," she says.

After lunch, a cuddle, and a nap, Tibor is up, wrapped in a white terrycloth robe, sitting at the piano again in the living room of their suite, Sally near him, a sketchpad in her lap, pencils in hand.

"Please," he says, turning his head. "It's hard to compete with that scratching."

Sally looks up. "It's very quiet, actually."

"Well, it's annoying me."

"How can I finish the portrait if you won't even let me sketch you?"

"Do it from memory," he orders, turns back to the keys, and retaliates with the Prokofiev toccata.

The recital is scheduled for nine p.m., Spanish time. At nine-twenty Tibor is still backstage, in an ancient room with photographs lining the walls. "Look," he says, pulling Sally by the hand to show her a young Ysaÿe, Galli-Curci as a girl, Josef Hofmann in knee pants, Casals in 1896 smoking a pipe, his cello beside him, and yes, there, Stephan in 1910, wearing a fedora, looking smart. An old man comes into the room, leaning on a cane, bows, and announces that it is he who will ring a bell to signal to the audience that the concert will begin. It has been his job for seventy years, "and I still love music," he says with a dry cough.

"Imagine that," Tibor says, as the man leaves. "Sally, I think I'm going to be sick—" He rushes into the toilet, Sally following. She holds his head as he leans over the bowl, an honor allocated to her in—where was it, how many days ago were they in Madrid at the Teatro Real when, cold with nerves, sweating with nausea, Tibor allowed Sally for the first time to watch, horrified, as he vomited before the .concert, his body wracked with spasms. In Barcelona, she rushed into the bathroom with him, put her two hands firmly on his temples, and,

181

miraculously, the urge to empty his stomach disappeared. And now, a second try, in Bilbao. "It worked again!" he says, smiling gratefully up at her, his lunch still in place, his nerves calmed as the old man rings the bell, rings and rings, and Tibor holds Sally's hand, kisses her, and whispers, "It's you I play for, only you."

After the concert, a cabaret. Castanets clicking, heels tapping, black lace and red roses flying. Teresa moves across the stage with her eyebrows raised, her lips pushed into a pout, a paragon of tension and grace. Julio strums his guitar with flamenco flair, watches the dancer like a trainer his fiercest tiger.

"Does she bite?" Sally whispers into Tibor's ear as he finishes a margarita, orders, with a snap of the fingers, another. The president of the Sociedad de Música de Bilbao leans over to Sally and tells her she really must try angulas, the local delicacy. His breath smells of old closets. Before she can say she has already had the pleasure, a plate of small wriggly gray creatures is placed before her. She smiles at El Presidente and turns back to watch as more dancers troop onto the platform, green, orange, purple petticoats whipping through smoky blue light.

After angulas, Sopa de Pescado a la Vasca, the special fish soup of the region, is served, while the entertainers take a break. Teresa heads toward their table, greeting Prince Aguila de Terreno y Orillar, Princess Orillar, El Presidente, and when she reaches out her hand toward Tibor, he rises to his feet, kisses her hand, and bows. From the way Teresa's eyes open wide, look into his, Sally has the distinct impression Tibor has frequented the Club Paco de Luca in the past.

"Do you know Teresa?" she asks, between nibbles of eel.

"Yes," he says, and when she looks at him, wanting an explanation, he speaks of closed chapters in forgotten books. Remembered chapters in new books open into her thoughts. Werner. She wonders what he is doing right now, as she sits, tired and overfed at two a.m. after a concert, at a table with people she's never met before and may never meet again. She imagines him, cigar in mouth, hunched over a typewriter at a desk in a Chelsea flat she has never seen, a sheet of white paper filling with words. She wonders what it would be like in that room, just her and Werner, quiet together, no castanets, no royal meals. . . .

"Well, did you?" Tibor is asking.

"Did I what?"

"Think the Schubert was OK?"

"Yes," she merely says, though she had been dazzled by his performance of the C-minor Sonata.

"I didn't. It felt flabby. That piece has to be pulled taut, ready to snap," he says, remembering Stephan as he stood over him, teaching it to him, yelling, "Must you land on the keys like a helicopter? Land with tension, like an animal stalking, ready to leap."

"Well, it didn't sound flabby to me," Sally says, "it sounded highly charged."

"Did it?" he asks again, brushing her temples with a kiss. "Did it really?"

"Yes," she says, as Teresa and company jump back onto the stage. Teeth flash, feet stomp, nasal high-pitched voices sing of lust and remorse, vengeance and death—a song of love.

It stands erect, waiting to be eaten. It's fondled, dipped in butter, soaked in vinaigrette, mixed with ham, painted with béarnaise and eaten with relish. It's the beginning of June, Spargel season in Schwetzingen, Germany. For a few brief weeks the white asparagus of the region is perfect, perfection itself, pure white spears of culinary pleasure. Everywhere heads are tilted back, mouths opened wide, and quivering tips of asparagus dangle into the abysses.

183

The markets are full of it, the restaurants are serving it; the bathrooms reek of its repercussions.

Tibor and Sally lunch on Spargel with béarnaise and boiled potatoes in the company of Herr Doktor Felix Vogelsang, the head of the Schwetzingen Festspiel. After lunch he offers to show them through the palace, quickly, of course, so Tibor will have plenty of time in the hall with the piano. Sally is delighted and Tibor grudgingly agrees.

A baroque castle, shaped in a semicircle, Schloss Schwetzingen is surrounded by extensive gardens, redolent of blossoms, resplendent with colors.

"Die Blumen, ach, the flowers are shining," Herr Doktor says as they walk through lilacs into rose gardens, sweet smells compensating for the Spargel.

"You can speak to me in German," Tibor says. "I know it."

"Ach, so, and other languages also?"

"Hungarian, French, English, Italian, German, and I can get by in Spanish."

"So ganz wendig, such versatility. Look," Vogelsang says, pointing, "there is it."

"Is what?" Tibor asks.

"The garlics." And Vogelsang tells them the story of the Baronin von Schwetzingen who hated her husband so much that she planted a bed of garlic, of which she consumed sufficient quantities to drive the Baron away.

At the hall, a gem of a baroque theater, Tibor tries the piano. "But it's fabulous," he says, surprised, after one phrase of Schumann's "Arabeske."

"So say all my artists. Your teacher was playing here on it in 1927, the program was—"

Tibor surges into "Carnaval," al più forte possibile, silencing the Doktor, blocking out the ghosts.

Sally heads toward the door, eager to wander in the gardens, homesick for her own, hoping she remembered to pack pastels, wanting a chance at the purple glow of lilacs, the blush of hydrangeas, the deep red of roses. But Tibor's voice makes her halt.

"Sally, I'm a little worried about 'Carnaval.' Do you mind listening a minute?" he asks.

"Of course not," she says and sits alone at the back of the hall, intentions drained to black and white. You can work later, she tells herself, you're needed here now. But as he plays she can't help seeing Werner, head bowed, lips pressed against rose petals, savoring smells and colors, a man who has time for variegations, a man whom, she reluctantly admits, she misses.

After practicing Tibor is ready for a nap, and wants Sally by his side. It's an important concert tonight, all Schumann, broadcast live on Westdeutsche Rundfunk, throughout Europe. Please, Sally. He looks at her and his eyes, flecked with green, signal distress, his hand, damp with nerves, tightens around her wrist. But as she walks at his side toward the hotel her thoughts trail behind, linger on an island four degrees north of the Tropic of Cancer. We never found those caves, she thinks. Perhaps it was a mistake to stop looking.

By June, the chestnut blossoms in Paris are past their prime. Browning at the edges, they droop, about to fall. Sally and Mireille walk along the Champs-Élysées, through the sculpture garden of the Élysée park, Mireille expounding. "You see, a woman's beauty corresponds to the stages of love in her life. . . ." Clearly Sally is in the blooming stage, Mireille is certain, and will reach her ultimate sometime in her thirty-sixth year, possibly thirty-seventh. Then, depending on this or that—exactly *what* is unclear—she will have the possibility of maintaining herself for a long time, at least until forty-five. Sally listens with the attentiveness of a convert while Mireille smooths her silk blouse and adjusts the gold and pearl chains that dangle across her neat bosom. Looking at least fifteen years younger than fifty-five, she still wears her hair loose, bouncing freely on her shoulders, and her tiny waist has resisted the ravages of middle age. Of course she diets with an ascetic ferocity, as must Sally when her time comes. Mireille does, however, indulge other appetites. Walking beside her, holding her hand, is Nicky, a dark, handsome, young poet; a very well-dressed poet.

"And tell me about Tibor," Mireille says, with no intention of letting her. "I've known him since he was thirteen, when he came to stay with Stephan, with whom I lived for the last ten years of his life. But of course you know about that."

Sally nods and Mireille goes on. "Stephan was a lion of a man, and a genius, le vrai génie, and so very kind and gentle. You should have seen him with Tibor, this pale, thin, frightened little boy who had the most enormous dark eyes. Stephan heard about him through the Red Cross. Word had already reached Paris that there was a child prodigy from Budapest stranded in Vienna. Stephan, who, as you know, was Hungarian, and fiercely nationalistic, took the first train out and brought Tibor back, along with his sister, Maya, a sweet girl, gentle, but also quite depressed. Well, you can imagine, leaving home, leaving everything behind, your parents, your life, everything. Because I was unwilling to risk having a baby myself when its father would be so, shall we say, mature, I was delighted at the idea of having young people around, young voices to cheer us, liven things up. But it was not a party. At first Tibor refused to speak. He just sat and stared. Even Maya couldn't reach him. But Stephan never gave up. He sat with him, hour after hour, beside him in the study, never saying a word. One day Stephan went to the music cabinet, took out some four-hand music, the Schubert Fantaisie, and began to play the *primo* part. Without saying a word, Tibor came to him on the piano bench, sat quietly beside him and began to play the *secondo* part. I stood at the doorway listening, and at the end Tibor turned to Stephan. Now he will weep, I thought, he will release all his grief, but I was wrong. In a quiet voice, a firm voice, one full of authority, Tibor said, 'Too fast.' I watched Stephan hold himself back from embracing the boy and he said instead, 'Do you think so? Maybe you are right. Let's try it again.' "

"How remarkable," Sally says, her voice catching in her throat. "Tibor has never talked to me about his Paris days."

"No, of course not. You see, Tibor is a very private man, so private in fact that—well, who am I to tell you?"

Mireille takes Sally's arm, walks between her and Nicky, pulling them both toward her.

"I don't mind your telling me about Tibor," Sally says. "Someone has to."

"Ah," Mireille says, giving Sally's arm a slight tug, "I thought so. Just like Stephan. I never felt I knew him. He could never be quite free enough with himself to suit me, but I believe his art took most of what he had to give. And yet I loved him. He had strength, he had character, he amused me, he made music for me, and if there were moments when I wanted something more, well, you can't expect one man to give you everything, can you?"

Mireille announces that there is a pebble in her shoe. Nicky bends down, offers his shoulder for her to lean on, raises her foot like an injured mare's, and removes the shoe, shaking it gently, side to side. Mireille's hand moves to the back of Nicky's neck, strokes him gently, appreciatively.

"You must enjoy what you have, for what it is," she whispers to Sally, "because nothing lasts, nothing."

"Come on, don't be shy," Tibor tells her, pulling her by the hand across the avenue Montaigne, through the gray-and-white portals of Christian Dior.

"But I'd rather see the exhibit at the Petit Palais with you," Sally says.

"We'll see it, we'll see it. This will only take a minute." He smiles and greets the salesgirls, leads Sally up the carpeted spiral staircase, and asks for Justine Chardot.

"Chéri," Justine says, clapping her hands, bouncing out from a dressing room, but stopping short when she sees his arm looped through another woman's. Sally is introduced, and if Justine is surprised or disappointed, she hides it with a shake of her short brown curls and asks, doucement, "What can we do for you?"

Tibor looks at Sally. "What would you like?" he asks, but she's already told him, and it doesn't come in sizes. Dressed in Indian cottons, she is perfectly comfortable, but if dressing her up in Diors will please Tibor, she won't deny him. Besides, it might even be fun. She stands tall, right arm behind her back, and says to Justine, "Perhaps something for the evening from your summer collection?"

Looking Sally up and down, Justine suggests an indigo chiffon, a stunning color to match Madame's eyes. Tibor sits in a gray velvet chair and smokes a cigarette while Sally changes, and waits for her to emerge through gray curtains. When she does, draped in indigo, and sweeps toward him, all gossamer, shimmering in the light, her golden hair trailing behind her like stardust, he is dazed, unable to speak.

"Do you like it, chéri?" Sally asks, twirling before him. He catches her right hand and presses it to his cheek, kisses it with such ardor that other shoppers, embarrassed by so much emotion, flee the room.

"Wear the green one," Tibor suggests later that day, nap time over, an evening stroll in order. Sally picks out a

188

green dress from the pile of five Diors that Tibor bought for her.

"The best woman deserves the best clothing," Tibor had said, and there in the showroom, for that moment, twirling through silk and georgette, she could only agree and gracefully accept.

"All these damned buttons," Sally says, turning her back on Tibor, "you know I can't manage them. Every time I wear this dress you'll have to do me up. I'm at your mercy."

"I'll be gentle," he says, kissing the nape of her neck, "I promise."

They descend from their rooms in the Plaza Athenée, stroll slowly down the palm-lined lobby. Heads turn. They amble down the avenue George V, admiring the grandeur, the hauteur, and after a nuzzle and an aperitif at Fouquet's, they take a taxi to the Bois de Boulogne for a walk around the lake. Late-afternoon sun drifts through trees, leaves flutter, birds are settling down. They follow a path along the edge of the lake. An evening breeze wrinkles the surface, and ducks swim past, boats glide by. Sally notices a couple in a rowboat, the woman rowing, wearing a bikini, her hair in rollers, covered with an Hermès scarf. The man leans back on his elbows, being rowed, his enormous belly shifting from side to side with each stroke of the oars. The woman is shouting at him, but he doesn't seem to hear her.

Tibor puts his arm around Sally's waist and she likes the feel of his rough afternoon chin brushing against her temple, she likes the comfortable way his hip leans into the hollow of her waist. They stop at a waterfall and watch green mossy water spill over fronds and branches, cascade onto lilies below. Pine trees seem to close around them, protect them, and they laugh and kiss, suspended for a moment in time, like two leaves at the crown of a waterfall, hovering above the swift flow.

OBSERVER LE PLUS GRAND SILENCE the sign says backstage at the Théâtre des Champs-Élysées. Hubert Dumont, Tibor's manager for France, kisses him on both cheeks, whispers "Merde," and, taking Sally's arm to show her into the hall, leaves Tibor to his grand silence. Tibor paces back and forth across the grimy boards of the backstage he has known so many years, first as a young man, holding Stephan's hand before his teacher went out to play.

"Maître," Tibor asked him there, "why don't they have a piano back here in the foyer des artistes, so you can warm up?"

"Warming up before a concert," Stephan had said, "is like doing breathing exercises before dying." His long fingers felt like icicles as they pressed against the back of Tibor's neck where they had affectionately wandered, his face was gray, and he couldn't stop yawning because, as he explained, when you are nervous, your body craves air. Tibor's stomach turned sympathetic somersaults, but when, a few minutes later, he sat up in the second tier and watched his teacher bound out like a lion onto that stage, Tibor's anxiety was replaced by confidence and pride because he knew, even then, that he, too, belonged to that supreme species.

Now standing backstage, some fifteen years after the death of Stephan Vlostid, Tibor tries to summon his teacher's spirit, his courage. But try as he might to envision the man as he was when they first met—robust, full of vitality, invincible—the image before him is Stephan at the end, frail, shrunken, propped up in his chair, eyes open wide, runny, unseeing. He could not hear, and his head jerked back and forth, like a parrot looking for seed.

"Maître," someone is saying to Tibor, repeating it, "Maître, c'est l'heure." A stagehand pulls his arm and he wakes up, cracks his knuckles, yawns, then rushes out of the shadows, as if from a haunted house, into the bright lights of center stage.

Only a few kilometers across the border and he'd be in Budapest. Tibor sits next to Sally in the Konditorei Demel, alternating sips of coffee and ice water, staring in the direction of Hungary. He wonders what the street where he lived looks like now, how big the oak trees of Buda would seem.

"Why don't we rent a car and go?" Sally suggests. "After all, you have a British passport."

"I can't. I just can't."

"You mean you won't. What could be so painful after all this time?"

"It's not just that. I'm playing Beethoven Three tomorrow night. I haven't played it in a year."

"But you know it backward."

"That's what I'm afraid of," he says, taking a bite of Sachertorte, offering her a taste.

"Then another time we should plan to make that trip."

"Perhaps."

Sally reaches for her cape, lets Tibor fasten it around her neck for her. It's the middle of June and cold, and they have been together for more than a month in fifteen different cities in five different countries. Today she woke in a panic, not knowing where she was. Tibor reached out to calm her, half-asleep. "Shh, we're in Vienna," he said, "we made it to Vienna." They walk along the Ringstrasse, Sally pointing out buildings and statues she's read about in her guidebook, Tibor listening tolerantly.

"You don't seem interested," Sally says.

"I'm not. I hate walking like this, without a purpose. I'm not a tourist, you know."

"Then why don't you go back to the hotel?"

"Because I said I'd go for a walk with you."

"Must you play the martyr?"

"Sally, please," Tibor says and, grabbing her roughly by the shoulder, pulls her close to his side. They walk, locked together, into the Stadtpark and stop at a Kinderspielplatz. Children play on bright-colored climbing toys. One little girl with long blond braids sits patiently on a swing, tapping her toes, whistling, waiting for a push. Tibor bends down and asks her in German if she'd like him to swing her, but she opens her eyes wide and runs away calling, "Mutti! Mutti!" Her mother picks her up, looks disapprovingly over her shoulder at Tibor.

"I'm losing my touch with women," he says.

"Sorry if I'm cramping your style," Sally says.

He shoves his fists into his coat pockets and kicks at a stone.

Passing the violin-playing statue of Johann Strauss on their way back, Sally holds on to the edges of her cape, twirls before him, humming a waltz. Is she taunting, is she teasing? Neither of them knows. But Tibor takes his hands out of his pockets and joins her, spinning her around, singing loudly, getting dizzy, as a woman in a loden coat stops to watch, removes her hat, and adjusts its feather.

In the lobby of the Imperial Hotel, Sally sketches a group of tourists at tea while Tibor takes a nap.

"I'm not tired," she had said.

"Mais un petit câlin?" Tibor asked in the babyish voice he's begun to use. But the idea of a little cuddle, a little loving, did not appeal.

"Later," she had said, summoning as much seduction as she could in her voice, and, grabbing pad and pencil, descended to the lobby.

Animated in conversation, one man is perched on the edge of his chair, arms in the air. A woman looks on skeptically, another with interest, while a second man leans back, fast asleep. Who is attached to whom? Sally wonders as she shades in their teacups. She closes her pad, walks around the hotel lobby, stopping for a minute at the telephones, three gold-edged glass booths. She could place a call to London, pay for it in cash, and Tibor would never know. Her heart beats madly for a minute while she imagines the conversation.

"Werner?"

"Yes. Sally, is it you, is it really you?"

"Yes, are you glad to hear from me?"

"Glad? I'm ecstatic. Where are you?"

"Vienna."

"Isn't it marvelous?"

"Is it? I don't know. I haven't seen a thing."

"You should be there with me. I'd take a few days off. I could show you Schönbrunn castle, the Palais Schwarzenberg, and I'd take you to see the Lippizaner stallions dance a perfect capriole just for you, and the woods where Brahms walked. Did Tibor tell you Stephan played for Brahms when he was a boy? Yes, they had lunch together. Brahms stuffed sardines into his mouth, and the oil dribbled down his beard. Sally, I could show you things. We could do such amazing things together, Sally—"

"Would you like to place a call?" an operator asks her from behind a walnut desk.

"No, danke," she answers and walks away from telephones toward the elevators. Upstairs, she quietly turns the key in the lock, closes the door silently so she will not wake Tibor, but she hears him talking. He's on the phone.

"No. Mozart wrote the C-minor Concerto fifteen years before Beethoven wrote his. Listen to the opening. . . . Do you hear that? He goes to a Neapolitan sixth, A-flat, in two bars, moves through a couple of diminished sevenths, and doesn't really reach C minor till bar thirteen. Very subtle.

193

Do you get it? What? Yes, you're right, exactly. All Beethoven does in his opening is state the key. You see how advanced Mozart was? So far beyond his— What? Yes, yes, you're right. Maybe, maybe. It's an interesting idea. Hold on, someone's here. It's Sally. Want to say hello?"

He greets her with a smile and offers her the phone. "It's Werner."

"Send him my regards," she says, rushing, as if in great need, to the bathroom.

She locks the door, sits on the toilet seat wondering which of them she's escaping from and why her cheeks are burning. She flushes and runs the cold water, splashes it on her face.

"Are you OK?" Tibor calls through the door.

"Yes, fine. I'm just coming out," she says and opens the door.

Tibor sits naked, legs crossed, on the bed, a Disque Bleu in his hand, wide awake, excited by the conversation.

"What did you and Werner talk about?" she asks casually, leaning over for Tibor to unhook her cape.

"About Beethoven's Third Concerto being retrogressive compared to K. four-nine-one."

"How arcane."

"Feeling excluded again? Or is it just your innate fondness for my friend shining through?"

"He's my friend, too," Sally says, turning away to hang up her cape.

"So I hear."

"And what's that supposed to mean?" she asks, holding on to the closet door.

"Only that he asked about you, sounded concerned about you, wanted to know if you're happy, as friends will."

"Oh," she says, pleased, plucking a pear from the basket of fruit courtesy DGG. "And what did you tell him?"

"I said you seem a bit remote, but that you're sketching a lot. I said you're probably finding it difficult to adjust to the constant disruptions of this kind of travel."

"Perceptive of you."

"Sally, come here," Tibor says, holding out a hand. She sits next to him on the bed and he strokes her fingers. "Do you want to go home?" he asks. "I'd understand if you did."

"No, I do not want to go home," she says, determined to make this work. "We'll be in London in a few weeks, anyhow."

"But there's still a lot of traveling ahead. Are you sure you've got the stamina for it?"

"I'm not as fragile as you like to think I am," she says.

"Darling, I don't think you're fragile at all. I just want what you want."

"And what about you? Would you like me to leave? You certainly act annoyed with me lately. I make too much noise, I'm in the way."

"Nonsense," Tibor says, shaking the hair out of his eyes. "Being with you has made all the difference. I'm calmer, I can really concentrate. Darling, I love being with you."

"Super. Then what's the problem?" she asks, rolling with Tibor onto the goose-down cloud of a comforter.

Tibor leans his head back during the long orchestral beginning of the first movement of Beethoven's Third Piano Concerto. Szabo's annual appearance with the Vienna Philharmonic has been sold out for months, and the public listens knowingly to *their* Beethoven played by *their* pianist in *their* special hall with *their* gold leaf, *their* crystal chandeliers, and *their* collective musical memories. Not a note will be missed. Tibor's eyes rest on the organ pipes rising stories high above him, move to the giant gold statues, naked women who seem to support the entire hall. Their gilded breasts loom above him, luring him from the music. He tries to concentrate.

This is Vienna, he tells himself, but he isn't the least bit nervous. He notices the conductor's shoes, wonders where he got them, then kicks his thoughts. Wake up! They're coming, those scales, C minor, clear as bells, with power, all the way up. Come on, come on, then the octave leaps. Come on, Szabo, this is Vienna!

The orchestra's grand pause. It's now or never, fly or crash. He plunges, swoops up the scales with the power of an eagle, gets the octave leaps like easy prey. He's Szabo, he's soaring. He holds the concerto securely, carries it off, but with no real appetite. He prods himself, he pushes, he rebukes, but still he has no hunger.

"How was it?" he asks Sally afterward, as he sits behind a table backstage and signs autographs for the dozens of silent fans who bow in his presence, flustered and awed, then scurry away.

"Superb," she says.

"Really?" he asks, unsure, hating himself for the easy conquest, feeling cheap when he accepts, signing a paper marked "Quittung," 96,000 Austrian schillings, in cash.

Next day on the plane to Bonn he reads a review in the *Neue Freie Presse*, slams it down onto his lap.

"Typical," he says, turning to Sally. "I play like a whore and the review says it sparkled with commitment. Trust a critic to praise you for the one performance you're ashamed of."

Tibor is particularly jolly this morning, the nineteenth of June, 1976. He prances in and out of the bathroom, cracks hard-boiled eggs on his forehead, downs his Orangensaft in one gulp.

"Are you rehearsing for a carnival?" Sally asks.

"No," he answers, tossing a scrunched paper napkin neatly into a wastebasket.

"Well, then," Sally says, "what are your plans for the day?"

The coldness in her voice chills his spirits, but he'll warm her up. "I have a meeting this morning, practice in the afternoon, and dinner with you, just the two of us, candles, wine. . . ." He takes her hand to kiss, but she pulls it away.

"If you're busy this morning, I'll go to the museum," she says, "and this afternoon I'll sit in the Stadtpark and sketch while you practice."

"Those drawings are really piling up. Maybe when we get back to London you should show them to Werner, have him write a text, collaborate on a book."

The suggestion irritates. It's so mild, his attitude, so neutral. She might as well sketch with invisible ink. If only he hated my work, she thinks, even that would be better. I'd have something to respond to. She feels the need to provoke him.

"Do you like my sketches?" she asks. "I mean, what do you really think of them?"

"I think they're great," he says, giving her nose a juicy kiss.

She persists. "You don't feel threatened by them or anything, do you?"

Tibor laughs. "You·should know me better by now. Nothing threatens me, because, outside of music, there's nothing that matters to me. Except, of course, you."

"Of course."

"I still say you should show them to Werner. It might be—"

"If they need a text, then the drawings are no good. They should speak for themselves. Besides, they're just studies."

"I see," he says, turning away, moving slowly toward the bathroom, uneasy with her response, but unable to identify the tone of her voice as discontented.

197

Sally spreads Pflaumenmus on her Vollkornbrot and bites hard. Why must I snap at him? she asks herself. And he says nothing, smiles, accepts my abuse, goes on adoring. She swallows and wishes he would stomp back out of the bathroom, stand before her, demand something from her, an explanation, anything. Doesn't he even hear the strain in her voice, or see the anger in her behavior, or sense her turning away from him? Is she his ideal, his perfect woman, helpless against the tyranny of his vision? And why, if they are together day and night, does she feel so alone?

She leafs through the pile of sketches she has made so far: a man waiting on a bridge in Barcelona, a child in Madrid holding his father's hand while the father talks to a friend, a girl waiting on a bench in Bilbao looking into the distance, bodies reclining on the Spanish Steps in Rome —pictures of expectation, inaction. What are these people waiting for, and is it they, or she, wanting something to happen? She might have drawn the movement on the beach in Barcelona, or the rush of crowds in Madrid, or captured some of the tension of Bilbao, or the vitality of street life in Rome. But no, she has marked time with people marking time.

Yet she has traveled, mile after mile, zigzagging through Europe at a dizzying speed. At least Tibor has his concerts, his footholds in this endless trail, but she scurries behind him, struggling to keep up, unsteady. Today they are in Frankfurt, tomorrow Cologne, the next day Essen and on and on. The disorientation, the fatigue, the deterioration, the anxiety—the life he leads has its limits, true, but are the limits in the life or in the man leading it? The thought grows inside, like a flu about to take hold, and she lies back on the bed, body aching, closes her eyes, listens to Tibor splashing at the basin.

He stands before the mirror in the bathroom, slicks back

his hair with two palms, and sighs. He soaps his chin for shaving and when he opens his mouth, a huge bubble starts to form. He should stamp his feet, grunt, make her rush in to see his transparent achievement, but she'd probably be annoyed, tell him to stop being childish, after all, it's only a bubble. He bursts it himself and looks for his razor. Her toothpaste lies without its top on the shelf, her brush, full of golden hair, beside it. She could be neater, he tells himself, but of course, with her hand . . . He scrapes at his upper lip, then wanders back into his thoughts. Why am I always making excuses for her? She's messy, but so what? Is that important? And she's been in a bad mood lately. But what can I do? I've got concerts to play, pieces to learn. It must be hard for her, tagging along, and I know she doesn't mean to be nasty. In some ways, it was better without her, wasn't it? More exciting, and I even played better before. A quick downward stroke and he cuts his neck, mutters as he applies pressure and a washcloth. He waits a few minutes. There. No sign of blood. He splashes after-shave on his cheeks, as music inundates his thoughts, pieces to practice, Bartók Second Concerto for Wuppertal, Schumann for Munich, the recital program for Berlin. He'd better call Conrad Diederich and change the Beethoven Sonata. He won't be ready for "Les Adieux" by the first of July. His head spins. He steadies it by brushing his hair, hard, then strides back into the bedroom, dresses without even noticing that Sally is still lying in bed. He hurries into the living room of their suite, sits at the piano, and pounds out scales.

Sally pulls a pillow over her head. She should get dressed, up and out of here, but her limbs ache, chest hurts, head throbs. If she asked, surely Tibor would stop, or maybe he would go to the hall to practice. She listens as he begins the Bartók, hears the dissonances, the augmented fourths, tritones, thought once, so Tibor told her, to be caused by the devil. Is this my little hell, then? she wonders, and lies very still, very penitent, aware that redemption will come only if she gets up and looks for it, but she cannot move.

Stitched onto cloth, the labors of Hercules hang along the walls of the hall in Munich dedicated to him, the Herkulessaal. Sally observes the tapestries, dulled by age but vivid with the strength of the man who felled the Boar of Erymanthus, who killed the Hydra of Lerna, who tamed the horses of Diomedes. Applause. Tibor rushes onto the stage, sits at the Piano of Steinway and takes on the Music of Schumann, lunging into the A-minor Concerto with the power of Hercules himself. Strange then, Sally thinks, that up close he is more like Sisyphus, each concert the rock, no performance ever quite reaching the pinnacle that satisfies him. She can admire his persistence, his energy, his courage, his drive, his stubborn faith. But, she wonders, is admiration equivalent to love? Aren't heroes best loved from a distance, a tapestry away, a stage apart? Up close, a hero, like a monster, loses his mastery, and in the end, aren't they one and the same?

On the bridge between the Intermezzo and the Allegro vivace Tibor steps into minor, back to major, now minor, then, head thrown back, black hair shaking, he canters off into Schumann's gallant theme, triumphant to the end.

Backstage, when all admirers have left, Sally sits beside Tibor on a faded green couch in a small stuffy room. Drenched in sweat, exhausted, he is depressed about his performance.

"Well, I loved it," Sally says, opening a window, sticking her head out over the courtyard of the Residenz below, an empty stone square where royalty once strolled.

What do you know about music anyhow? Tibor thinks, but says, "I've played it better."

"It's possible you have," Sally says, "but I still enjoyed this performance." She fingers a curtain, the color of sludge. "I can tell you something I don't enjoy," she says, wondering if she should but unable not to. "I do not enjoy your self-indulgent sulks, your negative attitude, or your self-obsessed way of life."

"Oh," he says, wiping at his forehead with a white towel. He's tired, and wonders why his hands felt trapped in molasses during those arpeggios in the last movement, why the entire performance had no Schwung, no sweep.

"Are you listening?" Sally asks.

"Yes," he says, not.

She sighs and turns away.

Why is she angry? he thinks. She's always angry with me and I haven't done a thing! I must try to cheer her up. Flinging the towel across the room, Tibor jumps to his feet, grabs Sally by the waist, and says, "Come, my love, I take you cigányozni, gypsying."

She is less than charmed. "But you'll like it, I promise," he says.

She looks up into his face and sees herself spread along the convex curve of his eyes, distorted, reflected as she feels. She backs away.

"What is it?" he asks.

"Nothing," she says, "and everything. I just feel all out of focus, that's all."

"Maybe you're tired."

"Maybe I am."

"Well, then, let's go back to the hotel. We'll have room service and go to bed."

"No," Sally says, "you go gypsying. I hate to spoil your fun."

Spoil it? he thinks. You positively ruin it. Yes, go to sleep. He needs some noise, some voices other than hers, some smiling, cheerful faces.

"I'll take you back," he says.

"Good-bye, then," Sally says on the corner of Maximilianstrasse. His sweat-soaked tails hang from her arm like a dead cat. She'll take them to the hotel, give them to the chambermaid, and tomorrow they will be revived.

"Tomorrow everything will be better," he tells Sally, blows her a kiss, and watches, hands stuffed into his pockets, as she walks quickly toward the Hotel Vierjahreszeiten, her head spangled by streetlights, topped with angel's hair. A moment's regret, a flicker of concern, and Tibor steps toward her, opens his mouth to call her back, but the revolving door has turned, and she is gone.

At the Alt Budapest the music stops when Tibor Szabo walks in the door, and a gigantic middle-aged man in white shirt, velvet knickers, and embroidered vest rushes toward him, violin held protectively high in the air. Bear hugs and back slaps over, Gyorgy Votor steps away to look at Tibor and says, plucking a string, "You could use a draft." They sit together at a wooden table, eat veal paprikásh, roar at each other in Hungarian, spill beer.

"Where are the girls?" Gyorgy asks, his round cheeks apple-red.

"There's only one now. She's at the hotel. Too tired."

"You fool. That's what happens when there is only one, fatigue, headaches. Women, like grapes, are best in bunches. Come, let's play."

Gyorgy wipes his mouth, taps his cimbalom player on the shoulder, points to Tibor, and the three mount a small stage, prepare to play.

Leaning his chin onto his violin, Gyorgy closes his eyes, strokes a lullaby out of the instrument, producing a sound that seems to come more from his throat than his hands. He sways back and forth, and the cimbalom player thrums accompanying chords, his sticks beating fast as bees' wings. Tibor closes his eyes and folds his hands in his lap, listens, until prodded by Gyorgy's bow, he opens his eyes, drapes his hands on the piano keys, takes up the melody of the altatódal, and improvises, twisting the song into different shapes. His thoughts move from Munich to Budapest, a kitchen table, Szusza's lap and her voice, pure, gentle, and her cool hand on his forehead.

"Now," Gyorgy says, after a rest and a beer, "something lively." Picking up the fiddle, he scrapes and scratches, leaps up and down the fingerboard, now a csárdás, now a keringö, Tibor following, the cimbalom player beating beside him like a heart gone wild. Now Tibor begins to feel at home, now his head rolls back, he laughs, he drinks a beer, another. He notices a woman alone at a table, joins her for a drink, asks her name, touches her knee. More music, more drinks, and by two a.m., head spinning, he can hardly remember where he is or in which direction the hotel can be found. Arm around Gyorgy, he staggers into the old town square, singing, laughing.

"Go now, back to your queen," Gyorgy says, pushing him away.

"Pig. You don't even invite me for a drink."

"Cad. You have a woman waiting."

"Let her wait, that's what they like to do," Tibor says. "Besides, the night is young."

They hail a taxi, drive off toward Schwabing, the part of town that defines night life, pulsating with action. By dawn Tibor is finally tired. He nudges Gyorgy's drowsing hulk, and with the help of two young women who seem to be with them, they find a taxi. Leaning against Gyorgy's shoulder, Tibor closes his eyes, his head spins back in time to a ride on a train toward the blue water of Lake Balaton, his father beside him, trees flickering past, and Maya opposite, embroidering on a small wooden hoop. It was vacation time, Eva would join them soon, and Tibor fell asleep in his father's arms, dreaming of cozy days ahead.

"Wake up, you cossack," Gyorgy says, pushing Tibor's head off his chest. Tibor rubs his eyes, steps out of the taxi, twirls through the revolving door of the hotel, wanders down corridors, stumbles into his room, and falls onto the bed next to Sally, fully dressed.

June 29, Copenhagen. The red banner above the Hotel d'Angleterre flickers in the wind like a dragon's tongue and Tibor enters, steady as Saint George.

"Are you alone, Maestro?" reception asks.

"Yes, why?"

"We have a reservation for two."

"Well, plans have changed," Tibor says, his voice gruffer than he intends. He grabs his key and walks too fast for the porter who huffs behind him carrying the bags. His suite, the two corner rooms on the fourth floor, looks out over the ornate dome of the Royal Theatre toward the sea. She would have loved this view, Tibor thinks, standing on the narrow balcony, watching people stream through the Kongens Nytorv, a pretty square in the center of the old town. One turning to the right and she'd be on the pedestrian mall, the Østergade, and a pleasant walk would bring her to the Glyptotek museum. He would be practicing next door at the Tivoli Concert Hall and they could meet at dusk, stroll through the Tivoli Gardens together, ride the roller coaster, watch Harlequin, Columbine, and Pierrot at the Commedia dell'arte theater, have a meal, and early to bed. . . . He closes the long French windows and sits at the piano, lifts the lid, wipes the keys with the palm of one hand. Who needs her, anyhow? He hasn't missed her one bit since she left, sneaking out like a thief as he lay dead-drunk in the hotel in Munich. She might have waited until he woke up, she might have seen if he needed anything, but she couldn't be bothered to talk to him face to face. She just left a note. His hand automatically reaches into the inside pocket of his jacket, removes a crumpled paper, opens it out, flattens it onto the mahogany music rack, reads it yet again.

> *Darling,*
>
> *Forgive me for rushing away like this. When you came in this morning and collapsed on the bed I felt such bitter conflicting thoughts, loving you, hating you, wanting to shake you awake, confront you. But what would I have said? There should be no accusations, no recriminations, no acrimonious words between us. I simply can find no place for myself in your life, nor, I realize with pain and despair, do I wish to. Forgive me, please.*
>
> *Sally*
>
> *P.S. I've left some bicarb for you in the bathroom.*

After three years together, is this how she says good-bye? How meager, how unfeeling. He crumples the paper up again, stuffs it back into his pocket as acid wells up in his throat. For the first time in weeks, he belches loudly. He's freer without her, isn't he? And there are plenty of others. In the four days since she left he can count eight, unless the Belgian twins, taken together, reduce the tally to seven. He shakes his hands, rolls up his sleeves, and tries to work. Female faces rise with his arpeggios. Kirsten, wasn't it? But Kirsten what? Without a last name, how can he look her up, and he's left his address book at home. How could he have known he'd need it?

It's hot. He takes off his jacket, drops it on the floor, where it rests like a dark puddle. He can't remember Copenhagen ever being so hot. The driver from the airport told him it's the English heat wave moving over. The

English would muck up Scandinavia for him, he wouldn't be surprised if Sally were personally responsible. The absurdity of the thought makes him laugh. He unbuttons his shirt collar. If not for the Mozart C-minor tomorrow night he could go out, watch girls in sundresses with bare shoulders and thinly clad hips swinging down the Østergade. But he'd better practice, he'd just better snap out of it and get to work. Or what? He could cancel the concert, say he is exhausted, get a doctor's note enforcing rest, everyone does it. But he isn't everyone. Tibor Szabo is solid, sturdy, nothing can shake him, certainly not one rather plain, even dull woman from England.

He practices the concerto Mozart wrote for himself to play in Vienna toward the end of his life, a turbulent, profound piece that never resolves its emotional tension, offers no happy ending. Tibor worries over the first-movement cadenza. Is it too brusque, is it too turgid? How can he tell? It's too hot to hear, and he's too tired to listen. He lies down on the sofa, stares into the large bouquet of roses in a blue enameled vase, a deep blue, the color of Sally's— Why won't she leave him alone? If he could just remember Kirsten's last name. Wait. Like a comet dropping into his head, it comes to him. He rushes through the room looking for a phone book, finds one, and with a flip of the pages he is by Kirsten's side, holding her hand, gazing into her pretty hazel eyes. At the Fiskehusets they savor tender bits of shellfish, drink wine, speak about his last visit over the nostalgic glow of candles, then back to the hotel and straight to bed. At two, with the Nordic day already dawning, he helps Kirsten into a taxi, waves good-bye, and runs around the square, and then once again, feeling fit, glad to be back in shape.

Onstage at the Tivoli Concert Hall, Tibor sits at the keyboard, head bowed, listening to the orchestra play Mozart's dark chromatic passages, jagged upward leaps.

He enters, alone, stating a new theme before being drawn into a troubled discussion with the orchestra. The Larghetto offers him some relief, but in the third movement, tonight, the last day of June, 1976, Tibor thrashes his way through the variations, clawing at them like a man dangling from a cliff, desperate but still determined. The final C-minor chord, and he has survived. Just.

Offstage, he needs to get out, flee the hall, the well-wishers, the autograph seekers, even the lovely Kirsten. He rushes down the stairs, out the stage door, and into the Tivoli Gardens, the vast amusement park that surrounds the hall. Swept up into a surging mass of people, children with balloons, old women with canes, a man with a dog, young people arm in arm, he listens to sounds collide —pipe organ, hurdy-gurdy, Strauss waltzes, jazz from the gazebo, ice-cream bells. But still the music he has just played reverberates inside him in a way that happened only once before—the first time he played after Stephan died. Usually music keeps its distance even as it enfolds him, usually he is involved yet apart, usually sensations are distilled. But tonight he can no more separate himself from the turbulence he has just expressed than could the composer. Moved, jolted, emotion ricocheting like shrapnel through his body, he rushes out of the Tivoli into dark streets. At the Nikolaj Church he turns right and stops at a canal, leans on a railing, watches tourist boats float by, guides pointing at magical spires and castles lit up in the night. He remembers a tall white boat he took once with Stephan, right here in Copenhagen, the night boat to Aarhus. On board at nine p.m., they dined together and then descended into the belly of the ship. He remembers sleeping in a small cabin, lulled by the knowledge that Stephan was next door and by the motion of the boat. That boat, so he's been told, is out of business. So many things are gone. Stephan. The boat. Sally.

The thought of her makes him reach inside his jacket,

touch the bulge of paper in his pocket. Her letter. He takes it and crushes it in his fist. He is about to drop it into the black water of the canal, but he can't. He holds on to it, squeezing tighter and tighter, his body beginning to shake. How could she, how could she? As he stands, shaking at water's edge, he finds himself actually considering the question. How could she, why did she, and is she really the only one at fault? She did, after all, have to make compromises to come on this trip, and she did, after all, try to keep up with the pace. She did try. And he? He changed nothing, he did not try to alter a thing—not the way he worked, or ate, or slept in the afternoon, or stayed up half the night. He expected her to fit in, but did he make room for her? No. Did he in any way try to accommodate her needs? No. Then of course she could not confront him, deaf as he's been, of course she could not show him his faults, blind as he is. Fool, he tells himself, bloody stupid fool. He opens her letter again. Darling. She called him darling. She still loves him, of course she does, and when she says she can find no place for herself in his life, well, of course she can't, he's given her none. Well, he will. He'll call her, apologize, tell her he's been a fool, beg her to return. No. He's always asking her to come to him.

He races back to the hotel, up to his room, paces back and forth, looks at the telephone. He could dial direct to Berlin. Conrad Diederich would answer. He can almost hear the voice, tense, prickling with control.

"Ja."

"Szabo here," Tibor would say.

"Na, ja, and how are you?"

"I'm terrible, actually."

There would be a pause of alarm. "What is it?"

What is it? Tibor tries to imagine the answer. It's Sally and me, it's my life, my whole life.

"It's bronchitis," he'd say, and cough. But then he'd

208

need a doctor's note, and he doesn't have a doctor. He thinks of Berlin, its gray streets, sterile new buildings, and bombed-out Kaiser Wilhelm Memorial Church in the center of the city, right on the Kurfürstendamm, preserved as a macabre monument of war and destruction. No, he will not go. And if he doesn't want to go to Berlin, he doesn't need an excuse. After all, he's Tibor Szabo.

He picks up the phone and calls the night clerk and asks him to book him on the first available flight to London in the morning. "What? Not until two p.m.? OK, OK. Anything. Just get me to London," he says, feeling airborne already—on tenuous wings, but he knows this is right. He'll surprise her, turn up at her door, tell her that he cannot bear being without her, that he loves her, what a selfish fool he's been. He'll change everything for her, cancel half his concerts, maybe all. He'll play when he likes and where he likes now. Maybe he'll even have his audiences come to him. He'll build a concert hall, his own, near Sally's studio, right on Hampstead Heath, and people will fly to London from all over the world to hear him. He's full of ideas; he can't wait to tell Sally, see her, hold her, be with her. It's the only thing that matters. He's aware that he's balancing on a very thin wire, dangling over some very deep and bottomless pit of consequences, but he's never been more sure of his footing. He can't possibly fall.

A late-day blaze of sun envelops Rosslyn Hill in Hampstead as Tibor climbs slowly up toward Willow Road.

"Drop me here," he had told the taxi driver at the corner of England's Lane and Haverstock Hill, wanting to walk, to feel light, free without the suitcases he couldn't be bothered to collect at Heathrow. Let them go to Singapore, he doesn't care, he will not be encumbered, not now, not anymore. He will arrive at Sally's doorstep, briefcase in

209

hand, like a normal man at the end of a normal day. She will open the door for him, gasp with delight, and, rising on her toes, throw her arms around his neck. Won't she? What if she's annoyed, what if she doesn't want to see him? He'll win her over, of course he will.

"A dozen roses, please," he says, stopping at a flower stall and, even though they're wilting, he chooses a red deep as rubies, and pays, agreeing that yes, the heat is beastly, but what can we do, just get on with it, what?

As he turns right onto Downshire Hill, jacket thrown casually across his shoulders, sweat begins to pour down his cheeks. He shivers in the heat, and wonders, for a split second, if he should have gone to Berlin. What if they sue him, cause a scandal? Who cares? He has to answer to no one now, only to himself, only to the woman he loves, because the only thing that matters is Sally and their life together.

Halfway down the road he breaks into a run, his briefcase banging against his leg, his jacket falling, the roses breaking, but he keeps going, he must reach her door.

Out of breath, he stops at the gate, wipes his forehead with a sleeve, and walks slowly, deliberately, toward the door. What if she's not at home? It's five-thirty, of course she'll be home, done working, through with tea. He rings the bell, his pulse throbbing, and waits, then rings again. No answer. He tries the door and, finding it open, pushes with one shoulder and enters. Familiar smells invade his nose, the lemon verbena furniture polish she uses, the oatmeal biscuits she bakes, the jasmine tea she drinks. She must be upstairs, maybe in the bath, her naked body covered with soap. He'll do her back for her, kiss her soapy neck, reach beneath the water for her; but at the foot of the stairs leading up to the bedroom he hears something. Laughter, hers, and then another voice, a deeper voice. He holds his breath and stands very still, certain he's imagined it, certain it's the people next door. Laughter again. He freezes and feels as if a hand has been clapped over his mouth, like Maya's that night in the swamp, and a voice inside tells him to be silent, don't make a sound, your life depends on it, *your life.*

He hears Sally's voice, it is hers, unmistakably, it is Sally Fraser, and she is upstairs right above him and there is someone with her—a man.

A flash of rage blinds him. He'll go to the kitchen, grab a knife, leap up the stairs, but he can't see to move, and he stands holding the banister, shaking with anger. The dignified thing to do would be to turn around, walk quietly out, and close the door behind him forever. That is what must be done. Instead, he feels one foot tentatively take the first step, the other the second, slowly he is moving up the stairs, quietly so the wood will not creak, the wood on which just two months ago Sally gave herself to him with such abandon. He stops at the bedroom door and listens again. She is making noises now, deep mewlings, like a stroked cat. Yes, she is noisy when it's good. The sounds of her pleasure detonate in his head, and with a rush of anger he kicks the door open and forces himself to look. Sally cries out and the man grabs for a lamp, then looks up and sees Tibor, eyes wide, staring at him.

Tibor blinks, and blinks again, and feels as if a knife has been hurled at him, pinning him against the doorway. He wants to crumple into a heap on the floor, faint, lose consciousness, not see what he sees, but he stands at the door, upright, fully awake, horrified.

"Werner?" he asks softly, hoping ludicrously it is not, knowing it is. He clutches at the wooden frame of the door, unable to take his eyes off them. Is that Sally, Sally Fraser, his Sally, the love of his life, the woman for whom he would give up everything, with Werner, Werner

Rawlings, his closest and dearest friend? Is that her body, gleaming with sweat, her cheeks, flushed with pleasure, and does that male body above her, buttocks in the air, limbs tangled in hers, belong to Werner Rawlings? They scramble to disengage, pull up sheets, as Tibor watches, strangely admiring the bodies, the firm flesh, the golden heads. How beautiful they are, he thinks, how innocent in their desire. He is embarrassed now that he has interrupted them, ashamed at having found them, like the time at Lake Balaton when Eva was reading to him, under their favorite tree, his head in her lap, and he could feel her belly rise and sink at each breath, and she stroked his head, and his long dark lashes fluttered against her wrist as she turned a page. It was perfect, peaceful, until his father sneaked up and, just for fun, threw a fish he had caught at them. It hit Eva under the chin, slithered into her blouse, still alive, still flapping for air. She screamed and stood up, hopping about, trying to dislodge the fish. Tibor and his father laughed mercilessly and when, in her panic, she pulled off her blouse, husband and son were suddenly quiet, standing together on the lavender-covered hill, admiring her torso, the small firm breasts, the creamy skin. The fish flapped once more on the ground and was still. "Monsters!" she shrieked at them, picked up her blouse, and holding it to her chest, turned and ran down the hill, sobbing. Imre told Tibor to stay behind and read the book and ran down the hill after Eva into their little cottage. But Tibor followed anyhow, silently, and holding his breath, peeked into their bedroom window and saw his mother crying on the bed, Imre gently patting her naked back. "Forgive me, little fish, my little fish," he heard his father say and he turned her over and made fishy faces for her and gave her fishy kisses and she laughed and pulled his head down onto her chest and his father pushed up her skirt and they lay together, flapping like one fish on the bed, and Tibor ran away into the woods at the top of the hill and felt sick and excited, confused and angry, almost as angry as he does now, as the image of Sally and Werner etches slowly, like acid, indelibly into his brain.

Werner is the first to speak. "It isn't what you think," he says.

Tibor hears the words, then hears them again, and begins to laugh, a slow chuckle. It's too funny—the startled lovers, the protestations of innocence—too funny for words, and Tibor has no words, he could not speak if he tried, nothing could possibly come out. He laughs, head spinning, and he leans back against the wall and his knees go weak as if hit from behind. He sinks slowly toward the floor, but like a tightly coiled spring suddenly released, he lunges forward in one convulsive movement toward the bed, and his hands are around Werner's neck, squeezing hard, harder. Sally yells, beats at Tibor's head with her fists. Werner makes grunting noises and his eyes bulge as he throws one leg around Tibor's back and flips him over onto the mattress, and yet hands tighten around Werner's neck. Sally pulls at Tibor's hair, but he knocks her away with a sweep of one arm. He hears her thump onto the floor, and turns to look. Lying there, naked, a terrified expression on her face, she looks so fragile, so small and pink, like a sea anemone washed onto shore. He hears someone gag, little barking noises, and he turns to see Werner slumping back onto pillows, his face dark blue, draining now to gray, now white, now some color coming back.

Tibor sits up, buries his face in his hands, and moans, wanting it all to disappear, please, someone, make it go away, please, all a bad dream, gone now. But he takes his hands away and they are still there, Sally tying a robe around her, a purple silk robe, the one he brought her

213

from Japan, and Werner, lying beside him, wrapped in sheets like a Roman emperor, weary but victorious. Sally sits down on the edge of the bed, between Tibor and Werner, her back to both. It is suddenly very hot, very quiet, very tense.

"Do you love him?" Tibor hears himself ask, not looking at Sally, and when she doesn't answer, he turns toward her, palm raised to strike. "Well, do you? Answer me!"

"I think," Sally says, moving her head with determined calm, meeting Tibor's raised hand with hers and slowly placing it on the bed, "it would be a good idea if the three of us went downstairs now."

"And what?" Tibor asks, pulling his hand away, standing up, turning like the prosecution to address them both. "Should we have tea and discuss our feelings, perhaps our needs? How very liberated of us, how very adult. No. There is no discussion here, no question of—"

"Now wait a minute," Sally interrupts, her voice rising. "I left you a letter, didn't I? I explained myself fully, I declared my freedom. How dare you break into my house like this? What claim do you have on me?"

"What claim?" Tibor repeats, softly, almost to himself. "Is love no claim?"

"Love?" Sally sneers. "You don't love me, you never have."

"Sally?" Tibor asks, wondering again if it really is Sally Fraser, this woman going red in the face, her body rigid with resentment.

"Don't Sally me, with that melancholy boyish Keats-like face of yours. It doesn't work anymore. I'm no longer interested, as I've told you. For Christ's sake, you have it in writing. Now get out, get out. Out!" She is shouting, her face crumpled into a fist of anger. She flings herself onto pillows, sobbing.

Forgive me, fish, my little fish, Tibor wants to say and

pat her back and make her stop, but he says instead, "You never told me, you never said you were unhappy, why didn't you tell me?"

"How could I tell you?" her muffled voice asks, between sobs. "There never was time, and there was no way to approach you, and I didn't want to disturb you, you always had to practice, you always had a concert." She hiccoughs. "Besides, it's too late."

Tibor reaches out to touch her, hesitates, then drops his hands to his sides. Werner coughs and he feels contrite at having attacked him. But with a flash of renewed anger, he digs his hands into his pockets, glares at Werner, and asks, very calmly, "Why?"

Werner rubs at his neck. "I didn't mean to," he says hoarsely, and coughs again. "I tried not to hurt you. I did, I swear I did. I would have come to you and talked to you openly if I could have, but it happened so suddenly, in Maspalomas. . . ."

"At Karl's house, when I was recording?" Tibor asks, sick at how obvious it is now, looking back.

"Yes, yes and no, and there was no time to talk to you and I went away and Sally tried . . ."

"I see," Tibor hisses, wanting to kill again as betrayal and rage tear at his chest, indignation burns in his eyes.

"It's not my fault," Sally says, sitting up, wanting Tibor to stop staring at her with hateful eyes. How could I have hurt him so much, how could I? she asks herself as she cries at him, "You pushed me away, you pushed me at Werner, you did, you did, it isn't my fault, it isn't. . . ."

There was a tree at Lake Balaton, a special tree where he sat with his mother, hour after hour, and she read to him, her voice gentle as the cotton clouds above them, their tree, their very special tree. . . .

The insistent memory sedates him for a minute, one hushed minute, like the eye of a storm passing over, and he holds his breath, unsure what he will do or what will happen next. Taking one last long look at Sally, then Werner, he turns, bolts down the stairs and trips on his briefcase at the bottom. He holds still and waits. They'll run after me and tell me it's all been a mistake, some terrible misunderstanding, he thinks, but there is silence upstairs. Slowly, Tibor picks up his briefcase, leaves roses scattered across the floor, red petals like drops of blood on the pale wood, and rushes out the door into a wall of heat.

He struggles up Willow Road, turns right onto Well Walk, past people sipping drinks, laughing, at tables outside a pub, past the house where, as Sally always told him, the painter Constable had lived. The large stone basin of Chalybeate Well, its once salubrious waters now dried up, is just ahead. He rushes at it, leans over the edge, retching, coughing. Raising his head, he sees an inscription chiseled into rock: "Drink, traveller, and with strength renewed, let a kind thought be given to her who has thy thirst subdued." He vomits, and pushes himself away, rushes on, across East Heath Road, past the red brick block of flats called the Pryors, into the deep woods beyond, running, until, chest bursting, head dazed, he stops beside a tree, leans his cheek against its warm dry bark. What time is it? Where is he? Why can he feel nothing but rage inside him, clawing at him, beating at his temples, devouring him? He has no thought, only image, Sally and Werner, naked flesh, hers, his. He throws himself against a low branch of the beech tree, leans against the parched and peeling trunk and feels numb everywhere. He has no sensations in his limbs, nothing, and yet he is crying. It seems to him there is a man leaning on a tree, weeping, and he wonders who it is, why he weeps, and why it seems to be he. Nothing makes sense now, there is nothing to be done, nothing.

A crackle of twigs and a couple approaches, holding hands. He will not be seen. He stands up, wipes his face on a sleeve, tucks his shirt into his pants, and rushes through the woods like a hunted deer, through the Vale of Health, toward Hampstead Village.

Someone is running. It must be he, his feet, his legs, his eyes that hurt when the last rays of the sun brand into them at the top of Spaniards Road. A taxi passes. Should he take it? Where would he go? He walks down the steep hill of Heath Street, and at the corner of the High Street the amber tiles of the underground station glow like burning coals. He hasn't used public transport in years. What does one do, where does one go? He wanders into the tube station. A few yards ahead, the doors of a lift open, invite him inside. He doesn't stop to buy a ticket and runs into the lift just as the doors clank shut, and he descends slowly into the ground, deeper, burying himself alive. Doors open again, and he follows a woman with two small children out of the lift, down a staircase, as a stale gust of wind from an arriving train blows in his face. Doors of the train open, and he climbs aboard. He'll go anywhere, what does it matter? Doors swoosh shut and he slumps onto a green-and-blue plaid seat next to a man who cleans his pipe, across from a boy in a yellow shirt who bites his lower lip, near three kids with orange knapsacks on their backs. Stations come and go, Belsize Park, Chalk Farm, Camden Town. The train hurtles through dark round tunnels and he is safe beneath the earth, leaving Hampstead, leaving Sally. He looks at a sign explaining what to do in case of suspicious packages. What does it matter if there are bombs? His life is blown to pieces already, and yet he is alive, twitching with pain. He must get away, that is the only thing to do, fast and far and now. Euston Station is next. He stands up, prepares to rush upstairs, take a taxi to Heathrow. But airports and airplanes will only remind him of her, and he sits down again, thwarted, staring straight ahead. His eyes rest on a map, focus on one dot marked Victoria Station. There are trains there, aren't there? "Trains," Stephan used to tell him, "are the fraying threads of a finer life." There are still trains, aren't there? And even if they are sordid and slow, they go everywhere, to Ankara, Kabul, Kathmandu, making their mark, taking their time, touching the earth, and the earth is his for the having. He is, after all, a free man with cash totaling £10,000 from his last three concerts in his briefcase, and he has a valid passport. He pulls at the arm of a boy with a knapsack.

"Victoria train station?" he asks like a foreigner.

"Follow me," the boy says as doors slide open at Euston Station and they change to the Victoria line. Oxford Circus, Green Park, Victoria Station. Tibor directs himself now, one foot after the other, down corridors, following signs for British Rail. When asked for his ticket at the tube exit, he reaches into his pocket and hands the man a five-pound note, rushes past him, up a final staircase, and finds himself in the middle of a vast gray space covered with steel and glass. It is hot and smells of hamburgers and moist embraces. Along a dirt-encrusted cement floor pigeons totter next to wet rivulets and baggage trolleys careen dangerously close. Tibor bumps into a large yellow litter box and, eyes down, stands still to get his balance as he watches feet pass, leather shoes, canvas shoes, round toes, pointed toes, sharp heels, a baby's sandals. He looks up and sees a large black board hanging in the center of the room. TIME NOW, bright letters say above a large illuminated clock. The time now is 20:11. He scans the board for a destination, but East Grinstead will not do, nor will Uckfield, Eastbourne, Horlay, or Ramsgate. New information twirls, letter by letter onto the screen under CONTINENTAL DEPARTURES. There is a night train to Paris leaving at 20:55. That's more like it. He dashes toward the

Seatrain ticket office, bumping into knapsacks and trolleys, and once there, he begs the four people in front of him in the queue to let him ahead of them, it is an emergency, please.

"No," the man behind the glass partition tells him, "there are no seats left on that train. Sorry."

"What about a sleeper, aren't there couchettes, anything, *please*?"

The man pokes at a computer. "Well, yes, one single-berth compartment in first class, but I'm afraid it will cost you, instead of the normal first class of forty-one pounds fifty-two pence, let me see . . ."

Tibor is peeling pound notes off a roll the size of a grapefruit, and pushing them through the glass partition.

"What name, sir?" he is asked.

What name, he wonders, wanting no one to know who he is or where he is going. "Stone," he says staunchly, "Mr. J."

"Very well," he is told, "here is your ticket and you have, I presume, a valid passport with appropriate—"

"Indeed," Tibor says, worried about what he will do when the name on the ticket doesn't match the one in his passport, but he'll think about that later.

"Bonsoir, suivez-moi, Mr. Stone," a man in brown uniform with a cap marked "Wagons-Lits" instructs at track seven. Tibor follows the man up the three steep iron steps onto the train and down a corridor to his cabin. The room is small, with a narrow bed, a washstand, a stainless steel tray and jug with one glass. The porter waits after being well tipped. He frowns and looks at Tibor, then at the name on the ticket, and at Tibor again. Then a smile curls on his face, and, touching Tibor's arm, he winks and says in a thick French accent, "I see, Maestro, that you wish to travel unnoticed."

"I beg your pardon?" Tibor asks, uneasy.

"It is natural, I understand completely. An artist of your stature is always being annoyed. Leave everything to me." Tibor nods, resigned to being discovered.

"Now can I get you anything? Some bottled water perhaps?" Tibor shakes his hair out of his eyes and sighs. "To tell you the truth, I am quite exhausted and wouldn't mind going to sleep right away. Will it be necessary to wake me at the border?"

"No, of course not. You give me the passport, and you will have it back in the morning. In fact, if I am not mistaken, tonight my friend, a great music lover, will be on duty at the French immigration. If I tell him who is on the car, he may not even look at the passport, but he will want to wake you for an autograph."

Tibor opens his mouth, but the porter puts up a reassuring hand. "I am joking, of course. Just give me the passport, and I will take care of it. And now, Maestro, did you pass customs here? Where shall I find your luggage?"

"I'm traveling light. Just this briefcase."

"Lucky man, all you need is music, I suppose. Well then, I will get some water for you and come back."

The porter returns in a few minutes carrying a bottle of Evian.

"That's very kind of you," Tibor says. "Thank you."

"But I am the one to be grateful," the porter says. "It is not every night I have on my train a passenger as famous as Maurizio Pollini."

Tibor smiles despite himself, pleased at the mistake. Yes, let them take him for Pollini, for Ashkenazy, Barenboim, or Brendel—there are many pianists as fine as Tibor Szabo. Szabo is replaceable, and no one will even notice that he's gone. To be an international star your light must be seen, and Szabo is taking the night train to Paris, first stop in his plunge into total eclipse.

The porter leaves, the door shuts, and Tibor sits on the edge of a small, hard bed, kicks off his shoes and lies on his back, hands under his head, staring at the ceiling. A sudden jerk forward, a whistle, a scrape of metal on metal and the train is moving, slowly inching forward, now gaining speed, now rattling toward the Channel. The heartbeat of wheels beneath him is some comfort and so is the air-conditioning that cools as they accelerate. He sits up and watches brick houses whiz past; a woman taking down wash in a garden, children playing in the final light of day; now fields appear, a cluster of cows, dark rolling hills. Out of the city at last, hurtling away, he can lie back, but he cannot sleep. He props himself up on an elbow, reaches for the water jug, and wishes, suddenly, for a sleeping pill. He hasn't had medicine in years, not even an aspirin, but then again, he has never had pain this deep, edging into his bones, seeping into the marrow. He rings for the porter and says, "I do hate to bother you, but I can't seem to get to sleep. You wouldn't by any chance have something, a pill, perhaps, to help me?"

The porter smiles. "I can never sleep on these clattering things myself. Here," he says, reaching into a pocket. "I'm only allowed to offer aspirin, but for you . . ." He winks. "Take some of these. Keep them."

Tibor looks at the bottle marked "Mogadon." "How many do I take?"

"One, two. But no more. Unless, of course, you plan to kill yourself." He laughs and tips his hat saying, "Call me, if you need anything else."

Tibor closes the door, opens the bottle quickly as if someone might see him, pops two pills into his mouth, takes a swig of Evian, and undresses, folding socks and trousers on the end of the bed. He crawls between the sheets and lies very still, listening to the wheels beat along the track, and waits like a humble suppliant to be granted sleep. The train seems to slow, it stops, and Tibor sits up, pushes back the curtains and squints out the window to see where they are. Distant houses are outlined on a hill. Why did they stop here? What could be wrong? Don't they know he has to get to Paris?

Stephan, he remembers being told, was once on a train in his own private car with his own piano, a bed, and a kitchen, traveling from Germany to Russia just before the Second World War. The train suddenly stopped in the middle of nowhere, and after some time, passengers began to disembark along the track to see what had happened. "I thought perhaps a cow had blocked our path," Stephan said, "or worse, that war had been declared, but then I saw the conductor of the train rushing toward me, his hands dripping blood. 'What is it?' I asked, and he motioned frantically toward the front of the train. I don't know why I went to look, perhaps to help, perhaps out of morbid curiosity, who knows. But there, lying in front of the train, was the body, or what was left of it, of a young woman. Her head was not mutilated at all, and she had shiny black hair, a perfectly lovely face, and her eyes were wide open and staring up at me, dark terrified eyes, the eyes of one betrayed. I later found out she had committed suicide, unrequited in love."

Forward motion again, and Tibor lies back and falls asleep thinking of wide dark eyes and severed arms, draped in white cloth, flapping on grass like broken wings.

"Maître!" the porter calls the next morning in the assured voice of a Frenchman returning to his own language, "c'est Paris! Dépêchez-vous! Si non, vous partirez pour l'Orient. . . ."

Tibor's eyelids flutter open. Paris? he thinks, his head heavy. He can hardly raise it from the pillow.

"Pollini!" the porter shouts and pounds on the door.

The train, the visit to Sally—it spills across Tibor like a bucket of cold water.

"Je m'en vais!" he yells back, and pours Evian into a glass, water from the jug into a bowl, splashes his face, manages to dress and brush his hair.

"Bonjour," he says to the porter while pressing pound notes into his hand.

The porter smiles and hands him his passport and ticket.

"Your friend at the French immigration," Tibor asks, wondering why the mistake in his identity was not discovered, "was he on duty?"

"No. And they are so lazy now at the border. They hardly even look at the passports for first-class couchettes, they flip through them. And can you imagine, I told one of them I had Pollini in my car and he said to me, 'Who is Pollini?' Qu'ils sont Philistins, n'est-ce pas?"

"Oui," Tibor agrees, a free man, and he walks briskly down the platform at the Gare St.-Lazare. A clock tells him it is 8:01, the pastel light trickling through the clouded glass above tells him it is morning, and the staccato voices, the smells of perfume, the stylish women tell him it is Paris. He enters the waiting room, La Salle des Pas Perdus, the Room of the Lost Steps, and stands for a minute under the big clock, the meeting place for all his student rendezvous. His heart beats fast as it did then, and he thinks of Annette, and he can almost see her walking toward him with that endearing little limp of hers. Annette, his first love, a soprano four years older than he, with her hair flaxen as Debussy's girl and her wide painted mouth and the laughter that spilled out in bright bursts, and how she held him close and showed him everything, and he kissed her leg, the short one, shrunken by polio, and told her it didn't matter, she was a beauty, a treasure. When she left to study in New York he was seventeen and

223

he begged Stephan to let him audition for Juilliard so he could follow. "Out of the question," Stephan had said. "I left Hungary for a contralto and I ended up holding her roses instead of her. Go practice, mon petit."

"Annette," Tibor sighs, each lost step leading him now down a flight of marble steps into the Cour de Rome, and out of habit from years past, he takes the rue du Rocher uphill, passing boys with leather book bags strapped to their backs, corduroy knee pants, shirts open, sleeves rolled up. The gutters still run with early-morning water and the hot air steams with moisture. Tibor removes his jacket and when he passes a woman with a long bread tucked under her arm, the fresh smell reminds him he has not eaten in more than a day. He reaches the rue de Madrid and takes the steps leading down under a dark steel bridge, heading, so he realizes, toward the Conservatoire de Musique. He enters at number 14, pushes the heavy glass door, walks past the austere bust of B. Sarrette, founder, and he stops, as he always did, to look at the bulletin board announcing competitions—Le Concours International Marguerite Long-Jacques Thibaud, Le Prix d'Europe, Le Leventritt—and his stomach tightens as it did years before and he wonders why there seemed so much to win, so much to lose. He walks on, into an open courtyard and takes the remembered thirty steps up to the main quadrangle. Relieved that no students are around, he walks down a pebbled path and stops at the small marble statue of Orpheus, curled on his side, holding his lyre, weeping.

"Attention!" he hears someone shout. Down the path a piano is being moved by men in blue coveralls. Legs removed, lid gone, the piano has been pulled apart, like Orpheus, who, so Stephan told him once as they stood together before this statue, was torn apart by the Thracian women. "But even as his decapitated head floated down the river Hebrus, still he sang," Stephan had said. "So you see, when there is that much music in you, it can never be silenced."

Mute, on a path leading nowhere, Tibor stands, faint with hunger, wondering if it is he, Tibor Szabo, who ever played the piano, and why he should have wanted to.

"Hey, you!" one of the movers calls and takes a pugnacious step toward Tibor, "this place is closed until eight forty-five. What are you looking for?"

"Rien," Tibor mutters, and walks back along the path, down the thirty steps, out the glass doors into the street. At the corner of the rue de Rome and the rue de Madrid, he is about to enter the café La Flûte de Pan, but he had better not—they just might remember him. Down the rue de Rome, descending to the river, he passes charcuteries, windows with white lace curtains, boulangeries, pâtisseries, dogs on leashes, motorbikes, a man with a purple scarf holding a baby, bicycles, delivery carts, fruit stands, fish stands. An old man with a cane hobbles past. Is it Janos, Janos Hartog, my friend from home? Tibor wonders, but the man is gone before he can call out to him. He is alone, weak with hunger. If he does not eat soon he may faint, so he stops at a café, stands inside at the steel bar, and orders une brioche et un petit crème. Gobbling the sweet bread, he stares into the mirror behind the bar and sees hollow eyes, a tight thin mouth, a dark beard beginning to sprout around the chin and he looks quickly away. Whose is this stranger's face and why is it attached to him? Sugar and caffeine flow in his system and he revives enough to pay and go on walking, but where? Away, just away, he tells himself, and he passes the Opéra, jostles through a morass of tourists on the rue de Rivoli, walks along the dusty paths of the Tuileries toward the Seine. At river's edge, thirsty, hot, exhausted, Tibor thinks of a shower and a tall cool drink, but where can he get them? Mireille would be delighted if he appeared at her door. "Comme tu es triste, mon chou," she would say, and pamper him, stuff him with bonbons and bavardages, stroke his forehead. But no. He does not want small talk or compassion. What consolation can there possibly be? His life is destroyed and he wanders on, alive but shattered, along the Seine, toward the Pont Neuf, then past the Hôtel de Ville, up the rue de Beaubourg. Here, in the Marais, he looks up at red-tiled roofs, ancient bricks, carved wood-work, intricate iron railings, and snakes his way along narrow sidewalks through a crowd that is bottlenecked to a standstill, then spills out onto an open plaza. Before him, displacing bricks and tiles and wood, is the new Centre Pompidou, an enormous modern structure with its func-tional apparatus exposed, like a man without flesh: arteries, muscles, sinews visible. Skinned alive himself, Tibor flinches and gapes at the building. In the space around him, jugglers and sword-swallowers appear, magi-cians and mimes, young street performers entertain the crowd like medieval beggars and troubadours, a Brueghel canvas in motion. Confused, dizzy from the heat, Tibor sees a group—members of that footloose international youth culture with their denims, backpacks, dope, and dreams—sitting on the pavement. He sinks down next to them, puts his briefcase across his folded knees, and doubles over.

"Hey, are you OK?" he is asked.

"Leave him alone," someone giggles. "Maybe he's meditating."

Tibor's ears buzz, he hears a voice, recognizes it as female, and feels a hand on his shoulder. It must be Sally, she's followed him, found him to tell him . . . He looks up, but there are no blue eyes, no shining golden hair. A young woman kneels in front of him, a mass of frizzy black hair around a pale, elongated face; two dark round eyes look into his.

"You're not OK, are you," she says, no question in her voice, and tugging at his hand, she instructs him, "Come on, get up, come with me."

Tibor Szabo, the international musical celebrity, is accustomed to attention, used to being picked up, but stardom seems light-years ago, and what would a woman want with him now? "You mean, you know who I am?" he asks.

"No," she says, helping him to his feet, "but I know you need a wash and a meal. Come on."

"Sabine," one of the boys sitting nearby calls out as she walks away, "where are you going?"

She tosses her head, offers no explanation, and waves. The boy leans back against a green knapsack and watches her go, a small frail girl in an orange sundress, leading a tall thin man through a swirling crowd.

"A man's character is his fate, do you believe that?" Sabine asks as she waters a pot of geraniums on the narrow terrace. Tibor sits on a folding wooden chair, his forehead pressed against the iron railing, and he stares at the street, the rue Rambuteau, four flights beneath them. Cheese is being delivered to a shop in large wooden wheels, a child reaches for a plum at the fruit stand, a truck passes with a picture plastered on its side, a girl in a bikini with the words DÉFENDEZ VOS INTÉRÊTS printed under her buttocks.

"Well, I do," Sabine answers herself and plucks a dead leaf from an ivy plant. Tibor scratches at his beard, which, now a week old, is black and thickening. He sighs.

Sabine climbs through the window into her apartment and returns with a bamboo tray stacked with sliced melon, strips of prosciutto, and two glasses of iced tea, a sprig of mint in each.

"If you don't eat," she says, leaning toward him across a small table covered with blue-flowered oilcloth, "you will disappear."

The pressure of the hot iron railing against his forehead is uncomfortable, but he does not move. He hears Sabine chewing, he smells the mint.

"I've been thinking," she says, "about what you should do. I mean, you can stay as long as you like."

Tibor shifts forward in his chair, closer to the railing. He sees a pigeon on a balcony two floors below. Sabine finishes her last bite of melon and reaches for a second plate, spears a slice of ham. If she had not seen the front page of *Le Figaro* the morning after she took Tibor home, she would have sent him on his way then, but "le plus fameux pianiste de son âge" is not a man to discard, especially when he is in obvious trouble.

"What happened?" she had asked him, dropping the newspaper in his lap. The astonished look on his face as he read the article, and read it again, turned slowly into anger. He threw the paper at the wall, then crumpled onto her bed, rolled onto his back, and stared at the ceiling.

"Tell me about it," Sabine urged and sat beside him. If, as the story implied, he was suicidal or having a breakdown, she would help him. She had already rescued him from the Beaubourg, she had recognized quality when she saw it—unlike her boorish young friends, who merely laughed. But Baronesse Sabine von Andernacht und Sonnenfels knew the minute she saw Tibor Szabo that he was an aristocrat or an artist, maybe both, and she took a chance, as she often did, by inviting him home. In bed, that first night, he said nothing, kissed her hands, and fell asleep, waking when she returned from her morning walk, paper in hand.

"Is it a woman?" Sabine had asked him, and he nodded. "Ah," she had said, with an air of precocious sophistication for a girl of nineteen. Having fled her family castle in Graz for a freer life in France, she knew about love and loss.

"She left you," Sabine guessed, "for another man."
Tibor nodded again.

"Well, she's a fool."

A wisp of a smile had flickered across Tibor's mouth and he reached out his hand, ran it gently over Sabine's pregnant belly.

"Where is the father?" he asked.

"He left me for another woman. Same story as yours," she answered. "But I'm not sad. No one owns anyone else. That's the way I look at it."

"It's not so easy for me," Tibor said.

"It wasn't so easy for me either, but it gets easier, each day, one by one. Slowly you start hurting less."

Tibor could imagine no end to the pain, and no end to the terrible relentless heat that parched, cracked, destroyed all thought.

"Can I stay with you?" he asked.

"Sure. But aren't there a lot of people looking for you? I mean, you might be causing someone grief."

"I doubt it," he said. "I'll pay you for the trouble."

"It's no trouble, and I don't need the money. You can stay if you like, and I won't tell anyone. Just tell me what you want for dinner, meat or fish?"

One week later, and Sabine is worried. Yesterday the concierge came up to fix the leak in the sink, saw Tibor, and acted suspicious. The police could turn up anytime. Then her family would find her and what would happen? Besides, Tibor just sits and stares and says nothing, and it's making her nervous. "You can stay here," Sabine says, "but I think it would be better if you moved on."

Tibor takes his head away from the railing and feels a slice of irritation, like a bandage being removed. "Why?"

"Because it's time, that's why. You can't sit here feeling sorry for yourself for the rest of your life. I mean, you've loved and lost, so what? There are people in worse shape than you, people without a roof over their heads, people starving to death. Children without parents." Sabine pats her belly and her eyes fill up like two flooded ponds.

"Don't, please don't," Tibor says, seeing incipient tears. He drops to his knees in front of her and presses his head to her belly, holds her tight. He feels the baby move, a small quick jab. Sabine wipes away her tears and Tibor pats her back, as he would Maya's on a cold night when they were alone and Maya said she could hear wolves howling. Wolves, so Szusza told them, lived in the hills of Buda and in the winter, if they got very hungry, they had been known to rush into town, which is why she often left a bowl of meat scraps outside the door of the apartment house.

"Sabine," Tibor says, holding her at arm's length, looking at her face blotched from crying—a child about to have another child. "Can't you go home to your family?" he asks. "Won't they forgive you, won't they take care of you?"

"No," Sabine says. "I've thought of it, of course. My father might have helped me, but he died two years ago, and my mother has a heart condition. This would kill her."

"Are you sure?"

Sabine shrugs and bites on a mint leaf, seeming suddenly older, determined. "I'll be OK," she says with a pallid smile. "Sometimes it seems hard, but I want this child and I can take care of it. I'll be OK. Honest."

Tibor hovers near her, unconvinced. "How can I help?" he asks.

"You can leave," she says softly. "I won't tell anyone you've been here. If you stay, and you're discovered here, my mother will find out about this." She rests one arm on the shelf of her belly.

"But where should I go?" Tibor asks, unable to think or plan.

"What about your family? Do you have parents?"

"A mother."

"And where is she?"

"Lausanne."

"Well, there you are."

Tibor looks perplexed. Wiping sweat from her forehead with the back of her wrist, Sabine says, "Don't you think your mother has seen the papers? She must know you're missing. She must be suffering, she must be worried. Go to her. She'll help you."

"But I'm thirty-three years old. I can't go to my mother and expect her to—"

"I'm giving you the same advice you've given me," Sabine says, "and it is the best advice. I can't take it, but if you can, if you possibly can, do. You are her son, aren't you? Can't you talk to her?"

"Talk to her?" Tibor repeats, trying to remember the last time he came to his mother with a problem. Problems were for Szusza or Maya, because Eva Szabo was always too busy, and he wouldn't dare bother her. Eva. He thinks of her in her straw hat, standing next to their summer cottage, a bouquet of just-picked wild flowers in her hand. When she closed her eyes and leaned forward to smell them, he thought he had never seen anyone so beautiful.

"How would I get to Lausanne?" he asks.

"Dead easy. By train."

"But they're searching for me, aren't they?"

"You have a beard and you've lost at least ten pounds. No one will recognize you. They hardly look· at passports on those trains, anyhow. I'll give you something to guarantee safe passage. I've used it myself."

Sabine opens a drawer, feels around, and pulls out a shiny black snakeskin passport cover. A gold eagle gleams at Tibor with the words THE UNITED STATES OF AMERICA beneath it.

"But . . ." he says.

"No buts. Just put your own passport inside this, and at the border, pretend you're asleep. They'll nudge you politely for your passport. Flash this at them, and they won't even look at it."

"And if they do?"

"You'll have your own passport inside. Yours is British, isn't it? To the Swiss, it's all the same thing."

Tibor laughs, it's such a mad idea, but Sabine wants him to leave and where can he go? There are hotels, of course, but the idea of being alone in some anonymous hotel room would remind him of being on tour, of being with Sally. Sally and Werner—the image of the two together will not leave his eyes even now, even after a week has passed. Spreading into the brain, it has taken hold like malignant cells, pernicious, deadly.

"There is a cure for it," his mother once assured him when, learning about cancer, he was afraid. "We only have to find it."

"And how will we find it?" he asked.

"We will look, we will not give up. We are nearly there."

Eva Szabo in her white uniform, hunched over a microscope, looking, looking. Tibor remembers standing in the doorway of her laboratory, afraid to disturb her, yet angry that she would not look up. "I'm here, Mama," he remembers wanting to scream, "I'm here!"

Sabine is placing a telephone back in its cradle. "I've called the station," she says. "Go to the Gare de Lyon. It only takes five hours, four stops—Dijon, Dôle, Frasne, Vallorbe, et voilà, Lausanne."

She hands him a slip of paper with the information neatly written down, then finds his briefcase and jacket, and he follows her slowly down four flights of spiral stairs. Out on the street Sabine looks at her watch and takes his arm. "I'll go with you to the station," she says. "We'll look like a couple, bearded man with pregnant wife. Come on."

Ten days had passed since Tibor Szabo disappeared, ten hot, heavy days, oozing by like lava, days that burned and smoldered. There was no way to avoid the molten heat. It followed Sally everywhere, scalding, scarring. Nothing brought relief, not changing clothes three times a day or taking showers or lying down. At the ironmonger's, when she asked for a fan, the proprietor mopped his brow with a rag and shrugged, "Madam, there is not a fan left in all of London."

"How well prepared we English are for these things," she sighed.

"But I am from Genoa," the man said, his upper lip beaded with perspiration.

Sally sat in her kitchen, fanning herself with a few pages of Werner's manuscript.

"Close the fridge door," she said as Werner reached in for more ice.

He poured himself some tonic and sat down opposite her, pointed at the ream of paper and asked, "What do you think of that section?"

"You're right," she said. "It does work better having the father keep quiet about Heinrich's child. I'm just confused a bit about motives."

"Whose?"

"Heinrich's. Clearly Magda is in love with him, not the father, so why does he have to expose the old man?"

Werner wiped at drops of water that condensed on the

outside of his glass. "I don't intend for motives to be clear. It's a character thing with him—he's driven to destroy his father."

"But—"

The phone rang. Motion froze, eyes stared.

"I'll get it," Sally said, breaking through.

"No," Werner said, "I will," and he rushed into the dining room.

Sally held her breath, but she could tell by the subdued tones that nothing had happened. When will it? she asked herself, and stood up, padded into the dining room on bare feet, waited for Werner to hang up. She looked wan in a cream-colored dress, bought that morning up the hill at a shop called Chic. In pale tiers, billowing out from two thin shoulder straps, it made her feel ridiculous, and the color washed her out, but the shop was hot, the dress was cool. One hundred and fifty pounds seemed extravagant for wisps of cloth, but it reminded her of her trip to Paris and she bought it, floated down the hill home in it, light as milkweed fluff.

She sank onto her knees on a large pillow and heard Werner say, "Talk to you later."

"Who was it?" she asked.

"No one."

She sighed. Werner wandered past her, stared out the front windows at the dry brown grass on the heath. "One match and it'd go up like kindling."

"I don't care if it does," Sally said, getting up, passing him on her way to the stairs. For the first time since Tibor disappeared, Sally climbed up to her studio. Although windows were open wide on both sides of the room, no air moved, and she sat down on the low stool in front of her easel.

"There is one thing I know—one thing I'm certain of," she said to Werner, who huffed up the stairs behind her. "Heat rises."

"Yes," he said, "but there's another absolute: Seasons change."

"When?" she asked, despondent.

"Soon."

Werner shuffled through some canvases stacked along the wall. "Nice," he said, looking at a still life.

"Dead leaves," Sally said from her perch. "Who cares about dead leaves?"

"Come on, Sally. Stop being apathetic."

"Well, what do you expect?" she asked, her voice bristling with tension.

"I expect—" He stopped and stood up, wiped his brow with a sleeve. "I have no expectations. I just think it's important right now for us to push depression aside."

"But it's depressing, deeply and painfully depressing." She picked up a brush and stroked away some moisture from her neck.

"Does that feel good?" he asked, flopping onto the floor next to her. Dressed in white, lying on his side, he was languid as a sybarite, but pleasure between them seemed a thing of the past. He had not reached out to touch her since Tibor's visit, nor had she made any approach. Consuming as their passion had been, it was killed by Tibor's discovery of it, like a fire stamped out.

"Did you call New York today?" Sally asked.

"Stop nagging at me," Werner snarled.

"If I annoy you so much, why don't you go away?"

"Will you stop asking questions?"

"Why should I? There are things to find out, things to understand, things to know. For instance—what if no one ever finds him?" She stood up and walked in front of Werner, the hem of her dress brushing against his face. He grabbed at it, like a cat at a cloth, and made her stand still. He opened his mouth to speak, but exasperation strangled words and he let go, rolled away from her.

235

Silence stretched between them, a long endless rope of silence.

"Talk to me," Sally pleaded at last, "answer me."

"I can't. I have no answers, not now, not until we find him."

She marched back and forth, bit at her lower lip. "Does everything hinge on finding him?" she asked. "And what about us, you and me? Were we drawn together only because of Tibor?"

Werner lay on his back and stared at the ceiling.

"Yes," Sally answered herself, "yes and no. There were things about it that had nothing to do with Tibor. You made me feel good, wonderful, in fact. And I felt known in a way I never have before."

Werner touched her ankle as she passed, raised himself onto his elbows, caught her eyes in his, smiled, but said nothing.

"And," Sally went on, looking away, "I was so monstrously jealous of your friendship with Tibor. I had no right. It's a deep bond. A long and profound connection."

"But it's severed," Werner pronounced. "And when I think of him wandering around somewhere, totally betrayed, I can't bear it."

"You can bear it because you have to, and so do I. We betrayed him, no doubt about it, but we haven't destroyed him."

"How can you be so sure? No one can find him, there are no hopeful leads. Every time the phone rings I'm sure it's news of a corpse."

"We have to find him, that's all," she said, and poked through canvases leaning against a wall, slid one out from behind the others, a huge surface, tightly stretched.

"It's unfinished," she said, stepping back to look at her portrait of Tibor. Werner stood up and moved next to Sally to look—a small figure seated at a large piano, hands just about to touch the keys, head turned toward the viewer as if suddenly disturbed. There is annoyance in his face and his eyes are narrowed. The piano seems to blossom in front of him, magically flowing from his hands, and it shines, black touched with gold, enormous, covering most of the canvas. Under its open lid, distorted figures from Tibor's life pour out, creatures cascading into an abyss. Sally is barely recognizable, brush in hand, a long, flowing amorphous figure, and Werner is bent over a desk with six arms coming out of his distended body. There is Stephan in tails and Zev clasping the cello in a lewd embrace and instruments spilling onto the ground, violins, broken flutes, a cacophonous vision.

"What's that?" Werner asked, pointing.

"Where?"

"That tiny thing in the corner."

"It's a woman without a face, a microscope in her hand, a straw hat on her head."

"God, is that good."

"Why?"

"He never had a clue who his mother was, and you've captured it all."

"Have I? Maybe it's also why he was unable to know me."

"What do you mean?"

"If he never understood his mother, he can never understand any other woman, and he's always looking for her. He left her when he was thirteen. He never had enough of her to be able to give her up."

"And maybe," Werner said, turning to Sally, "just maybe he would be compelled to make one last try, one final attempt to approach her. It's true he has always needed to worship a woman just as he did his mother, and he was looking for his mother in you."

"Sure. And I was looking for my father. Come on, we all do that."

"OK, we all do it. But maybe now, if finding us together pushed him to the edge, made him desperate, he will *really* look for his mother, one last time."

"When a man is desperate, he doesn't go to Mama."

"It depends on the man and the mother. Listen, just listen to me. He found us, right? He rushed off, right? What would he do, where would he go? He wanders in a state of shock and anger for a while. But then he begins to need comfort. Who can he go to? Why not Eva Szabo? Somehow he must have gotten out of the country, maybe by car, by ferry, by train. I don't think British subjects arriving in another Common Market country need landing cards. Maybe his arrival was unnoticed, or unrecorded. OK. He arrives somehow in France, he drives, he hitches, somehow he gets to Lausanne."

"But you talked to his mother today. She knows nothing."

"Yes," Werner said, excited now, as the faint glimmer of possibility brightened. "But she sounded tense. She could be hiding him. That's it. He's with her and she's hiding him."

Sally sat down hard on the stool and looked glum.

"You don't think so?" Werner asked.

"It's so unlikely, I just—"

"Unlikely, you said, you didn't say impossible. It is *possible* that he went to Lausanne. Sally, I'm going. Who knows what finding us together might have triggered inside him. I'm not sitting around waiting until I read his obituary."

"He's not going to commit suicide! We've been through that a million times. We've discussed it to death!"

"Well, I'm reconsidering. Look, he's a man of extremes, capable of violence, maybe even toward nimself."

"But he wouldn't try to kill himself!" Sally declared vehemently. Yet Werner's fears revived hers.

"Oh, God," she said in one sharp quick breath, and spun around toward Werner on the stool. "Then go to Lausanne. What are you waiting for?"

"It's me, Tibor. Mama, I'm here," he whispers into the intercom of her apartment on the avenue de Rumine. After a moment's hesitation, she buzzes him in, and when he reaches the fourth-floor landing out of breath, she is peering through a crack in the still-chained door.

A thin, bearded man in a crumpled suit peers back. "Are you alone?" he asks.

The voice is her son's, but she isn't sure. . . .

"Damn it, it's me, open the door." He twists his neck to flick hair out of his eyes and plants himself firmly before her.

At the clink of a chain, the door opens. Tibor steps inside. A small compact woman in a beige robe stands back to survey him.

"Why are you standing there gaping at me?" Tibor asks, holding out his arms. "Can't you even give me a kiss?" He rushes at her, picks her up, and hugs her so hard that, alarmed, she pushes against his shoulders to break away. He puts her down, and she notices, uneasily, that he is trembling, about to cry.

"Come, come and sit down," she says, pulls him by the hand, from the foyer to her sitting room, and points to a small brown sofa. He sits, he leans his head back. He sighs.

"Are you tired?" she asks. He doesn't speak or move. "You must have had a long trip," she says, trying to sound cheerful. "How about a glass of tea?"

He murmurs assent, and she walks into the kitchen to

put on the kettle and, sensing his agitation and distress, hurries back, afraid that he might leave. He stares at her, his eyes gleaming through two narrow slits.

"Are you glad to see me?" he asks softly.

"Of course, of course I am," she says, standing at the doorway, her hands folded like a singer about to begin an aria.

"Were you worried?" he asks, and wonders why she isn't weeping with delight and relief at his arrival.

"Yes, if you must know."

"If I must know? Of course I must know." He sits up to look at her, a woman with long gray hair pulled back into one tight braid, an old woman getting ready for bed. Like the map of her life, wrinkles are printed on her face and her skin has coarsened. She is in her sixties, the decay is normal, but when did she start to wrinkle, and at what point did her body spread, and where is Eva with the golden chignon and unmarked face, the woman who ran with him on the hills of Lake Balaton, who helped him catch butterflies and look for shells?

"How is it possible," he asks, "that time has passed and we are strangers?"

Eva waits. How shall she speak to him? How does he want to be answered?

"So," he says, watching her confusion. "As always, you have nothing to say to me."

She clears her throat. "In the past, I've had a great deal to say."

"In the past? That's good, Mama, but the past is past and this is the present, now, right *now*, and I want you to talk to me *now*."

"I will," she says, and defends herself with a smile, tucking a loose strand of hair behind one ear, "as soon as I make tea." She turns, like a young girl being coy, and disappears into the kitchen.

241

Spoons and cups rattle. Tibor puts his feet onto a wooden coffee table and surveys the room. Shelves of books cover one wall, and his father's photograph, framed in black, hangs on another, surrounded by small paintings, all by the same artist.

"I see that your friend Gustav never got beyond his abstract phase. It all looks like Kandinsky, bad Kandinsky."

Eva puts a tray down next to Tibor's scuffed shoes and pours two cups of tea. "Gustav Tomek is respected in some circles," she says.

"Your loyalty can only be attributed to love."

"Or friendship. There can be such a thing between a man and a woman, you know. Sugar?"

"No. Where is he?"

"Gustav? He's in Sankt Gallen, hanging an exhibition."

Tibor drinks the hot tea as if it's cool water and holds out his cup for more, wiping his beard with his free hand. "How long has it been now, I mean between you two?"

Eva tightens the sash of her robe. "You've never asked me these things before. Why do you need to know now?"

"Connections between people interest me, that's all. Loyalty interests me. Come on, how long?"

Eva stands up and opens a cabinet near the bookshelves, takes out a bottle of brandy. "Would you like some?" she asks. "It might help you relax."

"I don't need to relax. I'm fine, thank you."

"Are you? You don't show up for concerts, you disappear for ten days, you arrive at my door looking like a starving refugee. You don't seem fine to me at all."

"Well, it's all a big joke. Actually it's a publicity stunt. Some people will do anything for attention."

"Not Tibor Szabo," Eva says, and pours two glasses of brandy, sets them down on the coffee table, sits beside him.

"Mama," he murmurs, reaching for her hand, kissing it,

242

pressing it gently to his forehead as he did when he was little and he begged her to stroke his brow, please, just a little not for long just until my headache goes away Invented pains could not fool Eva, but she agreed anyhow and hummed and stroked him.

As if stung, Eva Szabo recoils.

"Why do you pull away?" Tibor asks, and his spurned voice hurts her, makes her want to explain, if she can.

"It's not you, it's just that it makes me remember."

Tibor drains his glass of brandy and pours himself a second. "Don't you have happy memories?"

"Of course, but . . ."

"I suppose having children was hard for you. Having *me*. I just got in your way, didn't I?"

Eva is annoyed. "You're asking me the questions of a fifteen-year-old."

"At fifteen I was in Paris, practicing, and you were in Hungary, remember? I couldn't ask you then. Can't I ask you now?"

Eva takes a sip of brandy and sits up straight. "Is it necessary?"

Tibor groans like a displeased teen-ager.

"There is no need to act so imperious," she says.

"Imperious? How can you possibly call me imperious?"

"Well, you are, you always have been."

"What?"

"Yes, you have, you've always been the little prince in the family, haven't you? Always the one who dictated what we did, the future king of the piano." Broken veins under the surface of her cheeks begin to redden and she raises her glass, takes another sip.

"Mama," Tibor says, patting her hand, "do you realize something? In the last twenty years I've seen you maybe two times a year, two brief visits a year, during which we said nothing hurtful to each other, nothing at all. Let's not start now. Please."

Eva leans against Tibor's chest and he closes his arms around her, rests his temple on her head. "Mama," he whispers, hugging her until both become disturbed, and he moves away.

He stands up and walks around the room, picking up a glass figurine, a picture of Maya and her children, a collection of dried flowers, a book about plants. Stopping at her small record collection, he flips through and asks, quietly, "Where are they?"

"Where are what?" Eva blows her nose with a lace handkerchief, tucks it into the sleeve of her bathrobe.

"My recordings. I've sent them all to you, I know I have. And where are they?"

"Gustav has them," she says, "and some of my other records. He has more time to listen than I do."

"But, Mama," Tibor moans, "my records! They were meant for you, not anyone else. How could you have given them away?" His forehead knots together and his eyes fill up with tears.

"Darling, I didn't mean to offend you, I just . . ."

But Tibor has turned away, wanders around the room, fingering a velvet curtain, a tasseled fringe on a lamp, touching Eva's life. He passes a desk piled high with papers and magazines and stops in front of a wooden chest, painted with bright-colored flowers.

"What's this?" he asks, pulling out packets of old letters tied in faded red ribbons. "Memorabilia, I presume," he answers himself and takes a letter at random, carefully unfolds the cracked yellowing page, and reads to himself:

August 10, 1952

Dearest Mama:

I don't think it's fair. Maya got to ride horseback all day. Papa will not let me. He says what if I fall and break an

arm. He says I have to respect my body and my talent.
What a lot of nonsense! Mama, please write to him and
tell him to let me ride a horse. I don't want to play the
piano if it means I can't ride a horse. Please, Mama.
I miss you so much. Why won't your laboratory give you
a holiday now? It's not fair. You must be very hot at home.
We have a nice breeze here. Lake Balaton is so pretty. You
and I could swim all day. Remember the lavender on the
hills? It's all in bloom. The color is your favorite. I'll send
you some if I remember to. There was a thunderstorm last
night. All the lights went out and we walked around with
candles. Papa pretended to be a ghost. He sang the
Erlkönig. It was scary. Do you think there is an Erlkönig
and does he really kill little boys? Papa says there's no
such thing, but I don't believe him. Why would Schubert
make a song about it if it's not true? I guess Papa's not so
mean. Except for the horses.
Please write to me, Mama. I miss you and send you
kisses.

Your loving son,
Tibka

"It's signed, 'your loving son,'" Tibor says, raising his
eyes to look at his mother.

"You wrote the sweetest letters," Eva says, sniffing. "I
kept them all."

"But not my records?"

"There is more of you in those torn pages than on a
plastic disc, more of you to keep."

Tibor wants to crush her to his breast but she is rising
nervously from the sofa, reaching behind a table to pull
out old scrapbooks, photo albums. "Come look," she says
and they sit together on the floor, rummaging through old
pictures, Tibor and Maya barefoot at the beach, Imre
carrying them piggyback, Grandpa Andras in his dress
suit, refusing to look at the camera.

245

"Remember how contemptuous he was? He said if God had intended the camera to be invented—"

"He would have sent a signed photograph with the Ten Commandments," Eva finishes for him. They laugh, and Tibor thinks of Grandpa Andras and his finger pointing at the sky and his violent arguments with Imre and how, as the Russians were coming, and they all huddled down in the basement with the Farkas family and the Kramers, it was Grandpa who slept with one end of a rope around his wrist, the other end tied to the door, so he would not be taken by surprise.

They are both silent until Eva gathers up the photos, the letters, the memories, and puts them back into the chest, closes the lid. She grimaces as she rises to her feet.

"Do you hurt?" Tibor asks.

"Just a bit. A touch of arthritis in the hip."

"But why didn't you tell me? I have a friend in the Canaries. They have wonderful cures there, mud baths, mineral waters. I'll send you and you'll be better in no time."

"Thank you," she says with a bittersweet smile, "but I can't really take the time."

"No. No, of course you can't." Tibor slumps back down onto the sofa.

"Is there something you want to tell me?" Eva asks.

"No, Mama." He folds his hands and looks up at her. "It's just that I've been in a turmoil lately, and I know all this fuss is being made to find me. But I'm not quite ready to come out and face it. So, please, don't tell anyone I'm here." His eyes plead with hers.

"But, darling, there's no use staying here. People drop by all the time. The police would find out in a flash. You'll have to go someplace else, someplace near, with a phone." She tightens the sash of her robe. "I have an idea. Take my car. I can easily get to work by tram. I have the key to Gustav's summer place near Villars. It's only a little cabin, but it's in the mountains and it's quiet. You can get food in the village. I promise not to tell anyone you're there. And I can call you every day." She steps toward him, somehow uneasy. "But are you sure you'll be all right? You won't do anything foolish, will you?"

Tibor smiles. "You sound like my mother." My mother, he thinks, Eva Szabo. Just a tired woman in a bathrobe ready for bed. What did I expect?

He stands up and puts his arms around her, holds her tight one long last time. Then Eva picks up her handbag, stirs around inside until she finds the key, holds it up like a magic silver fish. Wishing for silence and a soft bed, Tibor takes it.

"I'll write down the directions," Eva says. "It's easy, only takes a few hours. The key to the cabin is behind the first shutter of the window on the left of the front door. Can you remember that?"

"I can," he says, and stands looking at her for some time before he bends forward, kisses her lightly on the forehead and says, "Good-bye, Mama. I love you."

There is no sound at all. The cabin is dark and before he can reach for a lamp, the door bangs shut. Tibor takes one cautious step forward into the room. A sliver of moonlight lies on a table like a broken plate, two half-burned candles in brass holders beside it. He lights the candles, holds one up and looks around the room at a fireplace, a chair, a small chest of drawers, and a single bed with a rough wool coverlet. In an alcove he finds a wine rack, a small refrigerator, a two-burner stove, and a door leading into a bathroom. Colored bath oils and soft sponges line the edge of a deep tub and fluffy blue towels hang from hooks on the wooden walls. The old boy likes his bath, Tibor thinks, and turns on a tap, watches clear water run. He will have a bath, but first, some wine. He pulls out a bottle, dusts it off. Latour '72—'70 was a better year, but this will suffice. In a drawer near the stove he finds an opener, and carefully twists it into the top, pulls slowly, smells the cork. Satisfied, he walks back into the large room, places the bottle on the table. A glass would be useful, and he finds one on the mantelpiece, blows into it, rubs it on his sleeve.

He places his briefcase on the table and sits down, hands folded in his lap, waiting, as if about to begin a difficult piece. Then, raising his head confidently, he clicks the case open, removes his passport and money and places it next to a candle, watches a drop of wax trickle down the brass holder. He pulls out a pad of notepaper marked "Imperial Hotel Wien" and as he feels in the side pocket for his gold pen, a present from Sally, he touches a small glass bottle. Pills rattle. He holds it up to see how many, and decides there are enough. Sleeping pills from his trip to Paris will help him tonight. He wants to sleep, a deep sleep, an endless sleep.

He feels strangely calm as he picks up the pen to write. What shall he say and to whom? He chews on the end of the pen and tosses it back into the briefcase. No, he will not leave a note, there will be no ritual, no ceremony. This is a final performance and will speak for itself.

He drinks his first glass of wine seated at the table, and for his second, he moves to an upholstered chair. He is getting dizzy, and sits, trying to focus on a painting, blobs of green moving on a yellow background. His head is heavy and starts to droop, but he is not ready to sleep yet. He pushes himself out of the chair and runs a bath. Choosing blue oil, a cool blue, he pours it into the water, smelling the perfume of alpine flowers, stirs it around, wipes his hand on a towel, and undresses slowly, folding his clothes into a pile on the floor.

Candlelight flickers against his naked flesh as he stands beside the table, pours a handful of pills, tosses them into his mouth, washes them down with a swig of wine, now more pills, more wine until both are finished. Then he bends forward as if bowing and walks to the bathroom, flops into the tub. Water sloshes onto the floor and he leans his head back, stares at the ceiling. Bubbling up around his neck, water cools him, he is comfortable for the first time in days, he is weightless, floating, drifting. A face slides in front of his, disappears, comes back. It is a man, swimming underwater. He recognizes him now. It is Willy Kapell. They are face to face underwater, treading water, beautiful colored fish swim past, seaweed brushes against them. Tibor opens his mouth to speak. Only bubbles come out. Willy smiles, a calm smile, a peaceful smile, and swims away, looking over his shoulder, to see if Tibor will follow.

Wires dangle over his head. He tries to move but can't. "Shhh," someone says. A cool hand strokes his forehead and a face comes into view, blurs, fades away. He tries to imagine where he is and what has happened. He tries to differentiate parts of his body. The soft hand brushes across his brow again. Is it seaweed? Then where is Willy? He hears feet shuffle and voices whisper and he seems to be floating somewhere, suspended midair, and a faint blue light flickers into his half-closed eyes. Now he hears a tone, an intermittent buzz, a B-flat. What piece is this and who is playing? B-flat buzzes, one-two-three-four, the first measure of Mozart's last piano concerto, the heartbeat of the opening, buzzing, buzzing in his ear. He must sit up, he must get ready for his entrance, but his arms are pinned to his sides and he struggles to move, thrashing back and forth. He sees the keyboard in front of him. Slowly it starts to curve, to circle around him, closing in on him, tighter, tighter. He claws at the keys, his knuckles tearing, blood dripping onto the keys, dribbling into the cracks between them. Something sharp sticks into his arm and the nurse at the Centre Hospitaler Universitaire Vaudois in Lausanne says, "Shhh," and he falls into a deep mindless sleep.

"He did what?" Sally asks again, trembling, squeezing the receiver. "Speak up!"

"I don't want to shout," Werner says and leans against the wall of the waiting room. "He took an overdose, pills and alcohol."

"But you said his mother knew he was distraught. How could she have let him go off alone?"

"She said she was trying to help him, that he wanted to be alone, that he seemed OK. It's possible she didn't realize how deeply depressed he was. How do I know?"

"And brain damage, what about brain damage?"

"None. At least nothing showed up on the EEG. Lucky his foot kicked out the plug, or he would have drowned in the bath. And he vomited a lot of the . . . Look, Sally, it wasn't very pretty. But he's OK, he'll be OK."

"Why would he have tried it?" She chokes and rubs at one eye with a fist.

"Why does anyone ever try it? He was tired and upset and probably only half knew what he was doing."

"It's my fault."

"It's not. You're responsible only for yourself. What *he* did, *he* did. Besides, I don't believe he really wanted to, not really."

"Pills and alcohol. He was serious. Do you think he'll try it again?"

"No. He'll get help, he'll be OK. Look, they're letting me go in to see him now. Do you want me to give him a message?"

"A message?" Sally repeats, trying to formulate one. "Tell him, tell him I'm glad he's alive."

"That's all?"

"Yes. What am I supposed to say?"

"You're supposed to say what you mean."

"Well, that's what I mean. I'm glad he's alive, I am. Please tell him for me. I don't know what will happen when he's well. None of us do."

A nurse taps Werner on the shoulder. He presses his back into the cool tiles, pushes away from the wall with his foot as he says good-bye, hangs up the phone, and follows a starched white skirt down a quiet corridor.

252

><

Werner holds on to a metal railing and looks down at the bed. Eyes closed, wet hair spread out around his face, like a swimmer on his back, Tibor sleeps. The nurse checks the glucose drip, pulls up a chair, and motions for Werner to sit down, then leaves the room. There is a bruise on Tibor's face above the left temple, like a long dark fingerprint, and his sunken cheeks, sharp straight nose, thin dry lips are still as a mask. Leaning forward to see if he breathes, Werner watches the sheets slowly rise and fall, sees the two hands resting on either side, fingers curled, palms up. He hesitates, then slides his hand into one of Tibor's, squeezes gently. Like startled birds, Tibor's eyes flap open, he stares, his eyes close again, and his fingers tighten around Werner's. He pulls, he strains to sit up. Harnessed into the bed, he struggles like a horse with a heavy load, grunts, and lies back, breathing quickly, looking up at Werner with glazed eyes.

"Do you hear it?" Tibor asks, his voice rasping, his throat sore from the stomach pump.

"Hear what?"

"That note?" He presses Werner's hand, and they listen together.

There is the sound of a stretcher being wheeled down the hall, a man coughing in another room, the bing of the elevator signal.

"There," Tibor says, raising his head off the pillow, and he hums the note he hears, stops, and Werner hears it also, a faint sound, buzzing.

"It's the fluorescent lamp, that's all," Werner assures him.

"But it's B-flat, you know, like the opening of the last concerto."

"K. five-nine-five?"

"Good, Rawlings, you know your stuff."

253

Surprised to be recognized, Werner starts to pull his hand away, but Tibor squeezes harder, smiles, and listens, humming, while Werner watches, uneasy, eyes fixed on Tibor's bruise, a strange fingerprint, as if made by death itself.

"Can I tell you something?" Tibor asks. "And you won't laugh, promise?"

Werner nods.

Tibor lifts up his head, muscles in his neck straining. "I saw Willy Kapell."

"When?"

"Before. I wanted to go with him, you know, follow him. I tried. But he was swimming too fast. And then I came back."

"Came back where?"

"Here." Tibor looks confused and frowns. "What happened?" he asks.

"You took too many pills with too much wine."

Tibor squints, trying to remember. "Mother, I went to see my mother, and then . . ." Like a pile of stones when one is pulled out at the bottom, memory topples onto him, a crushing mass of recollection. He breathes quickly and snatches his hand out of Werner's.

"I trusted you," he whispers. "I really trusted you."

"I know you did," Werner says.

"And you must have been the one who found me. First you torture your victim, then you don't let him die. You're a cruel bastard, aren't you?"

"Am I?" Werner asks, the tips of his fingers turning white as they squeeze the railing. "Look, Szabo, you can blow your brains out the minute they release you from this hospital for all I give a damn. Another pianist down the drain—who cares? Sure, you'll be remembered for a while—memorial concerts, eulogies, inflated record sales—all the fame death can buy. But your memory will fade and only the loving few will play those records, weep to them as you do to Dinu Lipatti's. Do you think Lipatti wanted to die?"

"He had a family," Tibor snaps. "He had someone to play for."

"He played for the music, the music itself," Werner says and walks to the window, pulls back a buff-colored curtain, looks out at a courtyard filled with patients, some in wheelchairs, others in walkers, moving slowly back and forth under the spreading trees.

"I wonder how many of those people down there have heard you play and may never be well enough to hear you again," he says.

"Who cares?" Tibor mutters at Werner's back.

"They do." He turns and walks over to Tibor's bed, sits down again, and asks, "Did you ever stop to think what goes on out in that concert hall when you play?"

Tibor's eyes open and shut, try to take him in through the fog of drugs. "Are you going to preach at me?" he asks. "Because if you are, I'm ringing for the nurse."

"I have something to tell you, that's all."

Tibor turns his head away, looks back up. "I'm tied to the bed. Go ahead, talk."

"I was just wondering if you have any idea how many lives you make richer, how many lives you change? Take one, for instance, take mine. Did I ever tell you that before? No, of course not. You'd have laughed, brushed it off as so much fluff. But you did, Szabo, you turned my life around for me, you lifted me above the squalor of my little world." Werner reaches for the glass on the bedside table, takes a drink, wipes his chin with the back of his hand. "Look . . . we all have our own hideous mess to contend with," he says, and replaces the glass. "We pick through the garbage of our lives like ragmen looking for meaning, for answers, for hope. Life's full of struggle, contradiction, frustration. But music is more peaceful than life. And, besides, it doesn't preach or dictate or pretend to be right. It illustrates, it illuminates, but it resolves nothing, it offers no answers. And yet, played the way you can play, it lifts us above the dungheap of life. You have that power. If you deny your own strength, you betray your public—and if you do that, it's yourself you deceive."

Tibor watches droplets of glucose move like crystal beads through a clear plastic tube. "You're a fine one to speak of betrayal," he says softly.

"I'm not here to ask for your forgiveness," Werner says. "I've loved you and I've envied you. I've wanted what you have and I've caused you pain. For all of that, I'm sorry. But for never having told you what it's meant for me to listen to you make music, for that omission, I'm ashamed."

"It doesn't matter," Tibor says.

"It does. It matters to me, because I might not have had this chance."

Tibor struggles to say something, then reaches slowly up toward Werner, takes his head between his two hands, feels the thick curls, damp heat rising through them. He pulls him closer, places his lips on Werner's, a dry, quiet kiss and lets go.

Throat tight, Werner chews at the inside of his cheek, fights against tears that overpower his control. He wipes at his wet face with a sleeve.

"Here," Tibor says and hands him a bedside box of Kleenex. "Sally?" he asks. "How is she? Are you taking good care of her?"

Werner blows his nose. "Sally's taking care of herself these days," he says. "She's in London. I've got a message for you from her."

"You do?" Tibor asks, bracing himself to hear it.

"She says she's glad you're alive."

"That's all?"

"It's a lot, if you think about it," Werner says. "And when you start thinking, when your brain starts working again, try to remember you have some concerts coming up."

Tibor plucks at the sheet. "What makes you think I'll ever want to play again?"

"Because you're not ready for silence," Werner says, thumping his hands on the railing. "You have too much left to say. It's not time yet for you to join Kapell and Lipatti. And you know it."

A head crowned with a white cap pokes through the door.

"Mr. Rawlings, there's a call for you from New York, a Mr. Klein. Will you come to the desk?"

"Wait," Tibor says, stopping Werner. "Just tell me one thing. How did you find me? Did my mother call you?"

"No, I called *her*. She kept insisting she didn't know where you were, but I had a hunch and came to Lausanne anyhow. My sudden arrival frightened her, and she phoned the place you'd gone to. Then, when there was no answer, we called the police."

Tibor nods solemnly.

"But come to think of it," Werner says, a smile twisting on his face, "actually, it was the maître d' at the Jacaranda down the street from your house." He snatches a towel from the bedstand, drapes it over his arm and imitates. "'Your friend, Maestro Szabo, he probably go to the mountains to get away from the heat, no? Smart man, your friend.'"

Tibor grabs a corner of the towel and tugs at it. "You're a pretty smart bastard yourself," he says.

The patient lies wide-eyed at three a.m. His bedside light is on. The door is open.

"Would you like a pill to help you sleep?" a voice asks.

Tibor smiles wryly. "You ought to have a look at my chart, nurse."

"It's *doctor*," she says, then peers at the clipboard that dangles at the end of his bed. "Oh, Mr. Szabo, please excuse me." Embarrassed, she steps back, puts her hands in her pockets, takes them out. "I'm a great admirer of yours," she says. "I have all your records."

"You do?"

The doctor smiles, two dimples punctuating a pretty face. "It's quite an impressive discography, you know," she says. "Fifty-two recordings. No, wait." She raises a finger to her chin. "The complete Beethoven sonatas —fourteen discs, and that makes a total of sixty-six."

"So many?" Tibor asks. "I've never counted."

"Why should you? Records are for those who listen, not those who make them."

"You're absolutely right," Tibor says, looking up now with interest. Her long dark hair, pulled into a ponytail, falls over her shoulder like a question mark against her white smock. "What's your name?" he asks.

"Lise Bousard."

"Dr. Bousard, I have a recital here in Lausanne, let me see, on the third of September."

"I have a ticket. I bought it months ago, the day they went on sale."

"You did? I'm pleased."

"You're playing opus thirty-one, number two—my favorite sonata."

"Really? What do you like about it?"

"I don't think my opinion would interest you."

"But it would. It does. Tell me, please." He looks at her expectantly.

"I just think it's amazing. The year Beethoven wrote it he was deeply depressed, and yet he was able to create this piece, so original, so emotionally intense, from the opening recitative, the way it fans out, like a storm."

"It *is* the Tempest," Tibor says, pleased by her knowledge. He sits up, leans forward. "God, that finale! Nothing but sixteenth notes!"

"But it never sounds monotonous, does it? Not the way you play it, anyhow."

"Well, the cross-rhythms help."

"And, of course, the subtle melody," she adds. "It holds it all together, doesn't it?"

"Yes," he agrees, smiling. "But how is it that you know so much about music?"

"I don't really."

He looks at her in amused disbelief.

"Well, I studied piano," she admits, "in London, with Ilona Kabos."

"You must be good!"

"I was, but not anymore. I was *good*, but no more than that. I decided there were enough mediocre pianists in the world and I'd try to do something more useful with my life."

"That must have been difficult—a very brave decision," Tibor says as Lise pours ice water from a jug into a glass, places it on the table next to him. A distant rumbling distracts them both.

"Maybe it's a storm," she says, shaking a wet hand. "I

like them here, the way the clouds come racing over the mountains, the way it's so fresh afterward. Of course, we could use some rain to break this heat wave."

"I don't mind the heat, not really," Tibor says, lying back.

"You're used to it, bright lights on stage and everything," Lise says, tossing her hair back into place. "But it makes some of the patients here so uncomfortable. They suffer."

"I suppose they do," Tibor says, quietly, and points to the chair beside his bed, motions for her to sit down. She hesitates, then sits. Hands folded in her lap, she returns his smile, her cheeks glowing.

"Tell me something," Tibor requests, and props himself up on one elbow, turning toward her. "You're young and healthy. Isn't it difficult for you to work with all these sick people?"

"Sometimes." She looks down at her hands, folded the way she arranges the hands of the lifeless before they stiffen. "When patients get better, I feel enormous satisfaction. But when pain lingers and death is delayed, it all seems futile, miserable—even sordid." Removing her stethoscope, she folds it up, pushes it into a pocket, then reaches for a Kleenex and blots moisture from her neck. "There was a woman here this past spring . . ." Her voice dims as she wonders whether the story should be told.

"Tell me about her, please," Tibor urges.

"She was young," Lise begins, patting the moist Kleenex between her palms, "with two small children, a nice husband. She was dying and there was nothing to be done for her. Thin and frail, she never complained, and I had grown fond of her, so very fond. One night I went into her room and heard moans at each exhaled breath, soft sounds, like the cooing of a dove. 'What is it?' I asked her. 'Is it the pain? Can I help?' 'I'm singing,' she managed to say. 'Sing to me, now, please.' Maybe I should have rung for the emergency unit. I don't know. I have a terrible voice, but I started to sing, the first thing that came into my head, 'Im wunderschönen Monat Mai.' I repeated it over and over again. Her body relaxed, a smile dawned on her face, and finally she opened her eyes, very wide, and closed them forever. I just sat there, holding her hand, and I kept singing, over and over, 'In May, the loveliest of months, when all the flowers were in bloom, I felt love filling my heart . . . ' "

Lise looks at Tibor and shakes her head slowly back and forth. "I don't know," she whispers. "Maybe I should have rung that bell. She might have lived longer, a little longer." Her eyes sparkle in the shadows, question his.

"Lise," he answers, stopping to listen to the sound of her name, "you did the right thing."

"Do you think so?" She turns away and stares at the window, curtains puffed as a warm breeze begins to rise.

"You did the right thing," Tibor insists. "She was dying and you calmed her. You helped her."

"I didn't," Lise says. "The music did."

"Yes, the music." He pushes a damp lock of hair away from his eyes and lies back. "It can't change anything, can it? But it can ease the pain."

Lise sits quietly beside him awhile longer before she rises and bends over the bed reaching, out of habit, for the patient's wrist.

"I'm glad you'll be at my recital," Tibor says, and then he laughs. "God, I've said that a million times, but this time I'm serious."

"Are you? Why?"

"I am. Because I see the music will mean as much to you as it will to me. I'll try to play well."

"You always do," she says, looking at her watch, feeling his pulse. "Normal," she announces professionally, and lets go, but Tibor takes her hand, squeezes it gently, holds it for a moment in his. Then Lise turns and walks back toward the door, her perfume lingering, the scent of lavender.